RABBIS and GANGSTERS

T0159794

RABBIS and
GANGSTERS

a murder mystery novel

Philip Graubart

EXILE
editions

Fiction, Poetry, Translation, Drama and Nonfiction

Library and Archives Canada Cataloguing in Publication

Graubart, Philip
    Rabbis and gangsters : a murder mystery novel / Philip Graubart.

ISBN 978-1-55096-298-7

    I. Title.

PS3557.R3565R32 2012   813'.54   C2012-904786-4

Design and Composition by Hourglass Angels~mc
Typeset in Fairfield and Stone fonts at the Moons of Jupiter Studios
Printed by Imprimerie Gauvin

Published by Exile Editions Ltd ~ www.ExileEditions.com
144483 Southgate Road 14 – GD, Holstein ON, N0G 2A0
Printed and bound in Canada in 2012

Canadian sales: The Canadian Manda Group, 165 Dufferin Street,
Toronto ON M6K 3H6   www.mandagroup.com   416 516 0911

North American and international distribution, and U.S. sales:
Independent Publishers Group, 814 North Franklin Street,
Chicago IL 60610   www.ipgbook.com   toll free: 1 800 888 4741

For Susan, Benjamin and Ilan.
Thank you for the life we've built.

Contents

One

THE SCUMBAG

CHAPTER 1

Rabbi Yael Gold, thin, pale-skinned, attractive, thirty years old, skipped down the Desert Garden courthouse steps. She stopped when the thought hit her. "I'm in love with him," she whispered, irritated, amazed, then: "I'm late!" She took the steps two at a time, but stopped. Oh God. This can't be happening. Not again.

She pictured her husband of three years. No. I love Peter, I do. She glanced at her BlackBerry, saw the time, and again bounced down the broad staircase. I'll work this out later.

But before she'd gone down four steps, he – her boss, Rabbi Judah Loeb – was back in her brain, smiling shyly, covering her hand with his two soft, slender fists, the light shining off his silver hair; his blue eyes taking in her entire body, head to toe, as if evaluating every inch of her. Is that all this is, she wondered, just his touch, his silvery hair, his twinkling eyes, those things that captivate everyone who meets him? Yes, she answered, but tentatively. I'm really just another fan, a groupie. A congregant. And that's good, because that's not love. That's a crush. And I can live with a crush. My marriage can survive a crush.

She remembered the sessions with Dr. Martin, the gray-haired, bespectacled psychiatrist she'd seen briefly before accepting Peter's marriage proposal. "Crushes," he kept saying in a high, nasal voice – but actually *suggesting*, because he wasn't supposed to tell her anything, she was supposed to figure it all out herself. "Aren't these just crushes, all the different men you supposedly fall in love with every three months, like clockwork, whether you're in a relationship or not, whether you *want* to be in a relationship or not, whether or not this new feeling will lift you or ruin your life? Why do you have to use the word 'love' when, I might *suggest*, these are just crushes?"

"What's the difference?"

The old shrink squinted at her, impatient and tired, as if it wasn't worth the effort for him to answer something that anyone with any brains or emotional intelligence could work out on her own. "You're right," she added quickly, but just to get him to stop squinting at her. "They're just crushes. Schoolgirl crushes," she said, and he smiled. And I'm just a schoolgirl, she'd thought, at least for another month, until seminary ordination, when, at age twenty-seven, I'll finally graduate from the world of school for the first time since kindergarten.

She was sort of kidding about the "schoolgirl" comment, but it was at that very moment Yael decided to marry Peter. Maybe it's the being "in school," the perpetual adolescence, maybe that's my problem, she mused, not wanting to share such a risible analysis with the impatient Dr. Martin. Was junior high really so different than graduate school? At bottom, it's all about pleasing teachers and making friends. Maybe it really is possible to grow up, even at the rather advanced age of twenty-seven. She had, after all, really fallen for Peter. She loved him deeply even now, after nearly six years together, after cheating on him four times with four of the "clockwork crushes," and, more importantly, resisting the last four. That was the day, in Dr. Martin's office, she decided to say yes. She would marry Peter.

Amazingly, it worked. Mostly. Men – single and married, younger and older, with all manner of handshake grips, and colognes, and witty come-ons, and gleaming eyes, and bare or bearded cheeks – crossed her path, and every three months she'd look up and notice a particularly attractive jawline, or a toothy smile, or hair-part. Or she'd hear a melodic voice, an intelligent argument, or a funny line. And her old longing would resurface and, at least momentarily, she'd forget about Peter, push her long black hair out of her brown eyes, feel herself blush, and *respond*. But these days she'd been catching herself, well in time. Because, she knew, these were crushes, schoolgirl crushes, and she was no schoolgirl.

Of course, most of these men were congregants, and an aversion to entangling herself with parishioners, a repugnance at least as deep as her hatred of adultery, also kicked in, rescuing her from that deep and inscrutable hunger that had plagued her as long as she could remember. And her love for Peter only grew stronger.

But now, at the bottom of the courthouse steps, barely half an hour after persuading her fellow jurors to put away an obvious child molester, Rabbi Loeb's blue eyes stuck in her mind. No. She shook her head, as she reached the car and fumbled with her keys. It's still just a crush. Even though Judah wasn't some random male crossing her once-a-quarter radar screen – that deadly, once-in-three-months time when her senses suddenly and inexplicably became alert to mating signals. This was the man she'd worked closely with for three years, since he'd hired her, personally, not even consulting with his board. The man who knew her better than anyone except Peter, and in ways that Peter remained willfully ignorant of. Peter never imagined Yael as particularly adept at empathy or even listening, probably because she rarely exercised those skills with her husband, at least no more than he did with her. Peter hadn't seen her, for example, comforting the Levys last week after their second miscarriage, didn't notice Yael's tightly shut eyes well up with tears as she mouthed the line about God healing a broken womb. He hadn't heard her the day before when, shaking with nervousness, she'd spontaneously composed and sung a healing prayer for the ninety-two-year-old bed-bound Ellie Smith, who, as if in direct response, recovered from pneumonia the next day. When Yael told her husband these stories, he listened, but absently, strumming one of his exotic stringed instruments, humming a country and western klezmer mash up.

But Judah *knew*. He knew her professionally, which is to say he knew her as a pastor, as a *rabbi*, and being a rabbi was no small part of who she was.

But that's not it, she thought, not really, as she settled into the driver's seat, eager to get back to work after sitting through the gruesome two-week trial. It's his hands. His blue eyes, she thought, smiling and blushing, embarrassed even though there wasn't a soul around to see her. Blushing. Just like a schoolgirl. Just a crush.

She pulled her tan Tercel onto the Desert County highway, and quickly accelerated past eighty. She slid a Bruce Springsteen CD into the slot and cranked up the volume, hoping, with velocity, desert wind, and loud noise, to distract herself from thoughts of crushes and child molestation. She also hated to be late, and that worry gradually cleared her mind of other unwelcome thoughts. She pulled into her parking space with fifteen minutes to spare. Still, if only to hold on to the feeling of *rushing*, a feeling she frankly craved despite her protestations – certainly a feeling she enjoyed more than being in love with her married boss, the senior rabbi – she sprinted across the parking lot, burst through the side entrance of Congregation Anshei Emet, and jogged down the hallway, past the youth wing, towards Judah's office.

A fat, middle-aged man stood in her way. "What's your hurry, Rabbi Doll?"

Oh no, she thought, stopping in her tracks an instant before she would bowl him over. The scumbag. She shut her eyes and took a moment to sniff the air. Sweat, bourbon, a minty smell she associated, for no good reason, with heroin. The smells of Cantor Edgar Weinman. She looked him over. Same scaly, shiny bald head, same pale, fat face, same torn, brown corduroy jacket, same spotted, black wool pants, pulled up over a potbelly. Same smirk, same stink, same scumbag. "I was trying to get past you," she said.

"Oh, you know better than that," he said, his voice a rich, smooth baritone, as if he, once upon a time, might actually have been, as he claimed, a world-famous cantor. "You could never get past me, Baby Doll. You couldn't when you were three years old, and you can't now."

"Just watch me," she said.

"Guilty or not guilty?" she heard a voice say as, head down, her usual hurried position, she dashed into Anshei Emet's rabbinic suite. For an instant she thought, but I haven't even done anything yet. How could I be accused? But then, of course, she remembered the trial. She looked up into Charlotte's sunburned, grinning face.

"Guilty," Yael said, catching her breath. She moved the long hairs out of her eyes and forced a smile. "There wasn't much doubt. At least, not by me."

"Big-time criminal?" Charlotte shoved a thick, brown accordion file out of the way so she could look directly at Yael. Charlotte was Judah's personal assistant, though she also did secretarial work for Yael, who had no assistant. A dozen fat accordion files crowded Charlotte's reception desk: grant applications, graphs, arguments, e-mail, Power-Point slides, spreadsheets, all supporting the Reorganization, the subject of the big meeting. Yael had written three of the reports, staying up very late four nights in a row so she could get them done before jury duty. Judah insisted on thoroughness in his assignments, and Yael was anal herself in wanting to get the presentations exactly right, even though she'd been certain that no one but Judah would read them. Charlotte made copies of everything and sent them along to all members of the Reorganization committee. She kept the original files on her desk, where they now stood together like cardboard bricks, crowding out any other piece of business.

Yael chuckled. "Hardly. Child molester. Just a real nasty creep. Sort of reminded me…" she gestured to the hallway.

"Say no more," Charlotte answered. Yael knew that she shared her opinion of Cantor Weinman, though Charlotte didn't know the half of it. For reasons Yael could simply not imagine, Judah put up with, and even seemed to enjoy the company of Weinman, former cantor, present-day creep. Several times a week, she heard the two men laughing like schoolboys behind Judah's closed office door, and at least a half-dozen times she smelled cigar smoke wafting into her own office. The two were pals.

"Ready for the big meeting?" Charlotte drawled. Charlotte was from South Carolina, or maybe Tennessee. Yael could never remember.

"I broke several traffic laws to make it on time. Not to mention bullying the rest of the jury to *vote* already. I guess I'm ready. Anyone here yet?"

"Nope. But he wants you to go in as soon as you get here. He was hoping to spend some time alone with you. He told me to tell you that. Hey, why are you blushing?"

Damn. She'd never been able to stop herself from blushing. Since her marriage and job – since, in other words, she'd become a grown-up – she'd worked so hard to mask her emotional volatility, to present herself *professionally*, even to her husband, or brother, or best friends. The blushing always forced her to explain herself, to account for some inner chaos that she didn't fully understand and, in any case, desperately wanted to hide from the world. Now, with Charlotte, she didn't even bother explaining. She just scooted past the secretary, into the senior rabbi's office.

"Not guilty? I figured that's how you would vote. Was I wrong?"

She grinned, enjoying the sound of his voice, even as she marveled at how this man who knew her so well could get this one so wrong. Not guilty was definitely not her default option when judging anyone, particularly herself, particularly now that Judah's blue eyes shone at her and her pulse raced in response. She studied his thin fingers as they gripped his favorite uni-ball pen. Oh my. "It's good to see you," he said.

"Guilty," she answered. "In fact, I… well, I'll tell you about it later."

"Look forward to it," he said.

"Speaking of guilty, I ran into Edgar Weinman in the hallway."

He smiled, turning his head to the folders. It was his shy smile, the charming, half smile that made him look like he was sharing a guilty laugh with you, but only with *you*, his special friend. Yael figured he shared that smile with at least twenty people a day. It always worked with her. "Oh?" he said.

"Can't we get a court order or something? Get Javier to toss him out of the building?"

Javier was the synagogue security – a walkie-talkie toting guard, hired to placate preschool parents. He was well over 6 feet, and weighed a good 250 pounds, but Yael had never seen him walk through the parking lot without stopping to catch his breath. She figured, in a pinch, even Charlotte could knock the guy on his rear, certainly outrun him.

Judah looked right at her, the smile gone. "Toss him out? Why would we want to do that? You know, it was your husband who introduced him to me. After services, more than two years ago."

"He's a scumbag," she said, but softly, so he might miss the final word.

After a pause he laughed. "You know, I don't think I've ever heard you use that word. That's what Charlotte calls him, and Aviva. The scumbag. I don't think Aviva even knows his real name. Did you come up with that, Yael?"

She was definitely blushing, her cheeks burning, annoyance, even anger, blending with her obvious embarrassment. "I might have," she said, still keeping her voice quiet. "I'm sorry, Judah, but I'm not sure you really *know* him. And lately you're spending so much time with him…"

"I *know* him, Yael," he said in a steely, low, almost menacing voice, the one he used so rarely with the staff but that everyone recognized as the final word. Yael actually couldn't recall him ever using that voice with her. She looked down. He sighed. "Look, I'm aware of his past, and certainly aware of his present. But every rabbi, particularly rabbis in our situation, needs a project, don't you think, Yael? And he's not as bad as you think. He's trying. Listen, you call him a scumbag; you all do, and you're probably right. But isn't that exactly what we would call a *lamedvavnick*, at least at first? Maybe you're all correct; maybe he's just the classic scumbag, whatever that means. But I see something else. Maybe a *lamedvavnick*. Anyway, I have to try. Until I'm sure."

Yael was dumbstruck. Weinman, a *lamedvavnick* – one of the legendary thirty-six righteous who prevented God from destroying the world? Weinman, the alcoholic, gambler, drug addict, asshole? She didn't know what was more shocking, the very idea, or that Judah might say it, even *believe* it. Honestly, there were times when her boss's neo-Hasidic mumbo-jumbo, in her opinion his least attractive teaching stance, did nothing but piss her off. And what on earth was he talking about? He has to *try*? Try to do what? To reform the guy who calls her "Rabbi Doll," who stinks of whatever he's injected into his body that morning, and who told her all those horrible things about her father? To remove the scum from the bag? Dumbfounded, she could only change the subject.

"I was the holdout," she said.

"Hmm?"

"On the jury. I was the holdout. Everyone else was voting not guilty. I changed their minds. I wanted guilty."

Again, the smile, just a half grin but enough to warm the room. "Oh?"

"He was a child molester."

"Ah," Judah said. "That was the charge?"

"He was guilty. I convicted him."

"Of course." He studied her, briefly taking her all in, up and down, but just with his eyes, his face didn't move an inch. "I look forward to hearing about it." Which was his polite way of saying "not now," maybe not ever, meaning they should change the subject.

She nodded and took the binder she'd prepared from his desk.

"It's just that they'll be here any minute now," he said, motioning her to sit. "And I need to speak with you alone. But I do want to hear about the trial. And your courageous stand. Eleven angry men and one rabbi?"

She laughed. "More like one angry lady and eleven clueless women and men." She sat back in her chair, relaxing for the first time since she'd entered his presence. "So, what do you need to tell me?"

"You're my partner," he said. She waited. He'd said it before, usually as a prelude to assigning her some extraordinarily difficult task, like redesigning the preschool, or coming up with a single's program that could actually attract young singles, or officiating at a child's funeral. "You're my partner," he'd say; then present her with reams of paperwork, like applying for a grant that was due the next day; work that would keep her up until past midnight, past even Peter the musician's bedtime. "You're my partner," he'd say, as he'd head off for vacation, not available to preside at the Men's Club Torah Study. You're my partner, meaning I'm your boss, and you work for me. So she waited.

"That's it," he said. "That's all I wanted to say. That's what this is all about, Yael."

He leaned back. "These reports. The Reorganization. I'm doing it so we can truly become partners. It's not just a new organizational chart. Honestly, Yael, it's really about you, your role, finding your own voice of authority. You. Well, you and me. We're dividing responsibilities, pretty much down the middle. You handle your areas and I handle mine. We'll be partners, but really this time. I won't tell you what to do, and I mean, not at all, no more than you'll tell me. Yael, there are twelve binders on my desk, and many good people have been working on this for months, and this meeting could go on for hours. But it's really just about two words: we're partners. It's really just about you and me. Two rabbis, two professionals, with fully equal responsibilities and authority. That's my vision, Yael. I hope you share it."

Again, Yael didn't know what to say. True, that was the recommendation, and the two equal rabbis' business was implicit in all the slides and all the endless org charts. But, for so many reasons, it never occurred to Yael that Judah actually meant it when he wrote in the binder he'd composed, at the top of his ten pages, describing rabbinic duties: "Equal Partners." Judah had built this congregation in the desert; really, he'd built the entire Jewish community, the school, the JCC, the nursing home/senior center. When Rabbi Loeb had arrived in Desert County twenty years before, some 18,000 Jews called the gambling metropolis their home. But they were scattered across thirty miles, from the seedy inner city to the dozens of gated communities sprawling through the dry, desert suburbs. There were four local reform synagogues; large, gaudy, but spiritually empty. Factories, Judah had called them – cathedral factories, producing once a year high holiday pageants for all their members; and, for individual families, private adolescent shows called bar or bat mitzvahs, starring thirteen-year-olds reading meaningless Hebrew passages, and speeches composed by assistant rabbis.

Most of the new desert Jews hadn't even bothered with the factories. Their Jewish community had the lowest affiliation rate in the country, one of the lowest rates in the world. Then Judah took the job at the only Conservative congregation in the county, a small, downtown, 200-member community that, according to the other rabbis in town, had been dying since the day it had opened its doors.

"These were the original desert Jews, cowboys and cow-girls who moved here with the wagon trains, and opened failing dry-goods stores, or saloons. One of their great-grandfathers had been the first sheriff, as far as I know, the only Jewish sheriff in the West," Judah had told her when she'd interviewed for the job. "Which meant, naturally, that they were the only Jews without money in Desert County. But also the only Jews who still carried guns. Or came to services with whiskey on their breath. It was like preaching in a time warp, before the gaming industry, before all the mega-hospitals and law offices and real estate moguls. To be truthful, I probably liked it better back then. It was easier to find the *lamedvavnicks*. And the real villains."

Five years after Judah arrived, Anshei Emet had quadru-pled its membership. Two years later, now boasting of well over 1,000 families, the congregation made the move, out of the city, into Desert Garden, the latest of the suburbs to spread crablike to the north of the downtown casinos. Judah oversaw the construction of a Jewish campus: five white-washed, three-story, concrete structures with a Jewish day school, a kosher cafeteria, a nursing home, a federation building, a Jewish Community Center, all pentagonally arrayed around the gleaming highlight – Congregation Anshei Emet. Rabbi Judah Loeb now ran the biggest Jewish show in town.

What was his secret? "Get the fundamentals right," Judah had told her, when she asked at the interview. "Make sure there's a good school – doesn't have to be great, but good. Take care of the elderly. That's especially important for us, out here, with all the desert retirees. Offer quality education programs, no garbage, just quality. Work hard; that's especially important. And show up, day and night. That's the whole story. No one else was doing that. I got lucky."

But it wasn't just the work, and it was more than luck. Judah was *magnetic*. "He speaks softly but carries a big stick filled with sex appeal," was how Yael's husband had put it after listening to one sermon. "They come just to stare at his face, the gray hair wave, don't they? The shiny hair. Those eyes, Jesus. And to listen to that hushed, musical voice. Does it even matter what he says?"

"Oh, it matters," Yael had replied, and she believed it. Yes, he was theatrical, emotional, and charming. But she'd never heard such distilled wisdom, so much deep Jewish learning translated into lyrical English. She'd *learned* from him, thought differently about the world after listening to him. He had mastered the famous and obscure, the Talmud, and the Hasids, Kabbalah, and American-Jewish Literature. He had something to say and, in Yael's experience, that was a rare gift. She didn't claim to have it. Leave it to her husband to pinpoint the essential difference. "You're a great teacher, Yael," he told her one night when they were discussing just how Judah did what he did. "You're bright, you stay on message, you're pretty. But your students have to be in love with Judaism first, then they love you. But Judah, he gets them to fall in love with him, and then they fall in love with Judaism."

She'd thought about being hurt, but then she realized that he was, in his kindness, exaggerating her appeal. She knew that once they fell in love with Judaism they'd *like* her, but they didn't fall in love with her. But they did fall for Judah, whether or not they fell in love with Judaism. After all, here she was, sitting next to him, falling in love. Even if it was just another one of her schoolgirl crushes.

"I'm flattered, Judah," she said, wishing she could find the eloquence to match her feelings. "I want to be your partner."

"Education," he pronounced, his blue eyes boring into her, as if she were an audience of one at a Yom Kippur sermon. "That's you, from now on. You alone, and the team you build. I'm the pastor. You're the educator. Equal partners."

Equal partners. The phrase was absurd, from more perspectives than she could count. Salary? Respect from the board? Authority? Ridiculous. There was also something vaguely insulting in the whole presentation. Only *he* was the pastor? As if Yael didn't have what it takes to visit patients in the hospitals, to listen to their problems, to pray for them. Nevertheless, she found herself swept up by that big stick of his. She just nodded.

The big meeting went as predicted. No one had read the binders all that carefully; some glanced through them for the first time as Judah spoke. After less than an hour, they all agreed to Judah's plan. They trusted him completely. And, as he'd often reminded her, when you raise the money first, it's hard to argue. And he had raised the money, months ago.

The woman he'd raised it from, Addison Hart, lingered in Judah's doorway after the meeting, casting a round shadow on the white carpet. Seven months' pregnant, her belly filled the office entrance like a bottle-stop. Yael assumed she was waiting to speak alone with Judah. Three weeks earlier, Charlotte had confided to Yael that Addison and Judah were "plotting and planning" behind Judah's closed door nearly every evening, sometimes well past dark. But as Yael turned sideways and tried to slip her slender body past the protrusion blocking the doorway, Addison touched her arm.

"Lunch?" she whispered.

Yael paused – awkwardly, since they were standing belly to belly, or, more accurately, overflowing womb to tight stomach. She jumped as she felt Addison's baby kick. She thought about Peter, whom she hadn't really spoken to since the trial had begun, because she'd had to work most evenings after jury duty. She'd sort of promised him they'd have lunch together today, assuming the trial ended, as she'd predicted that morning.

But Addison bellied in closer, nearly crushing Yael, leaning face forward to whisper in the rabbi's ear. "Please," was what she said, but Yael heard it for what it was: a summons.

"Of course, Addison."

They ate at the Garden, one of the many posh, Beverly Hills-style bistros that lined Palm Boulevard, the Rodeo Drive of Desert Garden. Yael ordered a salad and iced tea, but barely ate, preferring to watch with envy while Addison gobbled down a steak with french fries. "Just wait 'til you're pregnant. A skinny girl, just like me – well, how I used to be – your doctor will order you to *gain* weight."

"Can't wait," Yael answered.

Addison raised an eyebrow, and Yael flinched. When it came to oversensitivity, Addison was in a category of her own. She noticed *everything*, any glance at a watch, any stifled yawn. Often, she stored the perceived slights and then later deployed them strategically. Three months earlier, she'd forced Yael to delay an already long-delayed vacation and officiate at the funeral of a friend, a non-member. "I don't want to ask Judah," she'd said coldly. "I don't want to explain to him why you won't do it, or why you so often look at your watch when I'm talking to you."

But now Addison just changed the subject. "So, guilty or not guilty?"

Yael chuckled. "Gosh, why does everyone ask me that? That's the fourth time today, and I just left the courthouse. I feel…"

Addison laughed. "Oh, it's all right. I already know. I just wanted to hear what you thought."

"What do you mean, 'I already know?'"

"Guilty. I already heard. Actually, I heard you made the difference."

Yael flicked hair out of her eyes. "Addison, how could you possibly know that? I only told one person, and he couldn't have told you because—"

"Judah didn't tell me."

"Then, how…?"

Addison smiled. "This is really about you. You know that, don't you?"

"The trial? How could that be about me? I don't understand…"

"No, no, I just changed the subject. Sorry, I'm really all over the place these days. It's like I'm about to die, not give birth. I'm losing patience with small talk. Getting to the point quicker, like I don't have time. I meant Judah's plan. Our plan. My plan. The Reorganization. It's about you."

"I don't agree with that. I know that's what Judah told me this morning, but a lot of roles are changing. Tzipporah is moving up to education director. We're hiring a new youth advisor. I don't see…"

"Oh, it's about you, Yael. Judah's made that clear to me all along. He has very strong feelings about you, you know."

"We're partners," Yael said, but softly. And, naturally, she was blushing.

"Oh, I wouldn't say that. You really think Judah could ever have a partner?"

"Well, actually, he told me—"

"He told *me* that you're more the administrative type. A manager. An executive. An administrator. You're not really a pastor."

Yael watched the pregnant woman chew on a french fry. She marveled at the fact they were the same age, born in the same part of the country; with their long, black hair, dark eyes, and normally petite builds, they even sort of looked alike. They were both married to professors at the university, their wedding anniversaries six months apart. But Yael knew no one in the congregation she liked less, no one, not even the old cowboys, with whom she had far less in common.

"Pardon me? I'm not a pastor?"

"Well, he said it, Yael, not me. But, I must say it sounds right to me. Sweetheart, you're not *warm*. You're not spiritual, are you? You're fabulous in so many ways. You're a wonderful teacher. But you don't project love. People don't warm to you. You're, well, you're cold. There's something about us you don't like. Probably it's our jobs. Do you disagree?"

She looked at her watch, not caring if Addison took offense. For this, she was missing lunch with her husband. "Of course I disagree. Is this why you wanted to have lunch, Addison? To tell me I'm not warm? That I'm not the pastor type? That I'm not spiritual?"

"Oh, no," she said, wiping her lips with her napkin. "Deep down, you know that already. And you must know how *I* feel about you. I just wanted to tell you what *Judah* thinks. I want to make sure that's clear. I think you know, now." She looked up and seemed surprised that Yael was staring at her. "Can you finish eating? I'm in kind of a hurry."

Yael fought with her husband when she finally made it home. He started in as soon as she mentioned her lunch with Addison. "Am I wrong," he said, scratching his beard, imitating thoughtfulness, "or did you promise to have lunch with me if the trial ended this morning? But you didn't, you had lunch with Addison Hart, at the Garden?"

"Actually, you are wrong," she said softly, trying to build up conviction. "I didn't *promise*. I said, I'd try – if the trial ended, if the meeting ended early, if I could – well, there were so many conditionals there, I don't see how you could call it a promise. Anyhow, I had such a terrible lunch meeting. Could we possibly postpone this until—"

Her BlackBerry vibrated. For some reason, her particular device generated a sound even when set on vibrate; it sounded louder than many ringtones. No one could fix it, not even her geek husband. "Damn," she whispered. He hated her phone interrupting their conversations. Answering it, he claimed, showed how much she disrespected him. But she had missed so much work because of the trial. She glanced at the number. It was Deborah Levine, the synagogue president. In the three years that Yael had worked at Anshei Emet, Deborah had never called her cellphone. "I'm so sorry, Peter, I just have to…" And she answered the phone.

"Lunch, tomorrow?" She looked up guiltily at Peter, but he turned away. "Uh, sure, Deborah." She replaced the BlackBerry in her purse and prepared herself for more combat. Instead, tears filled her eyes.

Peter embraced her. Just like that, dropping the argument, and holding her. They kissed for more than a few seconds.

"I was the holdout," she said. "I made them vote guilty. I wasn't leaving until we convicted that scum… the guy."

He released her and took a step backwards. "It was that child abuse case? I saw it in the newspapers."

She was about to say yes, but felt more tears coming. She knew she wouldn't be able to speak. She nodded. She'd been scrupulous about following the judge's instructions to say nothing to anyone about the case, not even to a spouse. Now, she could tell him. Only she couldn't speak.

"The five-year-old girl?" Peter asked. "It seemed like – well, was the damage permanent?"

"Probably not," she whispered, testing her voice. "Not physically. Still."

Peter touched her hair. "You forced the verdict, huh?"

She smiled, though she was still crying. "He was guilty," she croaked, and then broke down altogether. Peter again understood her need, this time to defer all conversation. She cried in his arms until she felt her eyelids puff up. She knew that in the morning it would look like someone had socked her in the eye.

"Do you think I'm a cold person?" she asked. "Not warm?" She wasn't crying anymore, not really, but tears still lingered, like eye drops. "Do you think I'm not spiritual?"

"Boy, that Addison Hart. There's a piece of work. Just what you needed, after that trial."

"You don't know," she said. "You don't know the half of it."

He nodded. "But you did it, huh? You found him guilty."

She looked him dead in the eye, the way, as she recalled, the young, female prosecutor had looked at the guilty defendant. The way, come to think of it, that the prosecutor had looked at Yael, at each juror, as she'd made her closing argument demanding a guilty verdict. "He was guilty," Yael told her husband. "He was a scumbag."

CHAPTER 2

Another day, another lunch on Palm Boulevard, this time at the French Gourmet, even pricier than the Garden, though the lunch menu – lacy cardboard, covered with blue ink, the size and feel of a wedding invitation – didn't seem to offer anything not stuffed into a croissant. Both Yael and Deborah ordered mozzarella sandwiches, and each of them ate exactly two bites before laying them down and sticking to raspberry iced tea.

"So, he was guilty," Deborah said.

"How does everyone…"

"Oh, Judah told me. He said you were the instigator; you pushed them. Doesn't surprise me. You've got that righteous indignation. That's why you and I get along so well."

"I never should have said that to Judah… to Rabbi Loeb. Now everyone will think I put the guy in jail! But he was clearly guilty. It wasn't me, it was the evidence. I just pointed out a few facts they'd overlooked. I wasn't out to *get* him, or anything." She was surprised to hear herself. She was almost shouting.

"Yael, you're turning red. You're misunderstanding me. I admire you. I admire what you did. I despise all criminals. You are a natural leader. You did a good thing."

Yael took a breath. "Sorry, I've been on edge. The trial. It wasn't an… it wasn't easy." The last thing she wanted was to lash out at Deborah Levine. For one thing, she *liked* Deborah. As wealthy and as philanthropic as Addison, Deborah stuck to simple gray business suits. And she never threw her weight around, never treated synagogue professionals, as Addison often did, as part of her own personal staff. She also had a dry, sometimes dark sense of humor, which Yael had always appreciated. During board meetings, Yael was often the only one in the room who could tell when Deborah was joking. Yael's giggle would be the signal that everyone else should laugh. Also, and for some reason this was important to Yael, Deborah wasn't a full-time philanthropist; she had a job, a career. She was the managing partner at Millstein and Ross, a law firm that helped mega-casinos evade taxes.

"I'm sure it wasn't easy," Deborah said, now all business, no joking around. "And I'm sorry to bother you today when I know you have so much to catch up on. But, frankly, I don't know where else to turn. I need to talk to someone – well, really to *you* – about Judah."

"Rabbi Loeb?" Yael was surprised. She was under the impression that Deborah and Judah were good friends; that Judah and his wife Aviva often socialized with Deborah and her husband Michael, a high-end criminal lawyer who'd been the synagogue president when Judah came to Desert County.

"Do you mind if I order a cocktail?" Yael watched while Deborah signaled to the waitress. In three years, and dozens of lunches and dinner parties, Yael had never seen Deborah drink alcohol. Now she ordered a gin and tonic.

"Do you think he's having an affair?" Deborah asked, after a lengthy draw on her drink.

"*What?* Deborah, I don't—"

"What did you and Addison Hart talk about yesterday, at your lunch?" She sipped again from her drink, then blinked twice quickly, but otherwise kept a straight face. For the first time, Yael noticed a single wrinkle under Deborah's left eye. Or was it a scratch?

"Deborah. Come on! What are you *saying?* We talked about, well, we didn't talk about *Judah*. We talked about… you know, it was just another chance for her to insult me. It seems to give her pleasure, more since she got pregnant."

"Yes, the pregnancy. Do you think Manny is really the father? Or maybe someone else? Someone we both know well? Oh, and isn't Tzipporah, our youth director, pregnant? How long has *she* been married? Who do you think's the father?"

"My *God!*" Yael nearly vaulted from the table. Only her morbid curiosity kept her on the seat, but she squirmed as if she were tied down and being tickled. "Is this a joke? Is that it? I'm just late in getting it?"

Deborah drained the rest of her drink with one long swallow. She looked at the glass. "It's no joke, Yael. Sorry. But it sure sounds like you don't know anything about it."

"Deborah, what on earth?"

She shook her head. "Sorry to blurt all this out. Not really like me, though I don't suppose I can blame the gin. I guess I can't ask you just to forget about it?"

"Deborah. I don't know how to respond." Until this moment, the three words Yael would have used to describe

Deborah would have been funny, intelligent, and *sober*. It was her essential sobriety that made her such an effective partner for the charismatic Judah, a man who came up with more ideas at breakfast than most rabbis pondered in a year. Deborah supported Judah by grounding him. But now, well now she was spouting nonsense; making outrageous charges. Judah, the father of Addison's baby? And Tzippi's? *Judah and Tzippi!* As if Judah were an ancient Oriental monarch, impregnating several concubines at a time, while still married to the queen. She put her hand to her mouth to cover up a gasp. "Honestly, I don't know how you can say these things. I'm pretty sure I should leave." But she didn't. It wasn't so easy to get up and walk out on her synagogue's president, someone she'd always trusted.

Deborah was still studying her glass, as if searching for more gin. "You know about confidentiality, Yael? Professional confidentiality?"

"Of course."

"Then maybe you understand that there's not much else I can tell you. It was probably wrong of me to approach you at all. But I just didn't…" She shook her head. "You should be ready, Yael. That's all I can say now. And think about us. What *we'll* need. How you'll help us get through. Get yourself ready. We'll all need to."

"For what, Deborah?"

But Deborah just took a napkin and wiped her eyes. "Thanks for lunch," she said, and gestured for the waitress to bring the bill.

Yael's next meeting of the day, as it happened, was with Tzipporah, the youth director. Under the reorganization, Tzipporah was being promoted to education director, a promotion that would include a considerable raise. Tzippi had been thrilled and proud when Yael brought up the possibility, and Yael was happy for her. But now, Yael couldn't help but remember her friend's first reaction. "This is from Judah?" she'd said, grinning. "Judah thinks I should be promoted?"

"You mean Rabbi Loeb?" Yael had said it lightly, but she meant the correction as a mild rebuke. She didn't think anyone on the staff should use Judah's first name when talking about him. She herself, a colleague who had more right than anyone to use the first name, was careful about sticking to the title. At the time, Tzipporah had just laughed and Yael dismissed it. After all, didn't most of the young women at Anshei Emet have some degree of crush on Judah? But now she wondered. Why was Tzipporah so quick to call the senior rabbi by his first name?

Not that she brought it up at their meeting. On the brief drive over from the restaurant, the late spring sun shining in her eyes as she headed west on Palm Boulevard, the only strategy she could come up with – the only "getting ready" she would allow herself – was to push Deborah's outrageous charges to the very bottom of her pile of thoughts. She knew that was impossible. Standing now before her friend, her hands shook as she noted the slight bulge in Tzipporah's belly. Bury the idea of Judah the adulterer, with the possible consequences squirming in Tzippi's womb, two feet away? Ignore the very thought? Impossible. But what else could she do? She couldn't exactly wonder out loud who the father was.

Nevertheless, the meeting went well. They discussed who to hire to take Tzipporah's place as youth director, and Yael showed Tzipporah how to fill out synagogue budget forms. It was only when she got up to leave that she asked, "Tzippi, are you pregnant?"

The younger woman blushed, but also smiled, widely. She'd recently cut her long black hair, and was now sporting brown eyeglasses. She looked wise, even professorial. "How did you know?" she asked.

"Oh, someone… it doesn't matter. *Mazel Tov!*" They hugged and, after Yael let go, Tzippi held on tightly for a few more awkward seconds.

"How long?" Yael asked.

"Twelve weeks. And before you do the math, I'll just tell you. It was the honeymoon. Not before."

"Ah ha," Yael answered. She'd officiated at Tzippi's and Tony's wedding, exactly twelve weeks ago; Tzippi had asked her, and not Judah, to perform the ceremony. While studying her friend's belly, Yael recalled the moment right before Tony reared back his foot and smashed the glass. Tzippi and Tony had looked at each other and grinned, not so much like lovers, but co-conspirators, as if they shared a bond – really a language, a grammar – no other human being could comprehend. It looked to Yael like they felt sorry for the rest of the world's clueless humans for not understanding what they understood. Yael sobbed out loud as Tony's shiny, rented shoe shattered the glass into shards. This, she thought, at least back then, was *adult* love, a love that had already transcended lust and adoration. She was, frankly, jealous, though at the same time deeply moved and happy for her friend.

She'd counseled the two of them in the six months leading to the wedding. That was standard practice for every couple she married, a task Yael didn't particularly enjoy, even as she understood its importance. She worked at it, compiling a growing list of trigger questions, and exercises, and cautionary words of wisdom. But her friendship with Tzippi and Tony made it awkward. She'd tossed back shots of slivovitz with them on Purim, shared too much wine with them, and then giggled at the shit-kicking crowd at Bootie's, a dusty country and western club Peter played every other Wednesday night. Once, she even confided in Tzippi her exasperation over Peter's refusal to look at a bank statement or a mortgage bill, or even a leaky pipe, as if these concerns of home and finance were for real grown-ups like Yael, not an eternal kid like himself. "He won't even try to grow up," Yael had complained. "For him, immaturity is an ideological stance."

"Oh, that's just men," Tzippi had said, but Yael knew better. It wasn't Tony, who the next day ended up repairing the leaky pipe. And it certainly wasn't Judah, the most mature human being Yael had ever met.

Anyway, even before the counseling sessions, Tzippi and Tony had already figured it all out. Finances? They bored Yael with a twenty-minute lecture – each speaking exactly half the time – of how they'd gradually merge their accounts. Children? They had a timeline, a plan, but, yes, of course they knew that when it came to getting pregnant, plans often didn't work out. So they had a plan for when the first plan failed. Infidelity? They stared at her and laughed. Impossible. Really. But, yes, if she insisted on speaking about it, they embraced human frailty. Forgiveness. They'd get through anything. Yael believed them. When it came to sharing household chores, Tony offered such wise and mathematically precise opinions that Yael fought the urge to grab a pad and write down what he was saying so she could share it word for word with Peter. Tzippi looked at Yael with a conspiratorial grin, as if to say, "See? There really is no one else like him!" For Yael, the counseling sessions revealed nothing amiss with Tzippi and Tony, but they did make her ponder her own marriage. She and her husband had yet to talk seriously about children. He refused to discuss finances. They did, of course, spend plenty of time on the subject of infidelity.

Yael adored Tzipporah, loved her laugh, her Westchester sophistication, her gentle fondness for all the teenagers she worked with, especially the shy ones. Tzipporah taught Yael about wines, encouraged her to reread Shakespeare. She was definitely more friend than congregant, more pal than colleague. Now, she tried to embrace Tzippi's extra measure of joy – new job, new baby! – or at least mimic the blissful, all-knowing look she'd seen on the day of the wedding. But Yael was a poor mimic.

"Is something wrong?" Tzippi asked, and stepped away, as if Yael had shoved her.

Yael looked at her tall, suddenly vivacious friend, so delighted and full of confidence. She considered what to say. Should she share Deborah's accusations? Tzippi, she might ask, are you sure it was Tony with you on your wedding night? Did you look carefully? It was dark, wasn't it?

"I'm sorry, Tzippi," she said. "I think the trial took more out of me than I realized. It was… it was child abuse."

"Oh!" She put her hand on her belly as if shielding the fetus. "My gosh! Guilty, or not guilty?"

"He was guilty. See, it wasn't clear at first. But he took the child's hand. She was five, a little girl. Then he took her other hand. He admitted that; he testified to it. And I could tell…" She shook her head, and glanced at her friend. Tzippi's pregnant glow had turned suddenly pale. She was staring, her mouth open.

"Yael, are you sure you're alright? Maybe you should go home."

"I'm fine, thanks. And I'm so happy for you. For you and Tony."

"Yael, you're trembling. And, my God, your color. I've seen you blush, but I've never seen this. I think you should go home."

"No, I'll just rinse off my face, and take a walk." Her voice cracked. She had to get out of there. "*Mazel Tov*, Tzippi."

"Yael. Go home!"

But she was already out the door. She decided to walk across the campus to her office. Maybe the red would drain from her cheeks. One thing for sure: no one would ever need a lie detector to see if she was telling the truth. They could just measure the color of her face.

She waved quickly to Charlotte at the front desk, shoved her key into the lock, then pushed open her office door.

And gasped. Aviva Loeb, Judah's wife, was sitting on her sofa, puffing on a cigarette.

"Aviva, what are you doing? There's no smoking in the synagogue! Are you looking for…? How did you get in here?"

The older woman exhaled smoke, then smiled guiltily. She didn't put out the cigarette. She was using Yael's desk mug – a birthday present from Judah – as an ashtray. There were, of course, no ashtrays on campus. Aviva crossed her legs, then fiddled with her curly, ginger-colored hair in a grotesque parody of primping. Yael flicked on the overhead lights. They illuminated the deep, coffee-colored bags under Aviva's eyes. "The door was unlocked, dear. I decided to wait for you in here."

Since the conclusion of jury duty, Yael was suddenly unsure about many areas of her life: her marriage, her boss, her career, one of her friendships. But she was sure of one thing: her office door was *not* unlocked. She always locked her door.

"Of course," she said. "What can I do for you? Aviva, can you please put out the cigarette?"

The rabbi's wife regarded the cigarette in her hand but made no move to extinguish it. Instead, she stopped puffing, letting it burn down. A piece of ash fell, missing the mug and hitting the coffee table. Yael thought about rushing out and finding Judah, but Aviva's sunken eyes held her.

"I need your help, Yael."

The rabbi stayed by the door, somehow afraid to cross the threshold, into the office. "Of course," she said softly. "Aviva, what's wrong?"

"Wrong? Why do you think something's wrong?"

Another ash dropped, this one missing the table altogether, landing on the white carpet. Aviva's hair hadn't been washed in some time, and there were bright red lipstick smudges on her lower lip and on her teeth. Aviva was no Addison, meticulous about her appearance, but she certainly cared about her looks and always presented herself with great attention to detail. She was, in fact, an attractive woman, with mid-length, curly hair, a clear complexion, and a former dancer's body – losing, with age, some of its slender sculpting, but still fit and angular at fifty. But now she looked awful, with those dark, stain-like spots under her bloodshot eyes, not covered by makeup, and what looked like the beginning of two pimples on her forehead.

"There's nothing *wrong*, dear. Really. I just haven't slept in a while. Insomnia. I've had it for years." Another ash fell, this one into the cup. Yael heard the sizzle, and wondered what manner of liquid was in the mug. Aviva glanced at the cigarette. She shook her head with surprise, then wrinkled her nose in disgust and disapproval, as if she'd just noticed it, as if someone else had been smoking – maybe Yael – but certainly not her. Much to Yael's great relief, she finally snuffed it out. "I'm planning a surprise party, Yael. For Judah."

Yael thought for a moment. "His birthday? But isn't that—?"

"Oh, no, not the birthday. The reorganization."

Yael finally entered the room. She removed her jacket, folded it carefully on one of the chairs across from her desk, and sat down next to Aviva on the sofa, breathing through her mouth to avoid the chimney smell. Yael despised cigarettes, and never much liked Aviva, who was regarded by most of the synagogue staff – if not the majority of congregants – as remote, even imperious. Still, the woman clearly needed her help, and she was, after all, the boss's wife. She pushed the tea mug ashtray out of the way with the back of her hand. "You're planning a surprise party for Judah in honor of the reorganization?"

"Why not? He's worked so hard on it."

Yael caught a whiff of some alcoholic substance. Was Aviva drunk? She thought of Deborah, downing a gin and tonic at lunch. Was that it? Had everyone suddenly decided to get drunk, all the time, every day, and indulge in mad speculations, bizarre behavior?

"I want you to help, Yael, because, after all, it's about you. The reorganization. Judah designed this just to advance your career. You know that don't you?"

What does one do with drunks? Yael was surprised to realize she had virtually no experience with inebriated folks showing up in her office. She supposed that was a blessing, but it left her puzzled right now, and worse, helpless. "Yes," she replied, "he told me that. But, Aviva, should I get Judah?" She touched the older woman's hand. "Will you wait right here? I'll run and—"

"No! Yael, it's a surprise! A *surprise* party. That means it's a secret. You can't *tell* Judah. I'm keeping a secret from *him*. For a change."

Now Yael definitely smelled the booze. It hit her full in the nostrils, along with the stale, smoky tang of cigarettes, a taste not unfamiliar to Yael from her college days. But she'd never really drank or hung around with boozers, so she had no idea what Aviva had imbibed, or when she'd started. She was about to reach for her BlackBerry and call Judah directly – she was afraid to leave Aviva alone – when the rabbi's wife struggled to her feet.

"Never mind," she said. "I can tell you're not the party type. Which, by the way, also sort of explains the reorganization, doesn't it? Gets you away from people, right, Yael? Celebrations, counseling, comforting? Not really your strength, huh?"

"Aviva, did I do something to you? Sit down, please. Do I need to apologize for something?"

But the older woman just leaned down and kissed Yael on the cheek. Yael nearly retched from the odor. "Of course not, sweetie," Aviva said. "What could you do to me?" She grabbed the tea mug and handed it to Yael, as if offering her a drink of ashes. Yael took it from her gently and placed it back on the table, while Aviva, with surprising quickness, stumbled out of the office.

Yael reached for her BlackBerry, waited a moment with her thumb hovering over Judah's photo, then pressed down. But without even a ring, all she got was voicemail. She didn't leave a message.

She walked out of her office and approached Charlotte, who was studying her computer screen. "Did you let Mrs. Loeb into my office?"

"Of course not, Yael. I would never unlock your office for anyone, not even Rabbi Loeb. I didn't even know she'd been there until I saw her walk out."

Yael considered that for a moment, wondering about the testy tone in the secretary's voice. "But haven't you been here all day?"

"Yael, you know, sometimes I go to the bathroom. I'm not the security guard."

"Of course. I'm sorry, Charlotte. I just don't understand how she got in."

"Well, doesn't Rabbi Loeb have a key?"

Yael regarded Charlotte closely. Was she accusing her of something? Was she implying that there was something wrong with her boss having a key to her office? "Yes, he does," she answered. "But I just can't imagine he'd give it to Aviva. Anyway, all she has to do is knock. It's not like I would tell her to go away."

"Yep," Charlotte said, turning back to her monitor. "It's a mystery. Let me know when you solve it."

Back in her office, she pressed Judah's name on her BlackBerry. But again there was no answer. She tried again, twice more and then gave up. She studied the numerous e-mails, texts, and phone messages she'd received in two weeks away from work. The Glatsteins, wanting to reschedule their son's bar mitzvah. The Evans, thanking her again for officiating at the funeral of their grandfather. The choir director, reminding her of their next rehearsal, a rehearsal Yael had no intention of attending. What did she know from choirs? Sandra Levy wanting to talk yet again about her miscarriage. Yael took a deep breath and divided the messages into categories – life cycle, counseling, administration, miscellaneous. She dove in.

Before leaving that evening, she stopped by Judah's office. The door was shut and the lights were out, but she knew that sometimes Judah liked to meditate in the dark. She put up her hand to knock, then the odor hit her. Not Aviva's boozy-cigarette mix, but the unmistakable stench of Weinman. She looked around quickly, sure that he was lurking somewhere in the foyer. Charlotte had left hours before, so Yael was all alone in the darkened hallway. She held her breath and surveyed the area, peering behind cabinets, under desks. No Cantor, just his essence, somehow both rotten and fresh, decaying but new. She considered the door. Inside, with Judah? It happened, much too often for Yael's comfort. But usually you could hear them, arguing, or yelling, or singing, or laughing like lunatics. But now just the smell, and a dark, quiet room. She was about to go ahead and knock but realized quickly that she couldn't face the scumbag, not tonight, not after dealing with the loopy, drunk Aviva, or the wacky Deborah. Instead, she went into the bathroom and grabbed the bottle of air freshener. She doused the hallway, replacing Weinman's nastiness with sickly-clean. Then she returned to her office and sniffed the air. Cigarette smoke lingered. She sprayed her office, wielding the aerosol can like a gun.

CHAPTER 3

On her drive home, the image of Tzippi and Tony hit her again, two decked-out connivers, grinning and winking under the *huppah*, the marriage canopy. She marveled that they'd only known each other six months before getting engaged, and then waited just three months before tying the knot. How could a nine-month couple develop such a confident, conspiratorial sympathy? She'd known Peter almost eight years now, and there were still vast areas of his psyche which remained black holes to her.

Yael had met her husband their senior year at Berkeley, at rehearsals for "The Grand Bowl," the Theatre Department's annual gala. Yael acted and sang, Peter played clarinet in the band. Yael noticed him right away because he was the only boy in the show who wore a yarmulke all the time. Apart from a few Black Muslims, he was the only guy she saw on the entire campus wearing a religious head covering. Peter's was a small, sky-blue knit kippah, quite unlike the large, colorful, multi-ornamented Egyptian-style caps favored by most of her male classmates at Hillel Academy, her high school. Actually, it wasn't the fact of the yarmulke that drew her; it was its lack of ostentation, the way it sat modestly on his big head of curly brown hair, looking slightly ridiculous, more like a beverage coaster than a hat.

Yael also noted that he was the second shyest person in the show, she being the first. He never clowned around with his fellow musicians during the long and numerous breaks; he either studied or, more often, took out a mandolin and played klezmer tunes. Yael walked past him several times during those breaks, fingering her Jewish star, or humming Jewish melodies, or muttering softly in Hebrew.

"It was your hips that got my attention, not the Jewish stuff," he told her later, the first time they'd spent the night together.

"Really! But you still didn't say anything."

"I didn't know what to say to those hips."

Finally, in the full throes of a crush, one day Yael interrupted the mandolin noodling and asked him the world's oldest question: where are you from? He smiled and put down the instrument. It was a long story.

"You haven't stopped talking since," she told him that night.

"Shy, but not quiet. That's me. You, too."

It was true. Once they discovered each other – once she found the four words they needed to open a conversation – their days and nights were filled with endless conversations, interrupted occasionally by meals and sex. Yael spoke about her life, growing up the daughter of a divorced rabbi, her strained relationship with her older brother, her love of performing, coupled with the unhappy fact that she was clearly good enough for college shows but definitely not talented enough to go professional. Peter responded enthusiastically, even wisely, but, except for his opening ten-minute soliloquy on where he was from, he barely spoke about himself. When he initiated conversation, it was often about pop culture, movies, TV or music. At first, Yael feared that he was a talented musician but a mediocre and incurious intellect, a charming enough combination, but, for her, not one that inspired a lifetime commitment. It was only after he shared some of his writings and compositions that she realized he was brilliant but also amazingly well read. In normal conversation he stuck to analyses of *Gilligan's Island*, or the latest Dave Matthews album, but alone in his room he composed lovely orchestral suites for mandolins, and wrote papers comparing Heidegger with Maimonides. "I'm kind of a savant," he told her. "When I read and write and play, I put my entire brain into what I'm doing, but it's like moving temporarily to a parallel universe where I exchange personalities and missions. It's like it's not really me doing all that deep thinking. When I'm done, I move back here, back home, and turn on the TV."

They got married four years after graduation, the summer Peter received his Ph.D. in musicology from NYU. A year later, after she graduated from the Jewish Theological Seminary, Yael assumed he'd want to stay in New York and pursue a career performing Jewish music on the mandolin and clarinet. But Peter told her to go ahead and apply to the huge congregation in Desert Garden; the university there had a decent enough music department. He received an offer before she did.

"I thought you wanted to play, write, record. I thought you didn't like teaching."

"Let's be honest here. For once. It's Jewish music. Even in New York, I'll never make enough to support us."

"I'll support you. I don't mind."

"I like the desert," he'd said, and grabbed his mandolin, the signal that he was done talking about himself. "Did you hear the new Wilco album?" he asked. "Listen to this riff."

She liked Wilco; she liked the riff. She enjoyed him when he waxed poetic about meaningless trivia. But this was their life. "Peter, this is Desert County. They don't put the word 'Desert' in every community down there for nothing. The culture is pretty far from New York, not to mention Odessa. Who will you play with? Who will you perform for? How will you share your gift?"

"I'll have students. I love teaching."

"You always told me you abhorred teaching."

"Really?" he said, not looking up. "I said that? Well, I do like making money, and the job pays well."

"Peter."

He removed his long, lovely fingers from his instrument and met her eye for the first time in the conversation. "Yael, you'll love it out there in the desert. You can go running at dawn, every day. You'll climb mountains at sunset. We'll look for coyotes together, and ancient Indian civilizations. I want to do this for *you*. And I'll be fine."

Yael stared at her husband. She wondered briefly if this was his insecurity, his fear (not, it must be said, unjustified) of losing her again to another crush. Give her the desert, a romantic landscape, perfect for her exercise cravings, her infatuation with the outdoors, and she'll give him her heart, forever. Was that the deal? She decided not to ask. Rabbi Loeb hadn't even offered her the job. But when he did, a week later, Peter immediately called the chair of the music department at Desert University and accepted the position.

Peter played for three bands in Desert County: clarinet for the Desert Klezmer All-Stars, a Jewish wedding/bar-mitzvah outfit; saxophone for Estancia, a Latin-jazz ensemble; and mandolin and banjo for the Desert City Cryers, a country and western group that played nearly every honky-tonk in the county, and actually recorded two albums in Bakersfield. Most weeks, Peter was out three, sometimes four nights, often not returning until early in the morning. When she could, when her schedule opened up, or when fatigue from overwork wasn't dragging her to bed, which wasn't often, Yael would drive to a club, a saloon, a *freilich,* or wherever he was appearing, and watch his supple fingers, moving either up and down the fretboard, or dancing along whatever reed was attached to his mouth. Wherever and whatever he played, the same sky-blue yarmulke bobbed up and down on his curly hair. He never complained about living in exile from the Jewish-American music centers, but then he never really complained about anything in his life, because that would mean talking about himself, or at least thinking about his dreams and aspirations, something Yael finally realized simply didn't interest him. They did fight, oh yes, but it was usually over her career, not his. Why was she always working so hard? Why didn't she ask for more money? Why did *she* have to stay out so late (for musicians, of course, that was understood)? Yael always caught a whiff of distrust in these questions, not necessarily suspicions of another man, though there was that, but fear that her passion, her attention, her interest was drifting, because that was always the symptom of the potential next phase, a new crush. Yael defended herself during these spats, which wasn't hard because she *did* love him, still, with a passion. She loved watching those thin fingers do their magic; she loved hearing him hold forth on the relative worth of the various *Star Trek* television shows; she loved listening to him practice on four instruments simultaneously while his computer honked out some electronic concoction; she loved watching him suck every emotion from his soul as he composed extraordinarily beautiful music, always on his mandolin. How many great composers, she wondered, composed on the mandolin? He was heavy and he was light and he was brilliant and he was mysterious. He never talked about himself, so she always had to pay careful attention, and her attention didn't waver. Until now, that is, until that moment on the courthouse steps.

He was waiting for her on the front porch, sitting in the dark, strumming on something she'd never seen before. It looked more animal than machine, like a two-headed mountain lion, with unkempt whiskers flying off in all directions, and Peter not so much playing as taming. Every three months or so, a new instrument appeared. Peter would take great delight in introducing Yael to the new acquisition, usually with a brief, witty lecture on the origins and development of the new thing in his hands. Tonight, though, Yael was not in the mood.

"Aren't you cold?" she asked, because it *was* cold, under fifty; it got cold in the desert, at night, even in late February. And he was sitting and strumming in the dark, barefoot, wearing only plaid boxer shorts, a white T-shirt and his blue, knit kippah. Yael pecked him quickly on the cheek, and whizzed past through the open door. She was, she decided, cold, much too cold to talk. She shut the screen door.

"It's a twelve-string malounka," Peter called out, as if that were the question she'd asked. "Greek, not really ancient; not old at all. Maybe 16th century, at the earliest. You're probably thinking klezmer – it's Greek and all – but I'm actually thinking of it for the Cryers. If you just play the top strings, it sounds like a double-barreled banjo. What do you think?" He picked the banjo part from "The Grievous Angel" by Graham Parsons. Graham himself, Peter had once instructed Yael, played the banjo on that record.

Yael decided not to engage in conversation through a screen door. She resisted the impulse to shut the thick, wooden front door – she was suddenly very cold, and somehow the sound of the malounka chilled her even more – because even her clueless husband would notice the rudeness in the gesture. But she didn't respond to his jabbering about banjos and country-rock legends. Instead, she opened the refrigerator, wondering about dinner, annoyed that Peter hadn't even thought to put on a pot of canned soup. She knew he could keep on playing and talking for hours until he got bored, and he didn't bore easily when it came to his own music or his many observations on pop culture. Under these circumstances, he didn't need her responses, he just wanted an audience, and even that wasn't entirely necessary.

But he surprised her this time by lugging the monster into the house, leaning it carefully against the wall, and embracing her gently from behind. "What's wrong?" he asked. "The trial? Do you want to tell me about the trial?"

She thought for a moment, while she rubbed his hand with hers, brushing against his wedding ring. The trial? Was that it? Did that account for the gloomy mood which suddenly felt like it had always been there, as much a part of her as her straight, black hair? But so much had happened since the trial: those awful lunches with Addison and Deborah; Aviva Loeb showing up in her office, drunk and smoking; Tzippi's pregnancy; the accusations against Judah. And, oh God, Judah – her feelings about Judah. Seeing – and smelling – the scumbag again after a two-week respite. She closed her eyes.

"Why don't we have a baby?" she asked.

He laughed. "You've got to be kidding. *That's* what's on your mind?"

She jerked away. "You think I'm kidding? I'm joking?"

He touched her shoulder. "We're *ready* to have a baby? Is that what you're saying? This would be a responsible thing to do? You're ready?"

"I'm not exactly fifteen years old," she said. "And we are married. I wouldn't call it *irresponsible* to start speaking about children."

"You're out every night, at a class, or a meeting, or whatever."

"So are you. Out every night. At a performance. Or whatever."

"Exactly."

She glared at him. She was astonished that he was still grinning, that he somehow hadn't realized that the conversation had moved way past banter. They were fighting, but he didn't know it yet. "Do you even want children?" she asked.

"Yael, I'm not even sure why…"

"What kind of father do you think you would be?"

He took a step back. "Yael, ordinarily, I would take that as a serious question. But do you hear how angry you are? What are you accusing me of? I've barely seen you in two weeks, and in our first conversation you wonder what kind of father I would be."

"Sorry," she said quickly, but mostly to fend off the calm lecture she knew was coming, how she didn't understand how hurtful a *tone* could be, how modulating a voice toward anger just provokes more anger. She took a breath. "I found out today that Tzipporah's pregnant. And I was just wondering why we don't even talk about having children. Every couple I marry has some plan. We never made a plan. Why do you think that is?"

He sat down. "Let's talk about it now. You're home, I'm home, we're both awake. The fact is, I've been meaning to bring it up. What an amazing coincidence. Let's talk about it now."

He pointed to the chair next to his. Yael sat, wondering what to say, wondering why she brought up the subject in the first place. Was this it? Was it as simple as a biological imperative? She needed a baby – in her body, growing inside her; outside her body, sucking on her breasts, something – some*one* – connected to her, to love, to nurture? That's what she wanted? She studied her husband's scraggly beard, wondering, as she often did, why it always looked so incomplete. "I... Peter... I think I want a baby," she said.

He smiled.

And then the air was filled with electronic music: the Hebrew song "Heivenu Shalom Aleichem." Yael's Black-Berry, the emergency number, known only to Peter, Judah, and Charlotte. "Please do *not* answer that," Peter said.

She glanced at the number. It was Charlotte's cellphone. Charlotte had been gone when Yael left for the day, so she wasn't calling from work.

"Yael," Peter said.

Her thumb hovered briefly over the device. She hit *ignore,* cutting off the music.

"Thank you," Peter said. "You were saying?"

"You know, I think you were right, at the beginning. It is the trial. It made me think about children, parenting. My parents. My father. And I just think..."

"Heivenu Shalom Aleichem" blared tenaciously, as if summoning them to a *horah.* To Yael, it seemed somehow louder this time, though she knew that wasn't possible. "Don't," Peter said.

She looked at the number. Charlotte, again. "Whoever it is can leave a message," Peter said in his quiet, wispy voice, a voice that somehow grew more insistent the softer it got. Peter, of course, was a genius with modulation. "We shouldn't put this off, Yael. You know that."

"Yes, but..."

"Yael."

The song played on. "I'm sorry, Peter, I'll just tell her..." She pressed the talk button.

"Yael!" It was Charlotte. Yael heard her voice several times a day, so she knew. But there was something high-pitched in the tone, as if she were on the verge of giggling hysterically. Yael also heard something else in the background, a soft buzzing, like wasps or a loud breeze, or someone whispering. "Yael, you'd better get over here! I'm at Judah's."

"Charlotte!"

"Yael, I can't tell you everything right now. But come!"

She looked at Peter, who'd leaned over to pick up the malounka. "Is this an emergency, Charlotte? Because, otherwise…"

"Aviva Loeb is dead."

"What!"

"She was murdered, Yael. Someone killed her! Rabbi Loeb needs you. And I need to *talk* with you."

"I'll be right there." She placed the BlackBerry on the table and slowly turned to face her husband. Peter was strumming the malounka and staring at Yael, his eyes wide with horror. Weird music – bent notes, atonal phrases – filled the air. "You heard?" she said.

"You'd better go."

"We'll talk later?"

He nodded. She was halfway out the door when she heard Peter's whine. "Yael," he called. She turned around. The music stopped.

"Who would kill Aviva Loeb?"

A thought danced through her head, several thoughts actually, images, ideas, distinct and specific, but none of them made it to her mouth.

"We'll talk later," she said, and ran to her car.

CHAPTER 4

"I've lost my soulmate, my *khaver rukhani* – my spiritual companion. I know just how the psalmist felt when he complained to God, 'You hid your face from me. I'm astonished.' I'm astonished at the ragged rip in my heart. It astonishes me. God's face is now hid from me. Aviva's gone, and I'm stupefied."

Yael was sitting in the second row of the sanctuary, Deborah on one side, Peter on the other. Aviva's sister sat directly in front of them. They all stared wide-eyed at the new widower, eulogizing his wife. Yael had thought, for a few moments at least, that she might be the one to offer the eulogy, or to conduct the funeral service. She assumed she'd participate in some way. She was, after all, the only other rabbi of the congregation, the only other clergy. But Judah's classmate Efraim Bergen was officiating. And Judah, despite his grief, or because of it, gave the only eulogy. As usual, he captured everyone in the packed sanctuary, on the strength of his words, certainly, but also through his gestures; the way he drew small circles with his thumb; the way he shut his blue eyes in between thoughts, as if channeling the angels; the magical way he managed to look everyone in the eye; the music in his voice, what Peter called his vocal blues scale. With tone alone, never mind the words, he articulated grief, then resignation, then rage, and then again grief. Bereft of his wife, he was still a master communicator, and Yael, despite her own breathless tears – more, of course, for him than for her – couldn't help but compare herself to the master, her boss. It was the right choice, she thought. I'd never be able to move these people with my words, my voice. And this congregation, these mourners, *wanted* to be moved.

She'd assumed that she and Judah would work out the funeral arrangements, along with Aviva's family. But even though she rushed to the Loeb house after speaking with Charlotte, she couldn't even get into the study to see Judah. Charlotte blocked the way. "I'm sorry, Yael. Rabbi Loeb gave me a list of people to let in to see him. You're not on the list. He said to tell everyone to please respect his grief and his privacy."

Yael wouldn't have been more surprised if Charlotte had spit on her nose. "But Charlotte, you called me! You said you needed to speak with me. You told me that Rabbi Loeb needed me. Anyway, the funeral arrangements. I have to…" She actually pushed the secretary out of the way, but Charlotte, thin, small, but wiry, was quicker and strong. She stretched her narrow, surprisingly lengthy arm against the door.

"Yael," she drawled, her Nashville accent suddenly prominent, "I'll tell him you'd paid your respects. But you can't go in, not right now. He insisted. Anyway, Rabbi Bergen's taking care of the arrangements."

"Oh. I thought…"

"Yael, you can go home. I only called you because you need to know. Isn't it obvious that you would need to know?

He didn't summon you. I'm sorry I gave you that impression. I'll let you know when he needs you."

Yael had noticed eight cars on the street and in the driveway, including Addison's black Mercedes. And she could hear voices, even laughter. Judah wasn't alone in there, bearing his grief in solitary meditation. He was with loved ones, his closest friends. And that, she realized, didn't include her. It might have been her imagination, but she could swear she caught a whiff of a familiar stench – Cantor Weinman. *He's in there, and I'm out here?* She quickly chased away the idea.

In the hallway, on her way out, she ran into Deborah. Her eyes were red and baggy, darting every which way, and her hair a sudden freak show of gray and brown wisps. Yael had never seen the synagogue president more discombobulated. She looked like a cocaine addict. The two embraced.

"I can't believe it. Yael, it's just too much for me to take in. I don't understand."

"Deborah, do you know when this happened? I left the synagogue two hours ago. I could swear Judah had already left. No one will tell me anything."

"I guess Judah got the call from the police at choir rehearsal. I think he was just leaving."

Yael thought for a second. The choir rehearsed in the school wing, on the opposite end of the campus from her office. Tzippi would have been there, singing with the choir. "Judah was at choir rehearsal?" she asked.

Deborah shut her bloodshot eyes briefly, then focused them on Yael. "Yeah, it was funny. Not his thing, right? But he said he wanted to check in, that he had some ideas. Anyway, how is he?"

"I don't know. Charlotte wouldn't let me in."

Deborah opened her mouth slowly and gaped, first at Yael, and then towards the study. "Charlotte wouldn't let you in? Charlotte?" Deborah shook her head so hard, it looked like she was shaking the demons from her brain. She appeared, suddenly, not just frazzled, but furious. "Yael, what the hell are they doing? Wait right here!"

She heard high voices, then shouting. But Deborah didn't get any farther than Yael. Her name wasn't on the list.

Driving east on Cactus Boulevard, heading home, Yael noticed Tzippi's red Toyota turn onto Judah's block. Yael pulled her car over and waited. She sat still, listening to an '80s alt-country compilation CD that Peter had burned for her. Tzippi, like her, would be turned away at the study door. She'd be back any second. But thirty minutes passed, and no red Toyota. So Yael turned around and drove back to Judah's. Tzippi's car sat empty in the driveway. She made it in, Yael thought. She talked her way past Charlotte, she, with her barely discernible fetus. Tzippi got in to see Judah. Not Yael.

She tried again the next day, but this time it was Shaina, Aviva's sister, who stood in the doorway – and not the doorway to the study this time; Shaina wouldn't even let her in the house. "I had to put Judah on Plaxiton," she explained. "It's an anti-anxiety medication. I'm a doctor, you know."

Maybe so, but now she resembled a professional bodyguard. Yael looked up at her face, studied her pale neck and guessed 6 feet, 200 pounds. With her thick, ginger-colored curls and wide green eyes, she looked like a steroid version of Aviva, without the worry wrinkle.

"Of course," Yael said. "But maybe if I could just…"

"Nope," Shaina said, now shutting the door and joining Yael outside. "No one." She smiled mirthlessly. "Doctor's orders," she said.

But as soon as Yael turned back toward her car, his voice reached her ears. "Yael." It was barely above a whisper, but the music was there, the *tone*. Pained. Welcoming. She faced him.

He looked dreadful. And wonderful. He hadn't shaved in at least two days. Yael was surprised to see that the stubble was reddish brown; a marked contrast to his silver hair, which needed cutting. He wore faded jeans and a black T-shirt; Yael had never seen him without a necktie. Sunglasses obscured his blue eyes; and so much of his appeal, at least to Yael, came from his eyes. Poorly dressed, badly groomed, Yael nearly gasped at the indignity of his appearance; this was a man who ordinarily took several seconds to straighten his tie before every appointment.

On the other hand: the stubble, the sunglasses, the black T-shirt covering a muscular chest. She couldn't help the thought; it escaped her like a burp, or gas: he looked like a movie star, a sexy leading man playing a grieving husband. He looked good.

"Thanks for coming, Yael."

"Judah." She squinted at him, trying to see past the shades into his eyes. "I don't know what to say. I'm – I'm sorry, Judah. I'm sorry for your loss."

He smiled sadly and nodded. "You're a good friend, Yael. I have a lot to say to you. But, now…" He turned up his hand, vaguely pointing at his sister-in-law, who was frowning fiercely. "Thank you for coming." Shaina took his arm and led him back into the house.

"Judah!" Yael called. He turned his head, but not his body. Shaina glared. "Do you need me to do anything for the funeral? I could read something or—"

"We've planned my sister's funeral," Shaina interrupted, tugging on Judah's arm. He opened his mouth as if to add something but then gave in, and allowed himself to be led. Shaina slammed the door.

Halfway through Judah's eulogy, as if a switch had been pulled, Yael broke down sobbing. It was the voice, not the words. She struggled to quiet herself and ended up squealing, while thick tears leaked from her eyes. Peter turned to her with surprise, then put his arm around her. She resisted resting her face on her husband's shoulder because she wanted to watch Judah speak.

"One," Judah, continued. "I learned what One meant, the Sacred Unity, the blending of souls, the shattering of differences, which obliterates separation and loneliness. Oh, Aviva! We were One, or, I should say, you made me feel the One. You made me whole. You integrated me, so I was one with myself, while I blended with you into the greater One." He stroked his red-brown stubble and fingered his torn tie, the garment he'd cut earlier to symbolize his grief. He shut his eyes and considered what to say next. "I don't feel the One anymore." He smiled ruefully, only now opening his eyes and peeking at the audience. He shook his head. "I'm like my tie." He showed it to the congregation, then grasped the two sides with both hands and ripped it once more. "Look!" he cried. "It's me!" Yael could swear he caught her eye. It felt like he was speaking directly to her, giving her the tie. She fought the urge to lift her hand toward him, to mimic a gesture of touch. His legs shook while he held out both ends of the tie to the crowd, an offering, a demonstration. He's going to fall, Yael thought, and steadied herself so she could leap up and catch him. But his classmate Rabbi Bergen grabbed his arm and led him back to his seat. The crowd murmured but then quieted when Tzippi, suddenly big-breasted, but not really showing, rose to chant the memorial prayer. Her soprano voice cracked several times. Before leading the mourner's kaddish, Rabbi Bergen reminded the crowd that the burial was private, but everyone was invited to Rabbi Loeb's home that evening for prayers.

"I thought you didn't like her," Peter whispered in Yael's ear as they walked out, his arm still around her shoulder "I've never seen you cry so much."

"I was crying for him!" she hissed, and untangled herself from his arm.

"Okay, sorry," he said, and his alto whine immediately pricked Yael's conscience. "I'm sorry, Peter," she said. "I honestly don't know why I was crying. I'm confused. I shouldn't take it out on you."

"Thank you for apologizing," he said coldly, then kissed her lightly on the cheek, and rushed off, leaving her alone.

He'd told her years ago that his best response to her snapping at him for no good reason was to kiss her and run away. That way they avoided a fight. She'd agreed, and this time was especially grateful. With Judah out indefinitely, she had a lot of work to do the rest of the day, and she wanted to be on time for the evening service at his house.

In fact, she thought she'd arrived early – a half an hour before the service was scheduled to begin. But the living room was already crowded with comforters milling around in dark business suits, trading jokes in soft voices, holding drinks. To Yael, these home mourning services – *shivah minyans*, in Hebrew – resembled low-key cocktail parties, particularly in affluent Desert Garden, where the French Gourmet often catered the affairs. It seemed like half the congregation was crammed into Judah's living room. She saw Deborah and her husband Michael standing in a corner, Michael finishing off his drink while Deborah stared into space, her makeup not quite obscuring the dark bags under her eyes. Yael also spotted Tzippi, without Tony, more to the center of the room, laughing hard at something someone said. She looked beautiful, Yael thought – straight and tall, like a model, with rosy cheeks, clear complexion, and those suddenly full breasts. Yael took a step toward her, scanning the crowd for Judah, then stopped in her tracks. The odor hit her first, followed by the revolting sight. Weinman, sitting on a chair right next to Judah's low stool, whispering in his ear, their knees practically touching. She shook her head. A wave of nausea hit her and she stepped backwards, as if the scumbag's essence carried a polar negative force, negative to her positive, evil to her good. What the hell is he doing here? she thought to herself, and then blushed because, for an instance, she thought she had whispered the question out loud. She wanted to flee, but heard Tzippi's voice calling her over. She waded through the crowd and stood next to Judah. His sunglasses were back on his face, and he showed no signs of acknowledging her presence. He was leaning his ear into Weinman's mouth, listening attentively. Yael glanced at Tzippi, who shrugged, then pecked Yael on the cheek.

Yael bent at her waist towards her boss. "Judah, I'm so sorry," she said, speaking into his other ear. He twitched suddenly, as if a mosquito had bitten him, and Yael jolted backwards.

"Yael," he said, and reached out his hand. She took it, thinking a handshake, but he held on, his long, skinny fingers caressing the back of her hand, not letting go. "My good friend." The stentorian tone was back in his voice, the confidence, the music in a major key. "My loyal colleague. You understand I'm so sorry you didn't lead the service today. But Aviva's sisters, they insisted on Efraim. It's no disrespect, Yael, no reflection on your ability. Or our friendship."

"Of course, Judah," she said, blushing. "Don't even think of it. It was the last thing on my mind," she said, lying. In fact, though she hated to admit it, she felt relieved. He does respect me, she thought. He does appreciate me.

"You'll have to take over now, Yael. You know I have full confidence in you."

"Thank you, Judah."

"It won't be for long. It's just the… shock. Jesus, the shock. The shock, I think is the worst thing. Don't you, Yael? I'll need some time. Perhaps… a few days."

A few days? she thought. After losing a wife of twenty-five years to murder? The traditional mourning period for every loss was a week. "Judah, you can take as long as—"

"This is bigger than both of us, Yael."

"Judah, I'm not sure…"

"Our synagogue. This work we do. Our work. It's sacred work, Yael. I think you know that." He peeled off his sunglasses. Yael drew back, expecting bloodshot eyes, but there wasn't a single drop of red in his baby blues. "It's bigger than me, certainly. Bigger than both of us."

"I know, Judah," she said, though she was not at all sure what he was getting at. Sure, they did sacred work, she supposed, but why remind her now, the day he'd buried his wife? And, after all, it was a just a synagogue, a congregation, in the suburbs, in the desert, in America. It wasn't the ancient Temple.

"Hey, Rabbi Doll, ain't you gonna say something to me?"

Almost on their own initiative, her eyes moved sideways and she saw the man, the fat cantor. He was smirking, leaning forward, his yellow teeth, his humpback nose, hovering dangerously close to her hips. Over the past fourteen months, since overcoming the raw hatred, the physical revulsion, since she'd realized that, for whatever reason, Judah would continue to tolerate his despicable presence, she'd responded to Weinman's approaches with wisecracks – jokes and puns that she'd hoped were cruel enough, devoid enough of warmth, to send the message that she still despised him, even though she couldn't ignore him, or slap him, or call the police. But now she couldn't think of anything to say, and wondered briefly what it would mean to kick in his ugly face, here at Judah's *shiva minyan*. As if daring her, he tilted his bald head questioningly and widened his smirk into a grin. "How's your dad, sweetie?" he asked. "Give him my regards?"

"Ed," Judah said. "Please."

"It's alright," Yael said, grateful that, for once, Judah intervened. She leaned down, kissed Judah on the cheek, and backed quickly away.

On the way out, after prayers, Deborah grabbed her arm. For several seconds the two women just looked at each other, as if uttering words would bring reality to the dark thoughts each knew the other held. Yael had always admired how young and healthy Deborah looked at age fifty-five, despite working more than full-time in a demanding job, despite raising four boys, despite serving in what was certainly the most stressful volunteer job in the Jewish community: synagogue president. But now, for the first time, Deborah looked her age. Yael noticed wrinkles on the older woman's forehead that she'd sworn she'd never seen and, of course, there were the red eyes and the bruise-like bags just underneath. "Deborah," she finally said, just to break the silence.

"You'd better get ready, Yael. I mean that. Talk to Peter."

Yael nodded.

"It's going to… it's going to hit the fan. You know what I mean?"

"I think so, Deborah." A murder investigation, Yael thought. It was probably a robbery, but still. Despite his assurances, Judah would be out of commission for some time now, leaving Yael in charge of a complex, confused, wounded congregation. And, of course, for two days now, buzzing in the back of her brain was her earlier conversation with Deborah. Judah. The women.

Deborah touched her shoulder. "I've always admired you, Yael. You're smart. You're competent. And you're even a little spiritual. You are, Yael. Please remember that. We'll need it." Tears filled Yael's eyes. Deborah tightened her grip. "We're going to need *you*, Yael."

Yael shook her head. She felt new sobs coming on and didn't want to hear her own squeals, especially not in front of Deborah. "I have to go home," she said.

"Yes, you do. Go home, Yael. Talk to your husband."

She turned around and left the house, determined to do just that. Go home, make up with Peter – though she couldn't remember why it was they needed to make up. And fortify herself for what she suspected was coming. But as she reached for her car door, another hand gripped her firmly on the arm.

"Ms. Gold?"

She turned, looked up, and blinked in surprise. The man leaning down to touch her shoulder was absurdly tall; Yael guessed 6 foot 9, but skinny, as if he were a teenager, still growing into his bulk. His scalp was smooth, tan, and shiny, but his sunburned face needed a shave. Yael recognized him right away. "You're the policeman," she said. "Epstein. From that child abuse case."

He smiled, but it was more an acknowledgement than a sign of warmth or familiarity. There was no friendship in the smile. "And you're juror number seven," he said. "I heard you single-handedly turned the jury around."

She blushed. "He was guilty."

He nodded. "Of course he was. And you don't even know the full story. I need to speak with you, Ms. Gold. I'm sorry; I should be saying *Rabbi* Gold. We didn't have women rabbis when I was growing up."

Yael wondered, as she had at the trial, whether the tall cop was Jewish. There was his name – Epstein – and his bumpy, formidable nose. But there weren't that many Jewish policemen, and even fewer Jews over 6 feet. Anyway, Yael was confused. "You want to talk to me about the case?" she asked. "But isn't it over? What, is he appealing?"

"No, no, not that case," he said, finally releasing her shoulder. "About *this* case." He gestured with his sharp-edged chin toward the house. "The Loeb case.

She suggested, more like implored, they meet tomorrow, maybe at a Starbucks near his office, but he insisted they talk now. And when she offered to get in her car and meet him at the Starbucks of his choice, he told her he really meant *now*, immediately, in this place. He guided her to his car, less than half a block away, and they both sat in the back. Yael caught the odor of stale coffee and cigarettes. Was he on a stakeout? How long had he been waiting for her? She declined his offer of chewing gum, but did accept a warm can of Diet Coke. "You do murders, too?" she asked.

He laughed. "This is the second homicide in four years in Desert Garden. Wouldn't be much work for a homicide department. There are ten detectives in the whole department, Ms. Gold. We all do all sorts of crime. Captain asked me to investigate this one 'cause it involves the synagogue. Besides, how'd you know it was a murder?"

Yael stared at him in the dark, looking for a smile, some sign that he was kidding. How'd she know it was a murder? Everyone knew it was a murder. It was the lead headline of the *Desert City Journal*: "Rabbi's Wife Strangled to Death." What kind of question was that? More importantly, to what kind of person did a cop ask a question like that? She thought for a moment. "Well, everyone knows."

"Everyone knows? What's that supposed to mean?"

"Well, just that."

"How did *you* find out, Ms. Gold. Let's stick to you. I mean Rabbi Gold. Sorry."

"It was the first thing Charlotte said when she called me…"

"Charlotte? Who's Charlotte?"

"You don't know who Charlotte is?"

"Please answer my questions, Ms. Gold."

He's asking questions he already knows the answers to, she thought, a sense of sick amazement growing in her head. And he knows I'm a rabbi, but he's deliberately provoking me. "Charlotte Millard. Rabbi Loeb's secretary. She called me that night."

"What night? And what time? Exactly."

He proceeded to shoot a series of questions her way, demanding precisely how Yael learned all the relevant facts, and insisting she fully account for her whereabouts for the past forty-eight hours. Yael was tired and rattled by the machine-gun, rat-a-tat volley of the questions, but she felt like she acquitted herself well. She told the story of how Aviva had showed up in her office, and recalled their conversation pretty much verbatim because it had seemed so strange. She remembered all the times and all the places. She was beginning to feel a bit more at ease, especially after Epstein offered – and she accepted – another can of Diet Coke. Until the detective said, "So, you really have no alibi to speak of."

Alibi? "I told you, I was with my husband when Charlotte called. Before that, I was in the office."

"Yes," he said quickly, and made a note in his book. "Your husband, Peter. The musician who also teaches. Now, Ms. Gold, are you having an affair with Rabbi Loeb?"

She fought the urge to throw the can of Coke in his face. Instead, she reached for the car door. She realized suddenly that she'd never even asked to see a badge. Was this really a cop? But then she remembered the trial, the abuse case. How could she have forgotten? She needed to sleep, to think. She was bone-tired. The caffeine in her Diet Cokes did nothing for her; if anything the drinks only heightened her weariness.

Epstein's long arm shot out, and held the door shut. "Do you need to speak to a lawyer, Ms. Gold?"

She shook her head vehemently, but in her mind she wondered, Was she a suspect? Clearly, she was. She was a suspect! "I am *not* having an affair with Judah," she spat out. "I mean with Rabbi Loeb. That's easy enough to prove. I'm offended that you would ask me, Detective. And please don't call me Ms. Gold."

"My apologies," he said quickly. "No offense intended."

She nodded, as if accepting his apology. No offense intended? Accusing her of adultery? Of murder? What on earth did he intend?

"I can go?" she asked.

"Of course," he said, as if it were the most obvious thing in the world, as if his large hand wasn't still clutching the door handle, preventing her from leaving. "But why do you say it would be easy enough to prove? That you're not having an affair? How do you *prove* that?"

He moved his arm and made no effort to stop her. "Just ask anyone," she said, and left the car. As she hurried away, she heard the detective slam the door shut.

Two

UNCLE FLAVIO

CHAPTER 1

When Yael first became reacquainted with Weinman, two years before Aviva's murder, she didn't call him scumbag; she called him Cantor Weinman. At first, she even liked him. Sort of. Or maybe felt sorry for him.

"I used to babysit you, kid. I changed your diapers." He'd phoned her at her office, six months after she moved to Desert County. "Tell me you remember me, please! Hey, how about this? I'll sing you something. You *loved* listening to me sing." He launched into "Varshe Mein." A spark went off in Yael's memory. She knew the song but didn't remember learning it, didn't remember knowing *any* Yiddish songs. The associations from the melody were both pleasant and unpleasant; she hummed along momentarily and then, for no reason she could imagine, squirmed in her seat. His voice, in fact, was lovely – rich, low, sad. So much different, she thought, than the high, jangly, upbeat melodies her husband always played. "I do remember that song!" she said, wondering why it simultaneously comforted her and filled her with anxiety.

"Ah, that was your lullaby, Doll. Hey, no offense, Rabbi. I used to call you Doll, just like your Dad. Maybe now I'll call you Rabbi Doll. But that was your lullaby, kid. I sang it to knock you out, when all else failed. Christ, it was hard to get you to sleep! Bedtimes were the worst for you. You were always calling for your *imma* and *abba*. But "Varshe Mein" did the trick – almost every time. Except when you started to cry just hearing it, 'cause you knew I was using it to get you to close those eyes."

"So that's how we know each other?" Yael asked. "You were my babysitter?"

"Babysitter? Jesus, you really don't remember, do you? I was the *hazzan* at your dad's *shul*. In Jersey, where you were born. For three years, 'til he had to leave. We were partners, he and I! Partners in crime, some would say. Oh, gosh, Doll, I adored your dad. Great, great man."

"Thanks. I agree. You know, it's funny, your voice sounds sort of familiar. And I love that song. But I don't remember the name 'Doll' at all." And I don't particularly like it, she thought, especially in combination with rabbi.

"Doll? Oh, that was my special name. Sometimes I called you Doll Face or Dolly, but mostly just Doll."

"I thought you said my father used it."

"Oh, he did, but only 'cause he heard it from me. Hey, why not ask him? He'd remember! Oh, shit, I can't believe I said that! Oh, God, what an insensitive thing to say! I'm so sorry, Doll. You can't really ask him anything now, can you?"

Two months ago Yael's father had finally received a diagnosis of Alzheimer's. His memory had been failing rapidly for six months. So, no, she couldn't ask him anything about old nicknames, or his early years in Jersey, or former colleagues. But Yael was puzzled. "How do you know about his condition? We've hardly told anyone."

"Hey, you can't keep a secret like that about your dad. He was a great man, Doll. Word gets out. Anyhow, after he was screwed over by those *momzers*, I tried to keep up. He was my hero, you know. I tell that to everyone I meet. Want to know about a great man? A *mensch*? A hero of the Jewish people? Abe Gold. That's what I say. Abe Gold! The name makes my heart sing, Doll. I even wrote some songs about him. Want to hear?"

"Well, I…"

"Hey, don't worry," he said, chuckling deeply, reminding Yael oddly of Santa Claus. "I wasn't going to sing again, over the phone. Since my stroke, I can only sing five minutes a day or I get these god-awful migraines. Haven't worked as a *hazzan* in over twenty years. But listen, Doll, I want to see you. My little Doll's a rabbi. Best looking rabbi of all time, probably, huh? The babe rabbi, am I right? Oh, I didn't mean it like that. Hey. That's the stroke talking, kid. I never remember to edit myself. Your dad was a deep thinker, an intellect, a *chacham*. That's probably you, too – even if you are great looking. Hey, didn't he ever talk about me? Cantor Weinman? Eddie Weinman? I'm telling you, we were *best* friends. He told me everything, and I mean everything, Doll. So what do you say? Got five minutes for your dad's old best friend? I'll tell you some stories, ones you probably don't even know, 'cause your dad was so modest. I'll sing you one of my tunes. Got ten minutes?"

"Uh, sure."

"Great. I'll be right over."

"No, no," she almost shouted into the phone. "I didn't mean right now. I can't do it today." In fact, this was the only light day on her calendar for the next two weeks. But for some reason she felt she needed preparation for a meeting with Cantor Weinman, or at least a chat with her brother or mother, just to verify that the guy was who he said he was.

"Of course," he said jovially, chuckling musically. "Hey, you're busy. You're the number two guy in the busiest, most successful *shul* in the world. What was I thinking? Right now! You're probably the hardest-working rabbi in show business. That slave driver boss of yours, he's probably got you holding the hands of all the rich *machers* in Desert County. He takes the super-rich ones, and you get the rich ones. That's your *shul*, am I right? The rich and the super-rich. I'm sorry to say I don't fit into either of those categories, Doll. Okay, not today. You're too busy for your old babysitter. Hey, how about tomorrow?"

She eyed the calendar on her computer screen, even though she knew it by heart. "Eight o'clock?" She said, thinking she could easily reschedule her weekly breakfast meeting with Tzippi.

"Eight p.m. it is. Thanks, Doll."

"No, I meant the morning!" she said quickly.

"Eight in the morning! *Gevalt.*"

"Well, it's just that…"

"Just joking with you, kid," he sang out. "I'm up by then. I'm always up. I never sleep," he said, and hung up.

At dinner, she tried to explain to Peter the unease she felt after speaking with Weinman. "It's bizarre," she said, "but I remember this odor. Not really a bad smell, but distinctive. Maybe it was a kind of shaving cream, or just his body."

"That's all you remember? A smell?" He poured her another glass of wine. They were enjoying a rare evening together. Usually she came home late and he was sleeping, or he was out performing until past midnight, and she was long asleep. Tonight they both made it home at 7:30, and neither was heading out after dinner. They celebrated by drinking a hundred-dollar bottle of French wine Yael's father had given them the day after the wedding, "*not* for a special occasion, but just to drink sometime to revel in being married to the one you love." The wedding, eight months before, had been the last good day for Yael's father. Two days later, he stopped recognizing most of his friends. Now, he only responded to his nurses. His neurologist, an old family friend, told Yael and her brother that he'd never witnessed such a rapid memory loss; that's why he still hesitated to call the ailment Alzheimer's, which progresses quickly, but not that quickly. "But what the hell," he'd told her, just last week. "It doesn't help him, what we call it."

"I was three years old last time I saw him," Yael answered. The wine tasted good, though she didn't know what a hundred-dollar wine was supposed to taste like. "I remembered the song he sang. I vaguely remember other songs. Sad melodies, pretty songs. A good voice. I think you'd like it." She shrugged. "Music and odor. That's all I remember." She sipped her wine. Her misgivings slowly dissolved in the glow of a slight intoxication. "I will call Arthur tonight, though. Make sure the guy's not a... I don't know that he was really a cantor. That we even knew him."

But Arthur, her brother, wasn't home when she called. She left a message, then curled up on the music room couch while Peter practiced the mandolin.

Hours later, she started awake, breathing rapidly, mouth dry, desperate for water. The details of the nightmare that woke her vanished as soon as she sat up. She vaguely recalled discordant ring tones, her husband pounding the mandolin strings. She also remembered a smell. She stumbled to the bedroom. "Why didn't you wake me up?" she demanded.

"Whoa, I tried to!" He shot up in bed, his arms outstretched as if he were defending himself from attack. It was only then Yael realized that her hands were balled into fists and that she was in a stance like a boxer, poised, ready with one foot in front of the other. She straightened out and dropped her arms. "You told me to go away, to leave you alone. Several times. I just gave up and went to bed."

She shook her head and tried to slow her breathing. "I don't remember."

"That was some bottle of wine," Peter said. "A hundred bucks."

"Yeah," she said, but didn't think it was just the wine. Something about Weinman, she thought, and then a memory hit her. A song. A different Yiddish song, jazzy, melancholy, bluesy, still lovely, but up-tempo. And vaguely menacing, but in the lyrics, not the melody. But how would she understand Yiddish lyrics? Something about seven brothers. She tried to hum the melody, or focus on a single word in the lyrics, but the memory fled. "Cantor Weinman," she said, as Peter lay back down. "I'm not sure I'm looking forward to seeing him."

But it wasn't so bad. She'd been right about the smell, it was him, but it had ripened over the years, soured, so while she wouldn't exactly say that the guy stank, she still wouldn't want to spend hours sitting next to him. It smelled like lemon-lime aftershave that had gone bad, turned slightly, though Yael didn't think that was possible. How could one can of aftershave last long enough to go rotten?

Otherwise, he didn't present a disagreeable appearance. He wore a faded white jacket, white slacks and a stained white tie; he looked like the head waiter in a seedy restaurant. He was large, his bulk hanging over the chair across from Yael's desk. His chubby cheeks were stubble-free, a black yarmulke sat awkwardly on his shiny scalp. Fat and bald, it struck a memory chord. As did his pale face, yellow teeth, the jack-o'lantern-like grin that one could also interpret as a mocking scowl.

The first thing he did was hand her a manila envelope stuffed with photos. There were more than a dozen of her, baby pictures; photos of her taking her first steps on chubby legs; posed shots of her showing off her first colorful dresses; candid shots of her howling in glee as her brother splashed water in her face at a baby pool. She looked happy in all the pictures, exceedingly so in some. The rest of the photos featured her brother and her parents. She nearly choked up at one shot of the entire family of four. They were crushed together in an intimate embrace, sitting on an old couch, waving to the camera, love and joy decorating their bright faces. Yael's parents divorced when she was five years old, so she doubted there were many photos like this.

"I took that one," Weinman said. He spoke with a sing-song tenor, like an opera soloist, each word portentous. He spoke as if he were performing. "You recognize the couch?"

Yael studied the photo. It was a turquoise sofa, with two worn, red pillows. Yael wouldn't exactly call it a memory, but a feeling of unease again flowed through her, along with a sense of comfort. She'd liked that couch, or at least she'd liked the pillows. She'd fallen asleep on it, her face buried in cushions, her feet in her father's lap. Yael looked at the cantor and nodded.

"Six months later, you were gone. Terrible thing. Not your dad's fault, not at all, not really, not in the slightest. He was a great man, never forget that, Doll. You don't mind if I call you Doll, do you, even though you're all grown up? A rabbi yet, my God! That was my name for you, kid. Your dad loved it when I called you that. Sometimes he used it, too."

"It's fine," she said. She was about to thank him for the photos, maneuver the conversation so she could bring up her busy schedule, when he struggled to his feet, pressing down hard on the arms of the chair, pushing himself up. Strangely, now that he was leaving, Yael wanted him to stay.

"Well, kid, I know you're busy. Hell, look at this place, busiest synagogue in North America. Your dad would be so damn proud of you, kid. *I'm* proud of you. But I don't want to take up your time."

"It's all right," Yael said.

"No, no, I'm an old man, and these are old memories, no damn use to you. No use to anyone, to tell you the goddamn truth. It's just that, well, kid, I've got some stories. And I love to tell stories. Especially about your old man, who was the greatest man I ever knew. Really. The greatest. You can tell the greatness of a man when he's been knocked around, when he makes the hard choices. And that was your dad. That's right when I knew him. So listen, Doll, if you ever want to hear some stories about a great man who happened to be your dad, give me a call, and I'll take you to lunch. And listen, kid, I know you've heard the gossip, the *drek*. I know you've heard the rumors, 'cause even though you were only three years old, you were the brightest three-year-old in Jersey, and they couldn't keep any secrets from Doll. This I know. So, if you want the *emes*, give me a call." He smiled – or scowled – yellow teeth shining. "Or don't. Water under the bridge. Let sleeping dogs lie. You're too busy. You don't want to hear it. Up to you."

And before she could protest or say goodbye, or, as she'd intended, ask him to sing the lullaby, he was out the door, moving his fat body with the grace and athleticism of a dancer, leaving only his odor behind.

That night, after a late social-action committee meeting, she finally got through to her brother. It was past ten in Desert Garden, past midnight in Cleveland, but she didn't want to let another day go by. He picked up on the fifth ring, groggy and confused, sounding oddly like their permanently addled father. After a quick apology she got right to the point, asking about the strange, fat, bald man with the photos, who claimed to have worked with their father. Arthur said nothing.

"Cantor Edgar Weinman," she said, repeating the name. "Odd duck? Beautiful voice?"

"I heard you. You woke me up to ask me about Eddie Weinman? From thirty years ago?"

"You were sleeping?" She heard stirring and mumbling in the background, certainly his wife Toby, possible one or even both of the three-year-old twins. Yael knew they regularly climbed into bed with their parents, either individually or as a pair. Arthur often spoke of buying two king-sized beds and binding them together to create the world's biggest mattress.

"Yael, call me in the morning."

"He said he has stories to tell."

"I bet he does."

"He's, well, I don't know exactly how to say this. I like him. But he scares me."

"Really? You're scared? You?"

"Well, maybe not so much scared. Creeped out, sort of. Concerned about what he's going to say. He keeps alluding to some scandal involving Dad, something that damaged Dad's reputation, maybe even got him fired. But he says he knows the truth. The *emes*."

"Shit, Yael. I'm going to call you in the morning. I will."

Yael doubted that he would. Certainly he would intend to, he would put it on his list of things to do. But since the birth of the twins, Yael's conversations with her brother went from once a week for at least forty-five minutes, to once a month, except for their all-business conversations about caring for their father. Both Arthur and Toby worked full-time at different accounting firms, both vying for partner-ships. They barely spoke to each other, much less the rest of their families. Arthur now took over a week to return a phone call from Yael, if he returned it at all. He was always full of apologies and reasonable excuses, which he delivered with the weariness of a man who rarely slept. Yael under-stood, even sympathized. Since moving to the desert, she knew how all-encompassing certain jobs could be, even without the added complication of two three-year-olds. Still, she resented him. She returned calls from him imme-diately, as soon as she got the message.

But he did call, the very next day, at six in the morning. "It's eight, Cleveland time," he told her. "I've been up for hours."

"Cantor Weinman," she said, stifling a yawn. "You called me back because of Cantor Weinman." She crept out of bed, careful not to wake Peter. She briefly wondered why Arthur called her cell, and not the home phone. She stood on the back patio in her bedtime shorts and T-shirt, and watched the sun rise over the Palomar Mountain.

"Listen," Arthur said, all business, no pleasantries, "you've got to keep in mind that I was only eleven or twelve. I barely remember him myself. And it was a confusing time, to say the least."

"Okay."

"Moving to Cleveland. The divorce. It's all jumbled up in my mind. I'm not sure about the chronology, and I'm pretty sure I don't want to try to nail it down. What would be the point?"

"Okay. But you called me back. At six in the morning. You've got something to say."

"I don't think you should talk to him again."

"Why?"

"You're afraid. You said so yourself. He scares you. He could be crazy. He could do you harm."

Yael was astonished. "Physical harm? Arthur, you're afraid for me? You mean, like, physically?"

"Of course."

"He's sixty-five years old. He must weigh 250 pounds. He can't work because he had a stroke. I think I can defend myself. Plus, he hasn't made the slightest threatening gesture, or said anything remotely dangerous."

"You're the one who said you were afraid. That's all I'm saying. Maybe you should trust that feeling."

"I'd had a bad dream. I don't like the way the guy smells. He creeps me out. But he doesn't look *dangerous*. What are you trying to tell me?" Yael was struck with the disconcerting and utterly unprecedented feeling that her brother was hiding something from her.

"Look, it's just some bad memories. And not memories of any specific incidences. Memories of unpleasant feelings. Feeling unsafe. That's what the name conjures up in my mind. Now that you mention it, yes, I even remember the smell, but it's not the odor that's important. I think you should stay away from him. Don't you have security guards in that place?"

"Security? You think I should have him beaten up? Arrested? For smelling bad? For giving me some photos I never saw?"

"Yael. Come on. You called me."

"Yes, but how come the first time I see happy pictures of our whole family – pictures of all of us together, smiling, enjoying ourselves – it's not from Mom or Dad, or from you, it's from Cantor Weinman? Why don't I know anything about our lives in New Jersey, the only time we were a complete family? Arthur, he's going to tell me things no one's ever told me."

"Yael, there's no—" But he was interrupted by a whiny scream. "Daaaaddy!" Elsa, Yael guessed, the louder, more aggressive and articulate of the twins. Then she heard a thwack – toddler flesh striking toddler flesh – and another, more insistent, but less tearful cry of "Daaaaddy!" Ilana, Yael realized, the more mature one, more passive, certainly the recipient of the slap, not the instigator. And then a hysterical, banshee-like howl, clearly from Elsa, the devious one, the aggressor. "Gotta go," Arthur said, weakly, his voice right in her ear, softer now than the baying of his daughters from another room. "Be careful," he said, instead of goodbye.

That night, after dinner, she asked Peter if he thought she should call Weinman and ask him to tell her stories about her father. They were slouching on the living-room sofa, the fake gas fire providing mostly light and not much heat. Yael was glancing over notes for a Friday night sermon, while Peter hummed softly, scanning a page of sheet music. Seemingly in response, Peter picked up his mandolin. "Listen to this," he said cheerily, smiling widely, as he launched into a bouncy, jazz version of the classic Jewish melody to the prayer *Adon Olam*. His blue knit yarmulke bobbed up and down on his brown, uncombed curls as his head swayed with the complicated rhythm.

A pet, Yael thought. I've got a pet instead of a husband. He's affectionate and performs brilliant tricks, but I can't talk to him. He doesn't listen to me. She watched his left hand fly up and down the tiny mandolin fretboard, marveling at how his or anyone's full-grown fingers could confidently grip the double strings in such small spaces. She enjoyed the melody – a blues variation on a tune she'd always despised – and was surprised to find herself pleased, rather than annoyed, that he'd completely ignored her question.

"That's your answer?" she asked when, with a note-bending, trilling flourish, he finished, five minutes later.

"Sorry, I had to get that out of the way. I can tell you liked it 'cause you didn't plug your ears. It's part of a series – jazz versions of famous prayers, written for bluegrass instruments. You did like it, didn't you?"

She shrugged, not wanting to encourage him, wondering if she needed to repeat her question. She decided to drop the subject, ignore the funny man she married, and return to her notes.

"Of course you should call him," he said.

She looked up, surprised.

"Of course?"

"What are you afraid of?"

"Did I say I was afraid? I'm not afraid of anything."

"Don't you want to hear his stories? Stories are important, Yael. Our identities are the sum total of the stories other people tell us about ourselves."

She stared at him. My darling savant, she thought. Stories are important. Of course they are. Stories create identity. The cantor would give her an identity, or at least reinforce the one she already enjoyed.

She watched as Peter picked up his mandolin and his flying fingers produced another melody, this time a jazz variation of the most droningly boring version of *Ein Keloheinu*, another famous hymn. To Yael's unrefined ears, it sounded inspired, the work of a genius.

CHAPTER 2

"Hey, Doll, I'm so grateful you invited me over. You don't know what it means to me, kid. When I look at your face, especially here in your office surrounded by these holy books, I see your dad. I really do. Oh, I know you're much better looking than him – you look more like a supermodel than a rabbi, you know that – but it doesn't matter. I look past your sexy lips, those hips, *gevalt,* your breasts, your body, and I just see one thing. Your dad."

"Uh, thanks," Yael answered. She'd called him less than half an hour ago, and suggested a meeting the next week, but he insisted on catching the next bus over so he could see her right away. She hesitated for a moment, then agreed, and cancelled her morning appointments. Now he sat across from her, settling his fleshy bottom into the office chair. The familiar rank smell wafted her way, but today the odor seemed less menacing, more familiar, even homey.

"Listen, before I start – before the stories – how about if I sing a song? Just to warm us up? Maybe "Varshe Mein" – you know, that lullaby I used to sing?"

Yael nodded, and the cantor sang. But the tears came even before the music. She'd choked up at the word "lullaby" and was bawling at the first note. She'd never heard anyone sing so beautifully. She'd never heard a more beautiful tune. But, again, it didn't comfort her, didn't inspire her. It saddened her and disturbed her, mostly because she didn't know why on earth she was crying. When he finished he smiled shyly, then shrugged. "I used to be a singer," he said. Yael nodded, and wiped her eyes. There was a story in that song, in the singing of it, but for now it eluded her.

He carried a worn leather valise, which he hefted with both hands so it landed with a plop on Yael's desk. At first he just stared at it, as if wondering where it had come from. "My files," he said, and sighed. "*Oy.* Newspaper clippings, some letters, two very interesting contracts." He shot Yael a look, frowning as his eyes twinkled, giving the impression of a gleeful sadness, or a sad glee. "It's not a pretty story, kid. Your dad, he got screwed badly, but you can read how it happened from this *drek* in my briefcase. He got fired from our congregation. Shitcanned. You know that don't you? I'm not the first to tell you, am I?"

"Of course not," she said, lying. It never occurred to her that her father had ever been fired from any job. She'd never conceived of her father being less than completely beloved by every congregation he'd ever served, and she'd never heard otherwise from her mother or brother. Several of her rabbinical school teachers had told her that he was among the best rabbis of his generation. Former congregants sang his praises whenever they'd run into Yael. Deeply spiritual, they'd say. Changed my life. Wise. Honest.

"He got canned. You know that. Not the first rabbi to lose his job, not the last. No great disgrace, really. Happens all the time. The question is, why? How is it that this good man lost his job, a good job, at a not-insignificant *shul*? And I'm asking myself now, should I be the one to tell you this here story? Should you hear it from me? Because Doll, Rabbi Doll, Yael, whatever you call yourself, I very much doubt that you've ever heard the *emes*. Maybe your brother told you something, maybe your mom said something else. Maybe your dad even had his version of events, though from what I understand, he never talked about it, not even to those who loved him the most. So, hey, do you want the truth? Because, you know, Yael, if I tell you, then you'll *know*." He played with the clasp on the briefcase with his thick hands, as if considering whether to open it and let the story out, or keep it shut, locking the story away. "If I tell you, then you'll know," he repeated. "So?"

She suddenly wanted this fat, unpleasant man out of her office. His scowling smile irritated her in the extreme; the tone of his voice made her uneasy. She remembered the frightened feeling from when she dreamt about him, even though she still couldn't recall a single detail from that nightmare. She sensed a stale but still potent menace wafting her way, along with the cantor's odor. But she did want to know. She leaned back in her desk chair, as if fortifying herself with distance. "Tell me the story," she said.

"No."

She glared at him, then stared at the briefcase. She thought about snatching it and calling Javier, the campus security guard, to remove the fat former cantor from the premises.

"I mean," he quickly added, "I'm not going to tell you right now. I want you to take the briefcase. Read what's in it. You're a busy girl, so take your time. Read first. Get a sense of how this *drek* was reported in the lamestream media. In other words, kid, get the story *they* told the world. Then we can talk. And don't forget to study the contracts. I'll come back in a week or so and fill in the rest. Okay, kid? We got us a deal?"

She was about to say, no, we do *not* got us a deal but, as swiftly as before, he danced his 250-pound body out the door, leaving nothing but his smell and the briefcase.

Yael grabbed a pen and used it to slide the valise toward her, like it was a weapon in an unsolved crime and she didn't want to leave fingerprints. She studied it. As far as she knew, and she knew very little about briefcases, it looked and smelled like genuine leather. Could Cantor Weinman once have been well-off enough to buy himself an expensive briefcase? He could certainly sing. Maybe he once made a good living. She was about to open the large metal buckle when she saw the monogrammed initials just below the gold clasp. A.G. Definitely not Edgar Weinman, but more than likely Abraham Gold. Her father. Somehow the cantor had acquired her father's fancy briefcase. The thought that an old and valuable possession of her father's sat on her desk, a remnant of his long and fruitful career, a career of which now not a single memory remained in his diseased brain, made Yael both anxious and sad. She considered booking a flight to Cleveland, flying out that very morning; hand her father the briefcase that night, and see which memory circuits it ignited behind his dead eyes. Maybe, she fantasized, he'd remember, and then *he* could tell her the story, the *emes*. She wouldn't have to learn it from whatever papers were in the briefcase, or from whatever exaggerated tales the fat cantor should choose to share. But this was a fantasy, and she knew it. There was no more talismanic, memory-provoking power in this briefcase than there was in her kiss, or her brother's touch, or the twins' tears. She clicked open the buckle and removed the contents.

Mostly it was *New York Times* articles, all copies. The first in the pile was a two-page obituary of Marco Gottlieb, a gangster who started his career as a hit man, and gradually worked his way up to boss of a multi-billion-dollar international drug enterprise headquartered in Newark, New Jersey. Gottlieb had been murdered, shot in the head – assassination style. According to the article, his gang consisted of Russian and Moroccan-born Jews, most of whom flitted back and forth between Israel and New Jersey. Gottlieb was Cuban-born. His father, the Russian Jew Flavio Gottlieb, had been one of Fidel Castro's chief spies until his death in 1994. Cuban money undoubtedly financed a good deal of the younger Gottlieb's business. Interestingly, government sources, according to the journalist who composed the obituary, sometimes mentioned the senior Gottlieb as involved in all sorts of Cuban dirty tricks across the globe, from assassinations, to fixing elections, to fomenting revolution in Africa. Flavio Gottlieb, the gangster-boss's father, had been one of the most clever, dangerous, and elusive characters in the Cold War.

A Jewish-Cuban gangster, with ties to Cuba's secret police, and son of a famous spy. Interesting to some, Yael supposed. Peter would get a kick out of it, particularly the spy story part; her husband loved spy stories. But she could care less. Why was she reading the obituary of a murdered monster?

She understood as soon as she reached the final sentence. "Funeral services will be conducted by Rabbi Abraham Gold at Congregation Darkei Shalom in Fairlawn, New Jersey."

That's why he got fired? Because he officiated at the funeral of a bad guy? But, *someone* had to lead the service, and the guy was Jewish. She quickly set aside the obituary and picked up the next article. It was a description of the funeral, and it quoted liberally from her father's eulogy. "The eyes of much of the country are on us now, as we pray for ease and rest for the soul of Marco Gottlieb. To some, he was an evil man, stuck in an evil business. But do I judge him? Should we judge him? Not I, not today." Yael winced. Her father, who judged her harshly whenever she spent even one minute less than the agreed-upon hour practicing the piano, who could make any adult in his several congregations reach deeper into his pocket at the *tsedakah* box with one judgmental glance, refused to judge a hired killer? And what did he mean "stuck in an evil business?" Stuck? Wasn't he the boss? Hadn't he, in any case, chosen that evil business years before? Still, this was his *funeral*. What was he supposed to say – good riddance to this bag of scum? He was technically correct; funerals were not the time for earthly judgments, certainly not from eulogizers. If that's what got him fired, it was unfair.

She stuffed the articles back in the leather case, and tried to focus on a Friday night sermon she was composing. As it happened, it was about Aaron and the Golden Calf and, therefore, about forgiving someone for a desperate, world-shattering sin. She thought about the numerous times Peter had forgiven her for her wandering eyes, and she had forgiven him for being an insensitive dork, and considered ways of alluding to these incidents in the sermon, without giving away any details. But she couldn't concentrate. She grabbed her BlackBerry, touched the green phone icon, pressed the anime drawing of her husband as a ninja warrior that he'd somehow downloaded onto her device.

"Ever hear of Flavio Gottlieb?" she asked.

"Greatest spy of all time."

"You believe that?"

"Who knows? Lots of folks do. But lots of folks like jazz fusion music, too, so what does that tell you?"

"How about Marco Gottlieb?"

"Marco? His son, the gangster? Of course. The *shande* to the *goyim*. The biggest embarrassment for the Jews of his time. Who hasn't heard of him? One of the truly great Jewish criminals."

Yael sighed. Who didn't know that? "Guess who officiated at his funeral?"

"I don't know. The Lubavitcher Rebbe?"

"Close. Abraham Gold." She told him about the newspaper articles Weinman had left for her.

"Hmm. Wow. Well, somebody had to do it, right? It's like medical treatment. The Hippocratic oath. You're not allowed to refuse, are you, even for a *shande*?"

"I think it got him fired. In Fairlawn."

"Really? That doesn't sound right."

"It may have been something he said at the service. He told everyone it wasn't right to judge the guy. But how can you not judge a killer? The greatest Jewish criminal of our time."

"Uh, well, not necessarily *the* greatest. But what else was he going to say at the funeral? It's not like he could ignore the issue. Everyone knew who Marco was."

Yael smiled through a yawn. Every once in a while she was reminded why she married Peter. Like many twins she read about, she and her admittedly weird husband, given the identical set of facts, often jumped to the exact same conclusion. Of course her father urged the mourners not to judge. What else was he going to say at a funeral? Both she and Peter immediately cut to the heart of the issue, even if her father's board of directors in Fairlawn hadn't quite seen it that way.

"But I guess his board of directors didn't quite see it that way," Peter continued.

"What? Did I just say that?"

"No, no. It's just the logical thing to say. It's probably what you were thinking."

She was about to snap at him; ask him how he could *know* what she was thinking. But she realized that would be the fatigue talking, an achy weariness that was just now revealing itself, though Yael knew it had been lurking since her first vague nightmare about Weinman. She wondered briefly if she was pregnant, but dismissed the idea. "I'm so tired," she told her husband. "And I've got so much work to do. But I think I'd better call Arthur. I just need to track this down. There's something that's haunting me in this story, starting with this creep, the supposed cantor. I was just starting to like him, at least a little. He sings so beautifully.

But then he hands me these articles. The Gottliebs – these great spies, these murderers. What am I supposed to do with all this?"

"Listen, why don't you let me do a little research? I'm not getting anywhere on this tune I've been composing. I need a distraction, some fun. And I've been interested in Marco Gottlieb for years. Now that you mention it, I think I may even have read an article at some point about his funeral. You go back to your real work. Let me see what I can find out."

Yael smiled again, and knew her husband would spend the next several hours – maybe the next several days – googling away without, of course, using Google at all but other "faster, more penetrating" search engines. There were sometimes advantages to being married to a classic OCD case, even when his obsessions encompassed assassinations and famous Cuban gangsters. In any case, she suspected she'd get more out of her geek soulmate than her brother, who always seemed to change the subject whenever she wanted to talk about the time before her parents' divorce.

She left later that day before dark, early enough, she judged, to take her favorite route, a bike path that cut through two scruffy, desert hills. The trail wasn't lit up at night, so Yael never used it on her half-mile walks home after sunset, fearing wild animals, or even muggers. Most days she trudged home along the narrow strip of sidewalk that accompanied well-lit Desert Canyon Boulevard. Instead of sage and hyacinth, diesel fuel and melting tar assaulted her nostrils.

McDonald's arches and Pizza Hut signs decorated the city landscape, not rolling hills, cacti, or the occasional coyote. Instead of desert pinks – the setting sun bouncing off the white boulders – endless city lights illuminated the concrete condo developments that stretched into the desert as far as the eye could see. Yael was surprised after moving to Desert Garden at the bland ugliness of her new, expensive neighborhood. She expected beautiful sunsets, desert vistas, sand dunes, pink rocks, oddly shaped trees, wild flowers, exotic animals. Instead, she encountered one gated monstrosity after another, all the same off-white color, all built in exactly the same neo-Hispanic style, all with Spanish names (Hacienda del Sol, Hacienda Caliente, Vista del Montana), all filled with English-speaking whites, mostly from the Midwest. The roads in Desert County were almost all flat and straight, and featured no natural wonders more impressive than brown dirt, and knee-high scrub brush. Ugly.

Except, of course, for the casinos: the baroque, bizarre, burlesque pleasure palaces thirty miles to the east – the ersatz Venice, the fake New York, the Disneyesque, Blade Runner, misty world of orgiastic colors and sensual sounds. The Strip. Downtown Desert City. The castles of an industry that, at least indirectly, paid her salary and Judah's, and everyone who worked at Anshei Emet.

But Yael never went there; she stayed in her soulless suburb. Soulless, in fact, was the first word to pop into her head (and, as it happened, Peter's head) on her first drive down Desert Canyon Boulevard. An odd word, she acknowledged, for a rabbi to label her new flock's hometown, but for Yael it fit more and more as the months went by and she settled in. Somehow, the glitzy downtown hotels sucked all the soul out of the suburbs. She'd moved to a soulless place.

Anyway, there were only a few genuinely beautiful spots in Desert Garden, and the bike path was one of them. The hills obscured entirely the view of the road, and even the sounds of automobiles only snuck through in small doses, mixing, even harmonizing with the sounds of owls, the whistling wind, and coyote calls. On cloudy winter days, the sunsets were indeed spectacular, the sun falling beneath the hills in explosions of color. The scrubby landscape featured all manner of usually hidden desert varmints, like voles and chipmunks and porcupines; Yael even once spotted a rattlesnake, and was struck not only at her fear, which was genuine and sharp, but by her admiration for the thing's beauty, its scaly, deep yellow, the brown diamond spots, its graceful speed, as it slithered away just as Yael was about to run as fast as she could in the opposite direction.

That late afternoon, an unseasonably brisk day in March, the sun and clouds showed every sign of cooperating in producing a lovely sunset. And the desert smells – the sage, the mint, fox dung – were especially pungent. Yael spotted a coyote in the distance, heading up the hill, probably for the road where a passing car would throw it some food. The wind blew through the sagebrush, producing a low whine – A-flat, her husband had told her, a bluesy jazz key that reminded him of New York. Yael had finished writing her sermon, had made her phone calls, attended her meetings, had accomplished everything on her to-do list, done her bit for the Jewish people. The air was cold and pleasant, the odors a nice mix of animal and vegetation, with almost no hint of car exhaust.

She stopped suddenly. A new smell had invaded the mix. Stale aftershave. Body odor, only partially covered by lemon-lime antiperspirant. Weinman. Was he following her, stalking her? She sniffed the air and looked around. The sun was still out but sinking, and the light was fading. But there was no place to lurk – no boulders, no trees – and the smell was suddenly gone. She stood stock-still, like the time she spotted the rattlesnake, ready to run, ready to jump, ready for anything. Then she laughed at herself. He's just a crazy old guy with a genuine affection for her father. He had a stroke, for God's sake. He's no physical threat, and even psychologically, really, where was the menace? The knowledge that her father had once, in an honorable career, been fired, and even at that for a mistake in judgment, using perhaps too strong language in a funeral for a bad man, trying to make the best of an awful situation? There was nothing fearsome in this knowledge and, for that matter, there was nothing remotely frightening about Weinman. He was actually funny and charming, if, yes, a little creepy. He's no rattlesnake, Yael told herself. Nevertheless, she hurried home, enjoying the view a little less than usual.

She expected to find Peter on the computer, lost in a true-crime blog, or surfing through his favorite obscure search engines, unknown except to his fellow savants. But she found him at the kitchen island, carefully measuring olive oil and balsamic vinegar and mixing it into a large green salad. He'd made dinner: grilled tuna, baguettes, and salad. Yael also spotted her favorite desert, banana cream pie, on the counter. Either, she concluded, he got bored quickly because he found nothing, and decided to put his restless energy into a meal he knew Yael would appreciate, or he had something unpleasant to tell her and wanted to make it go down easy, using her favorite foods, cooked in her favorite ways. She decided not to ask until after the scrumptious salad, after the perfectly done tuna steak, after she'd taken one bite of the banana cream pie.

"So? The greatest Jewish criminal mind of all time? Was my father fired because of him?"

"Well," he answered, putting down his fork. "I don't think it was the funeral per se." He regarded her, tilting his head. "I wonder how much of this you actually know, but maybe forgot."

"Forgot?"

"Well, it's just hard for me to believe that no one ever told you. And, you know, people forget unpleasant things. Look at you and Cantor Weinman."

"I was three years old the last time I saw him."

"I remember everything from when I was three."

"Please, just tell me, Peter."

"You really never heard of Marco Gottlieb? The name?"

"Peter, I never heard of him. I don't follow the careers of Jewish gangsters. I'm not well-versed in assassinations. These are just not interests of mine. Peter, what exactly are you trying to tell me?"

"You never saw the name until today? Until you read the articles from Weinman?"

"I never saw the name until today."

"See, I find that hard to believe."

Yael felt herself growing red, not from embarrassment, but, to her astonishment, rage. Rage! She was furious at her strange husband. She clenched her fists. "Why not?"

"Because Marco Gottlieb was your father's first cousin."

CHAPTER 3

Yael felt the color quickly drain from her face, along with her sudden and inexplicable anger. She looked down at her napkin. Out of the corner of her eye, she saw Peter studying her. "You really didn't know, Yael?" Peter asked. "Because there's something about your look, like you remember *something*."

"I don't..." She snapped her head up. "How many times do I have to tell you?" she said. She took a breath. "God, I'm sorry. What is the matter with me? You're just trying to help."

"It's okay, it's okay," he said, quickly. "I understand."

"Marco Gottlieb," she said. "His real last name was Gold?"

"Well, not quite. The original name in Poland was apparently Golodevzky. The Cuban side of the family, for some reason, chose Gottlieb, but your grandfather picked Gold. Yael, I'm sorry to keep asking, but this information was ridiculously easy to obtain. You really never knew any of this? Even the name Golodevzky?"

She shook her head. "My father never discussed his family. My impression was that everyone except his parents died in Europe, in the Holocaust. His father, my grandfather, died of pneumonia, in Chicago, when my dad was a kid, a long time before I was born. His mother was killed in a bus accident when he was twelve. I always thought this was all

98

too painful for him to talk about, so I never asked. And now it's too late."

"Well, it's never too late when you've got Google. Or, better, Geekster, or Findem. But, anyway, you want the whole story? Do you want to know?"

Why was everyone suddenly asking her if she wanted to know the "story?" As if the story could traumatize, or steal her innocence, or provoke permanent hatred or revulsion. Did everyone see her as essentially vulnerable? Too frail for this dirty world? Of course she wanted to know the story, if it were truly her story.

But first she needed a drink. She asked Peter if there was any gin left from the bottle they'd received from their neighbors as a housewarming gift, six months earlier. He looked at her. "Hasn't been opened," he said.

"Open it."

Peter held forth, his lovely fingers dancing at his notebook keyboard, while Yael sat next to him on a folding chair, and sipped the first gin and tonic (really, gin and seltzer, with lemon) that Peter had ever mixed. "First thing we have to do is get to Findem. Now, it's not exactly a legal website, so the URL changes every day. So you have to Google it to get it, and sometimes – " his fingers floated across the keys " – Okay, there it is. Findem. Now I type in Marco Gottlieb and Cuba and Flavio. Okay." He studied the screen. Yael sipped her drink. "Of course, we ignore Wikipedia, so I'll scroll down, uh, and there it is, the definitive article, excellently sourced, well-written. Thing is, it's in Spanish. So I have to copy then paste parts of it, and then Google the whole thing so I can…"

"Peter."

"That'll just take a second. This way we can use the translate function and read in English. Uh oh, now Google's not finding the Spanish article. But that's okay, I'll go to Geekster—"

"Peter."

He quickly removed his hands from the keyboard but kept his eyes on the screen. "Yes?"

"Could you just tell me? I'll trust everything you say. I don't need to know how you got the information."

He frowned and turned to look at her, his eyes drooping in what Yael recognized as his hound-dog look, wounded, sad. At first Yael thought he was offended, but at a closer glance, after another sip of gin, she realized he was concerned for her. He was convinced she would take the news badly. How sweet.

"Please, Peter."

He nodded slowly, and removed a single sheet of paper from the desk drawer. Yael noticed that the text was handwritten, not printed. At some point, Peter had jotted it down from the computer screen. "Flavio Gottlieb – Golodevzky – was your grandfather Alexander's brother. There were eight of them altogether, seven brothers, one sister."

"I was told seven."

"Eight. Do you want me to show you how I know?"

She held up her hand. "No. Just go on, please."

"Isaac, Daniel, Samuel, Jacob, and Ignatz were murdered at Treblinka."

"Yes, I'd heard that. But to me they were never anything other than the five brothers. The five who stayed. The five who got killed. I couldn't even tell you if you got the names right."

"Oh, I did. I checked in a couple of places. First the YIVO website, then the *Arbeit…*"

"Okay, okay, Peter."

"Okay. But there was another brother, Flavio, who left even before your grandfather Alexander. Flavio – well, it wasn't Flavio then, it was Moishe – Moishe took a boat from Odessa to Havana in 1922."

"But why Cuba? He couldn't get in to the United States?"

Peter sighed. "Not exactly. Apparently, he was *sent* to Cuba. By Soviet Communists. He was sent there to foment revolution."

"Peter. C'mon."

"Well, that partially explains why you never heard of him. He was a revolutionary. They weren't so rare in those days, even among the Jews. He was a communist agent, not a person your family would embrace with pride. Now, listen, do you want the whole story? Or should I cut to the chase?"

Yael polished off her drink. She felt simultaneously relieved and exhilarated, as if she were embarking on a sea voyage to parts unknown just as she received a clean bill of health after a lengthy illness. She knew the giddy, nonsensical feeling was coming from nowhere but the gin, and wondered why she didn't drink every day. Why didn't everyone drink every day? It was fabulous! "How about something in between?"

"Moishe changed his name to Flavio and opened a tailor shop in downtown Havana. He mostly mended military uniforms, and in his spare time fomented communist revolution. He met Castro right after World War II, when Fidel came into his shop to get his pants widened. He was the official tailor of the revolution."

"Peter, I'm drunk. But I'm not in the mood for jokes."

"It's no joke. That was his title. Remember, this was a proletarian uprising. Tailors were *valued*, like bricklayers, and farmers. Castro admired people who worked with their hands. Anyway, it was a front. He was mostly a propagandist and intelligence officer."

"So he really was a spy? My uncle, the spy?"

"Great-uncle, actually. And, yes, a spy, but not just any spy. Chief spy. He was Castro's chief spy. He became the head of his secret police. But I'm getting ahead of myself. The Communist Party was outlawed in 1950, and Flavio was deported. He spent ten years in Moscow."

"Learning Russian sewing techniques."

"Undoubtedly. But probably also learning something about creating a communist internal security apparatus. There's some evidence that he also spent time in East Germany; maybe he even slipped back to Stashov, in Poland, his hometown. He returned to Cuba in 1960, and took over his old tailor shop. He went back to mending uniforms. But now he had a few other jobs."

"Head of the secret police?"

"And chief Communist Party propagandist. He wrote several of Castro's first speeches as president, the five-, six-hour masterpieces. But I forgot the most important part. In

1935, he married Ester, a nice Jewish girl from Havana. Sometime later, it's weird, but it's not exactly clear when, they had a baby. A son."

"Marco?"

"*Exactamente*. But in 1950, Ester and Marco didn't go to Russia with Flavio. Flavio was deported, not them. With Papa Flavio away, Marco fell in with a bad crowd as a teenager. Drinking, petty theft, a lot of fights. Didn't want to take over the tailor shop. Castro came down from the hills one time to bawl him out, but it didn't do any good. Make a long story short, he became a criminal. He started out smuggling rum, but later switched to marijuana and heroin. Fidel expelled him in 1960, right after his dad returned. Ended up in Miami, and then Jersey, where he built up a major criminal enterprise. Mostly drugs, but also a kind of Murder Incorporated, with Jewish hit men from Morocco and Russia."

"Until he was murdered himself, and my father officiated at his funeral. Who killed him, by the way?"

"The *Times* said it was the Italian Mafia. The Gambinos."

Yael leaned back in her chair and put her bare feet in Peter's lap. He massaged the skin in between her toes. She closed her eyes and concentrated, swaying her head slightly, as if in time to some imaginary music. "So. My father clearly knew Marco was his cousin. Somewhere along the line, Grandpa must have told him that he was related to gangsters and spies. But no one ever told me. Well, why should they? It's pretty unpleasant stuff. I always thought we came from an illustrious line of rabbis. I even made a family tree in school with, I don't know, dozens of rabbis. But I didn't know about this more eccentric branch. Too bad. It would have livened up the project. But obviously, they wanted to keep it a secret. But now *you* know. And me. And Cantor Weinman, I guess. And Geekster and Google and Findem and Wikipedia. And anyone in the world who really wants to know. You say it was the Gambinos who knocked off Marco?" She hiccuped, and wondered if she could ask Peter to make her another drink. She also marveled at her quick use of gangster terminology. Knocked off?

"Yes, according to the mainstream media." Peter opened his desk drawer, and carefully replaced the piece of paper. The Starship Defiant – Peter's favorite screensaver – zoomed in and out of focus. Peter stared at the monitor.

"The mainstream media." What an interesting phrase, Yael thought. She wondered when it entered the lexicon. And hadn't she just heard it that day? She remembered. From Weinman. No, he'd actually said lamestream media. Whatever. She raised her eyebrows and removed her feet from her husband's lap. She pointed at him, almost brushing his cheek with her finger. "Does that mean you have your own story?"

"Just rumors. Stuff floating around on various blogs. Geekster's a great search engine." He looked at her. "Want to hear?"

"Please stop asking me if I want to hear. I'll tell you exactly when I stop wanting to hear. I want to hear."

"Want another drink?"

"I desperately want another drink, but I'm not sure I'd survive. Peter, please just tell me what the not-so-mainstream media say about my gangster cousin."

"He killed Kennedy."

She blinked twice. "You're insane. You've lost your freaking mind."

"You wanted to hear."

Feeling a headache coming on, she rubbed her temples. She wondered what a hangover felt like. She'd never had one. Could you get a hangover ten minutes after finishing a drink?

"Please," she said.

He reached for the desk drawer, then looked at his hand and retracted it, changing his mind. He'd memorized the material. "One key date to remember is May 12, 1959. Remember where Flavio was living then?"

"Havana. He moved back after the revolution, to help his buddy Fidel."

"No, you weren't listening. He moved back in February, 1960, six months after Fidel took over. On May 12, 1959, Flavio was still living in Moscow. He checked out a book from the Gorky Public Library. *Don Quixote* in the original Spanish. That day, according to a website I mostly trust, another person checked a book out of the same library. *The Idiot* in the original Russian, even though there's no evidence that he could read Russian that well. Guess who checked out that book?"

"Guess? I'm supposed to guess who checked out a book in 1959, in Moscow?"

"Lee Harvey Oswald."

"Peter."

"I'm telling you the story! You said you wanted to know."

"My great-uncle met Lee Harvey Oswald in Moscow."

"Well, I would phrase it differently. I would say that there's some evidence from non-mainstream sources that your uncle Flavio perhaps knew Lee Harvey Oswald. But keep in mind, this isn't an official version. This isn't the Warren Commission. Okay, that's May 12, 1959. Let's go to March 3, 1960. Where's Flavio?"

"Back in Cuba. Reunited with his no-good son."

"Exactly. Back in his tailor shop. Did I mention that the tailor shop was right next door to the new Nomiente Building? The Cuban secret police? Guess who was arrested and interrogated by the Cuban secret police on March 3?"

"Captain James T. Kirk."

"Close. Jack Ruby. You know, the guy who shot Oswald."

A beat of silence. Peter was clearly waiting for a reaction, like "gee whiz," or "holy moly," or "Jesus Christ." But the gin buzz was sadly, oddly wearing off. She was becoming more irritated, more drunk. "Peter," she said. "I think it's time you got to the point."

"Well, Ruby had been there before the revolution, to drum up business. He owned a strip club, and he was interested in gambling. He stayed on for a few months after the revolution to see if Fidel's regime would still be open to American tourists having the kind of fun that would be illegal in the U.S. But like a lot of visiting Americans, he was detained. Now, if he were just some ordinary hustler, Flavio never would have met him. But – okay, we're conjecturing here."

"*We* are?"

"Well, not us, not you and me. I'm just reporting what I read. But, well, obviously Ruby was something other than just a hustler. He murdered the man who supposedly murdered Kennedy. My theory – I mean, not my theory, just sort of the general consensus among people who think about these kinds of things – is that Flavio himself interrogated Ruby. Think about it. That would mean that Flavio Gottlieb, the founder and head of the Cuban secret police, and, incidentally, your great-uncle, was acquainted with *both* Lee Harvey Oswald and Jack Ruby. Now, you know about Operation Mongoose? You do, don't you? I don't have to waste time telling you about Operation Mongoose?"

She carefully considered what to say. "Peter, I will get the bottle of gin and hit you over the head with it if you don't clearly and succinctly explain to me what you mean by Operation Mongoose."

He reached forward and his fingers flew along the keyboard. Yael heard the shut-down music. This was unusual; Peter almost never turned his computer off; he preferred it ready for business, in the middle of the night, returning from a gig or first thing in the morning or right before bed, always; he didn't like to wait when hooking up to his virtual world. He stood up slowly, stretched his lean body, reaching his long arms over his head. Yael figured he'd had enough, enough of taking her tipsy abuse, enough journeying through the mucky Internet rumors about her family, enough of her. She figured he was either leaving her once and for all, or going to bed. But he said, "Wait here," and walked quickly to the kitchen. He returned with two bottles

– gin and seltzer – and another glass. He mixed a drink for Yael and poured himself straight gin. He took a sip. "Operation Mongoose?" he said. She nodded, wide-eyed. She'd never seen him drink anything stronger than beer or wine.

"It was a CIA operation to assassinate Cuba's communist leadership. Most people – well, people who know something about it – think that Castro was the only target. Not true. The idea was to knock off all the leaders."

"But why?"

He shrugged. "Cheaper than invading. Regime change. Things haven't changed that much. Anyway, there's no official list of targets. The government still doesn't even acknowledge that the operation existed. But we know what they tried to do to Castro, the exploding pens, the poison tobacco. We don't know how they tried to kill the others, or even who the others were. But it seems likely that Flavio would have been a target. He was not only Castro's most important spy, he was his propagandist, his best speechwriter. He was *very* important. If Operation Mongoose targeted *anyone* besides Castro, it would have been Flavio. That means the U.S. government tried to kill your uncle."

Yael resisted the impulse to fling her drink, at him, at his computer, at the wall. Instead, she sipped from it and almost instantly felt better. She nodded. "Continue."

"For me, one of the most plausible JFK assassination conspiracy theories – now, remember, 'plausible' doesn't mean true, in this context it just means not ridiculous – has always been that the Cubans decided to kill Kennedy in retaliation for Operation Mongoose. Even before researching your uncle Flavio, that theory made sense to me, at least a lot more sense than 'the CIA did it,' or 'Jimmy Hoffa did it' or Richard Nixon or Lyndon Johnson. That stuff is wacko." He took another sip of gin. "But Castro had a clear motive. Not just revenge, but deterrence. He was sending a message. You try to kill me, I'll try to kill you. Maybe he didn't even know it would work. He just wanted to send the message. Now, remember, it's just a theory. You understand that, right? A little less wacky than some of the other theories, but still just a theory?"

Yael nodded slowly.

"Okay, but let's go with the theory for a moment. Now, this just occurred to me today, on my computer, researching Uncle Flavio. If 'the Cubans did it' theory is correct, who would have planned it? Who would have given the actual order? Who would have found the assassins?"

"Uncle Flavio. My grandfather's brother. My uncle killed JFK?"

"Okay, it's just a theory. I'm not Oliver Stone. But, well, yes. He was the chief spy, so Castro could easily have handed off the job to him. But more importantly, he was in the Gorky Library the same *day* as Oswald. Six months later, he probably interrogated Jack Ruby. He himself was a target of Operation Mongoose. A lot of coincidences here."

"That's why my dad was fired," Yael mused, then hiccuped. "Because his uncle killed the president. *My* uncle. I guess you can't blame them." She winced, hiccuped again and took another sip. She liked gin.

Peter looked at her. "You're joking?"

"I'm drunk. Sort of. But. I mean. Is it possible?"

109

"Oh, I doubt it. That was 1979. No Internet. No world-wide community of conspiracy theorists. Flavio Gottlieb was still alive, still working in his tailor shop and hiding all his secrets. I doubt anyone on the board of your dad's synagogue stumbled on the truth. Marco Gottlieb was a pretty notorious gangster. That was probably enough. But there's a little more." He opened his mouth as if about to say something, then closed it, pulled his neck back, and looked at her.

"Please, do *not* ask me if I want to hear."

"Operation Mongoose! Back to Operation Mongoose. Who do you think the CIA used to attempt the assassinations? After all, in the early '60s, agents weren't professional assassins. They were mostly lawyers and accountants. So they hired the real thing. Mobsters. Real hired killers."

"This is true? This is true what you're telling me now? Or just geekster talk? Geekapedia. This is truth?"

Peter opened his mouth, tilted his head and put his finger to his lips, in the pose of a thinker. "What is 'truth?'" he asked.

"Peter."

"Listen, if you're going to ask questions like that, what's the point in having this conversation? I'm not the History Channel. I'm telling you what I find on my screen."

She nodded. Fair enough, she thought. She had, after all, married him, just him, and not, for example, some normal person.

"So it was mobsters. Murder Incorporated. So, when Castro and Flavio decide to turn the tables, who do they hire to do their dirty work? Flavio's a tailor. Castro's running the country. Who's going to pull the trigger?"

"Oswald. You already told me, Flavio met with Oswald in Moscow."

He shook his head. "Yael. The average length of all the thousands of books about the Kennedy assassination is approximately 800 pages. Do you want all the information, now, tonight? Because I could do that. You know I could do that."

"No, no. Please continue."

"Let's stop being naïve. If we're entering the world of the theorists, let's enter all the way. Even you know that in that world, Oswald had a gun, he pulled a trigger, but he was *not* the lone shooter. He was not the true assassin. Yael, really, even you know that. Or, let me say, even you're familiar with that theory."

"How about if I just don't talk?"

"Excellent. Okay, so Oswald was a patsy. Flavio set him up. Later, Flavio somehow convinced his old friend Jack Ruby to kill Oswald, because he was afraid he would crack. But this takes me back to my original question. Who – *besides* Oswald – would Flavio hire to do the killing? He'd need a professional. The CIA hired professionals. So would Flavio. But he had one close at hand."

Marco, Yael thought. But let Peter say it. She'd promised not to talk.

"Marco," he said. "Marco Gottlieb assassinated our thirty-fifth president. Your cousin killed JFK, and your father officiated at the funeral. In some ways, that makes your dad a kind of an accessory after the fact."

Yael closed one eye, and squinted with the other at her dork of a husband. "How did this happen?" she slurred. "How did God let this happen? How did I marry a freaking maniac? You're a lunatic."

"No. No. No, it's not that. Well, actually, I was joking."

"You were joking. *Joking*. About Flavio? About this whole thing?" Lunatic was too gentle a word. She felt her body heat rising through the dim fog of the gin, felt an angry blush coloring her cheeks.

"Of course not! I couldn't invent all that. I was joking about the accessory part. I thought you needed to lighten up."

"Lighten up." Is that what she needed? She looked at her watch. Just past ten; a reasonable hour, for a change. What she needed now, suddenly, desperately, was sleep. Her drink and a half had moved her past tipsy, past drunk; she was heading for the passing-out stage. She put down her glass and mumbled "going to bed."

When the phone woke her the next morning, she vaguely remembered Peter following her upstairs, remembered the shower water pounding on her head keeping her awake, remembered collapsing naked into the bed, remembered dreaming that her brother Arthur had killed the current president and was hiding out, along with Toby and the twins, in their home in the desert. That dream was so vivid she was convinced it was Arthur's call that shattered her sleep. She didn't even look at the caller ID, just rolled over, picked up the phone and whispered, "Arthur?"

But it wasn't her brother. "I need to see you! *Today!*"

Weinman. She drew the sheet around her breasts, unwilling to speak with him while uncovered. She sniffed the air, as if expecting his smell. "Why today? I thought you were going to wait until I called you. Didn't you say it was all just water under the bridge?"

"More like under the sewer. You read the articles?"

"Of course."

"I need to see you. You need the whole story. Not just the mainstream media. The *emes*."

Lord, she thought. Save me from the *emes*. Let the *emes* be a bad dream. She longed for the mainstream media. "I don't care about any of this," she whispered, still clinging to the hope that she wouldn't wake Peter. She knew she should tiptoe out of the room and talk on the kitchen phone, but the thought of spending even an instant naked with Weinman on the line made her skin crawl. "It happened a long time ago. It doesn't matter any more."

"It's your father. It's your family. You should know!"

"You stay away from me," she hissed, stopping herself just before blurting out "you creep." What, she wondered, had happened? One day ago, she'd sort of liked the guy. He was a link to her ailing father, an old friend. Sad, yes, pathetic, even smelly, but still an old friend. And now? He's evil, she thought, then blushed; the heat, like bugs, crawling up and down her skin. Evil? Where did that word come from? How could she think that? How could she know that?

"I'll be at your office in an hour!" he wheezed. "There are some things you need to know, Yael. It's time. It's time for the true story."

She crept out of bed, showered and dressed. No headache, she thought, no nausea. Maybe dread is the secret. No mere hangover could compete with the foreboding that filled her soul at the thought of seeing the fat cantor once again settling his bulk into her office chair. She should, she knew, call Javier the security guard, call the cops, remove the man from her synagogue, from her life. And maybe she would, after he talked. Because as much as she longed suddenly to see him led away in handcuffs, she knew there was more to the story, something involving her, her father, and the cantor, something, despite last night's drunken hijinks, that had absolutely nothing to do with the CIA or JFK or Castro. The story, she thought. Her story. Of course she wanted to hear it, Peter had told her. It was her story. And Peter, for all his eccentricities, knew her. Knew that she needed to know.

She considered walking along the bike path to work; feeling the cool air, listening to the birds, watching the pink light bounce off the brown soil. But she was in a hurry, so she drove along Desert Canyon Boulevard. She stopped at McDonald's, for coffee.

He was waiting outside the administration building, holding a steaming Venti Starbucks cup in one hand, and a brown bag in the other. His bald head glistened with sweat. Red blotches covered his cheeks, as if someone had slapped and pinched his chubby face. Or maybe it was just sunburn. "Door was locked," he said.

"I would hope so." She wondered how he got past the gate; then realized that it was only set up to stop cars or trucks. Anyone could walk through. And the guard didn't arrive until 7:30. She led him to her office, then hurried to sit behind the desk; she wanted a hard wood barrier between her and the old guy. Only after settling herself in her chair, tightly gripping the ends of her desk, did she allow herself a full look at the man. He smirked at her, smiling with a closed mouth, and held a scone out for her to take. Evil, she thought, as she shook her head, refusing his gift. She stifled a chuckle. What had she been thinking? Evil? The guy was a joke, a sad, sick has-been. She'd sort of *liked* him, especially his singing voice. She'd drunk too much last night, spent way too much time on ridiculous theories. He was a pain in the neck, an irritant, not evil.

"So you know?"

She breathed in slowly, testing the air. Suddenly, even the smell wasn't so bad. "He officiated at the funeral of a gangster. So what? Someone had to do it."

"A gangster. Just a gangster? He was your cousin!"

She shrugged. "Again, so what? They fired him for that? It's their loss. He was a good man. You said so yourself."

"I think you're missing something. You're missing the essential point about the gangster. Should I fill you in?"

"Yeah, he killed Kennedy. So what?" The deep smell of Starbucks coffee mixed with the cantor's odors, producing a truly nauseating effect. She swore she would never go to Starbucks again.

"What are you talking about? Killed Kennedy? Are you crazy?"

"Could you just leave? Please? I don't want trouble with you. You knew my father. You worked with him. That's wonderful. But could you leave? I really don't want to have you arrested."

"But you're missing the point! You don't have the story!"

She sighed and picked up her phone. "Our security staff is definitely here by now. Please, Cantor Weinman. Just get up and walk out. I don't want to do this."

"But it wasn't the fact that he was a gangster! That was the *fable*, the excuse they used, the mainstream media. You're missing the real story! The *emes*."

She took a breath. He was going to tell her, so why not ask? "Which is?"

"He was *shtupping* the gangster's wife!" he screamed, sweat and spit spraying Yael's desk, leaving a bubbly puddle. "He was *shtupping* his own cousin's wife. He was having a fucking affair with her! That's why they fired him, Doll! That's the story!"

She put down the phone. Heat, this time white, not red, hotter than anything she'd ever felt, rose from her bowels, through her heart to her cheeks, whitening her face. Rage, murderous and clean, rushed through her veins. She stared at the abominable, execrable, demonic figure in front of her, the very picture of evil, and her hands moved towards the scissors lying on her desk, next to the scumbag's puddle of unholy fluids. Weinman smirked again, winking his bloodshot eye, as if daring Yael to do the darkest deed she could imagine. But by the time she'd grasped the sharp object, lifted it and pointed it, dagger-like, at his heart, he'd risen from the chair and pirouetted toward the exit. As the door slammed shut, she slowly brought the gleaming scissors to her eyes, wondering what on earth she was planning to do with them, even as, deep down, she knew. She knew.

CHAPTER 4

That night, while Peter picked his banjo at the Hoosegow Grill and Tavern with the Desert Cryers, Yael called her brother. She closed her eyes while waiting for him to pick up, and imagined snow falling in wet clumps on his Beachwood, Ohio home. Whenever Yael thought about Cleveland and its suburbs, even if it was summer, she thought about snow. Somehow, all her childhood memories had been chilled by Cleveland's dirty white winters; as they wound their way through the sun-drenched warmth of Desert County, they reached her flash-frozen. Learning to ride a bike, her first fist fight with her best friend, fumbling her lines in *How to Succeed in Business*, kissing her non-Jewish boyfriend – it seemed like they all happened in the middle of blizzards, her ears and nose stinging with cold, her hands numb, her gloves somehow always lost. She'd never felt at home in the North Country of Cleveland. It was as if the snow and ice prevented her from growing roots. She'd fled after graduating from Hillel Academy in the eastern suburb of Beachwood; she entered Berkeley, and that very autumn called herself a Californian. Her brother, on the other hand, finished his four years at the equally frigid University of Chicago, and then, as if released from prison, returned home, to Cleveland.

"How's the weather?" she asked when he answered, skipping "Hello."

"Sunny and warm."

"You're kidding." She tried to imagine it. She couldn't.

"Actually, yes, I am kidding. It's snowing. Third night in a row. It's also past eleven. "

"Sorry, but whenever I call earlier in the day, the twins start jumping and squealing after three minutes."

He sighed. "You're right. They give me exactly three minutes on the phone. No more. I guess I should be grateful for that."

Yael had intended to be cross with her brother, maybe even to bully him a little with her little girl charm; she knew that to him she'd always be a little girl. She wanted the truth and had sensed that in their last conversation he was keeping something from her. But picturing the twins melted her heart and filled her with guilt. She'd only seen them three times in two years. She knew how difficult it was for her brother's suddenly full family to travel, but she'd only made the trip to Cleveland once, for the double baby-naming, forcing the four of them to fly to New York last spring for the Seder. She was a workaholic; she knew that. As much as she adored her nieces, and genuinely liked Toby, her sister-in-law, she hated taking any time off. It was a trait she'd inherited from her father.

"I met Cantor Weinman again," she said.

A pause, maybe just for breath. "Yael," Arthur said, "when was the last time we saw each other?"

She thought for a moment. "You came to my rabbinical school graduation, in New York. Just you, no screeching monsters, I mean no cute darlings. That was nice. Six months ago."

"Too long. You know, I've never seen your new house. Plus, I've never been to Desert County. I'd love to check out the casinos, the Strip. I think I need to fly out there."

"Oh? Well, Passover's in about six weeks. You all can—"

"No, I think it needs to be sooner."

"Oh?"

"What are you doing tomorrow?"

Twenty hours later, they were hiking together up Mt. Kisko. She wanted to show her older brother her favorite view in the world, the sun setting over Desert Valley, when the entire landscape – sand, scrub brush, cacti, coyotes, lizards – turned inexplicably pink. The locals, in fact, called it the "Pink Time," and nowhere was it pinker than Mt. Kisko at sunset. She was grateful that her brother had been joking about the casinos and the Strip. He had no interest in the glitz, but did want to see the desert, the real thing, not a tourist spot. Yael despised the Strip in almost exactly reverse proportion to how much she loved hiking in the desert.

A love-hate relationship, in fact, pretty much summed up how she felt about living in Desert County. For Yael, the casinos – what the locals called the "gaming industry," a good twenty miles to the north, but still the central economic reality for her community – symbolized the absolute apex of human corruption. A naked appeal to greed wrapped up in pride and lust, but lightly disguised as good clean fun, for the whole family! Yael and Peter visited the Strip their first week in town. Benny Hertz, a past synagogue president, guided them, starting with his own outfit, "The Megalopolis," a super-casino patterned after the Chinese cities of Beijing and Shanghai. He proudly paraded them through "Dragon Garden" with its 50-foot-high plastic azaleas; the Lego "Forbidden City," built exactly to a 360:1 scale, and, of course, the fake bamboo slot machines as far as the eye could ever see, even with binoculars. Peter whispered to her that it was as if the world's most beautiful prostitute had covered herself up with a sickening amount of the priciest perfume and the gaudiest makeup. Doesn't matter how much perfume and makeup these people use, he'd said, it's still a syphilitic whore. Yael had visited the Strip exactly twice more since moving to Desert County – once to show her mother, who'd loved it and had to be coerced away from the slot machines, and once, to take Peter's parents who'd pleaded to be driven back to the clean desert after five minutes.

Arthur didn't even ask about the Strip after dropping off his bags at her house. He'd read about the Pink on the airplane. According to the *Hidden Desert County* book, they could make it now, if they hurried. Did Yael have any flashlights? The book said to take flashlights.

The Pink did its work, both on Arthur and Yael. Arthur gasped as the sun dipped past Mt. Arnold, and it was as if they'd been transported to a new planet called Pink. The pebbles, his canteen, the skin on the back of his hand – all turned pink. Yael whispered a prayer – the *shehecheyanu*, a prayer uttered at special occasions, a prayer thanking God for keeping us alive to witness this moment, lines

Yael recited often in her official capacity, but really only meant when she experienced the Pink. By unspoken mutual consent, they didn't start talking until the way back down, as if the Pink, not to mention the other later luminosities – the eerie blend of oranges and greens when the sun reflected off the pines; the browns and golds of the stones in the canyons, where, from the heights of Mt. Kisko, the entire footpath looked suddenly like a copperhead snake, scaly and beautiful – would distract them from their important business. But almost as soon as the sun disappeared, and Arthur flicked on his flashlight, he asked, "Did you ever hear about the diary? 'Chronicles of a Broken Marriage?' Did Mom or Dad ever tell you?"

Yael took a sip from her water bottle. She motioned for her brother to start back down the path, and then she followed. "Let's start with the assumption that I don't know anything. That's been working well lately."

Arthur kicked a stone. They stopped to listen to it bounce through the boulders to the valley below, the sound growing oddly louder as the rock traveled farther, as if desert mountains had their own laws of physics.

"I found Dad's diary," he said. "I was snooping through their drawers, looking for *Penthouse*. He kept it in a box of personalized stationery, on these cream-colored papers with his name embossed on the top of each page. I was eleven, so you were, I don't know…"

"Two," Yael whispered, as if she were talking to herself. She wondered how Arthur could forget that she was born in the same month as him, nine years later. She always felt that the number nine was the central feature in their relationship. They were the same person, only nine years apart. The world happened to her nine years later. Whenever she remembered an incident in her older brother's life, she calculated his age at the time, and then subtracted the number nine.

"Yeah, two. So I couldn't share my discovery with you. Do you want me to tell you now? Do you want to know?"

That question, again. Was knowledge really so damaging, or did she simply appear weak to everyone around her? But all she said was, "Of course."

"He was having an affair."

"With his cousin's wife. The gangster's wife."

"So he did tell you. Cantor Weinman. I was afraid of that."

"But why would you be afraid? Why is it so awful for me to know the truth?"

"That was the worst day of my life, finding that diary, finding out about Dad. And Mom. I don't think I've really recovered from the disillusionment. I wanted to spare you."

"You were eleven. A little boy. I'm twenty-eight."

"Of course. But I don't remember myself as eleven, as a little boy. I remember it like yesterday. Like *I* found the thing, not some eleven-year-old."

"So he got fired because of the affair? Is that what happened?"

He sighed. "It's so… Yael, it's complicated. There's more to the story. There are so many details. I'm not even sure I remember it clearly."

"Please don't tell me it involves the assassination of President Kennedy."

He chuckled. "Huh? Oh, it's not that complicated. But, hey, I'm glad you can joke about it." He laughed again. "The Kennedy assassination. I guess that gives the whole thing some perspective."

"Okay," she said, relieved, sort of. "Go on."

He spoke in a rush, his words punctuated only occasionally by hard breaths as he hurried down the mountainside, not quite jogging, but fast, graceful like a deer. Yael struggled to keep up. "Well, keep in mind that I didn't just read the diary that one time. Once I found it, I couldn't stay away. I snuck into their room every day. It was like the most addictive soap opera you could imagine, but I *knew* the characters. I was one of the characters! And it really was like a serial romance, or tragedy – a distinct story, with a beginning, middle, climax, and sort of an ending. It occurred to me more than once that he was making the whole thing up, that he was just writing a novel. He even gave it a title – 'Chronicles of a Broken Marriage.' Maybe he was writing it for me, his one reader. But real life matched up too closely with the story. He'd write about a fight at the marriage counselor's office, and I'd hear them whispering about it the next day. I read about him slapping Mom, and I saw the bruise…"

"Whoa!" she said, putting out an arm, stopping his descent. "Let's please just sit down." The moon, three-quarters full, craggy and pockmarked, shimmered with such silver brilliance that it was almost painful to look at. The bright stars overwhelmed the night. Yael and her brother clicked off their flashlights; it was light enough without them. They found a boulder with two flat spaces, perfect for a couple, as if it had been designed as a couch for two shy lovers, or a brother and sister long overdue for a talk.

Her father, Arthur said softly as if still guarding a secret, had slapped her mother. For some reason, that one revelation, in a day full of them, stopped Yael cold, stole her breath away. Now she understood why everyone asked her if she wanted to know. Maybe she didn't. But she couldn't stop now. "Start at the beginning," she whispered.

"The beginning." He looked up and did a double take, as if seeing stars for the first time. Yael recognized the feeling. The first time she'd seen the desert sky – the bruises and pimples on the face of the white moon, the constellations, Pegasus, Orion, the Big Dipper, more vivid than planetarium displays, each star looking not only close enough to touch but dangerous, as though it would burn your fingers if you even put out your hand – convinced her that, until her move to Desert County, she'd never really seen stars, never knew the moon.

"That's not so easy," her brother continued. "*I* didn't start reading from the beginning, so… well, she – the other woman, his cousin's wife – came to see him one day. In his office. It was like a pastoral visit. Her name was Yelena. I'm pretty sure she was born in Russia. Anyway, she was afraid of her husband. I think he was beating her up. Or, at least threatening her."

"His cousin? The gangster?"

"Our cousin, Yael. Yes, the gangster. Funny, how you keep using that word 'gangster.' But this isn't a rap song. He was a vicious killer. Did Weinman tell you everything he did? Everything?"

"Uh, well, I found out. I think."

He nodded. Yael could see the wrinkles on his face, the hills and crevices of his cheeks, and they reminded her of the moon. She felt like she'd never seen her brother this clearly, not even in the brightest light. "That's how it started," he said. "She came to him for counseling about her husband, our cousin Marcus. The man terrified her. I think she was afraid he would kill her. At that point, he'd already killed a lot of people."

"So Dad slept with her? To, what, *reassure* her?"

"Wow, you really want to skip to the end! But, yeah, I guess that's how it ended up, except for this one detail: he fell in love with her. He really did. And she fell in love with him. It went on for just a few months, but it was a hot time."

Now Yael really did wonder how much she wanted – needed – to know. She decided to hold back on the comments and questions. Let him tell the story. Who knew when he'd ever talk about this stuff again?

"The hardest thing for me was finding Mom's suicide note." He looked at her. She winced, but grabbed the boulder, not wanting Arthur to see her tremble. Then she nodded. "It wasn't the actual note, but Dad copied it verbatim into his diary. 'I can't go on.' That's what it said. I found it the day after he transcribed it. 'I can't live with a cheating husband. The only reason I haven't done it up to now is because of the kids.'"

"It?" Yael said, then regretted the interruption.

"Suicide. The only reason she hadn't committed suicide yet was because of us. You and me."

She nodded and exhaled with caution, as if, without extra care, her exhaled breaths would become tears, or shouts of rage. She considered her mother's note. "The only reason I haven't done it up to now is because of the kids." There were, of course, multiple ways of interpreting those words. But this was Arthur's story, and she would let him tell it.

"When I read it, I ran to find Mom. That was stupid because I'd seen her that morning, so obviously she hadn't killed herself. All she'd done was write a note that Dad found. Did he stop her in the nick of time? Was she just playing with the idea, writing her own journal? I don't know, Dad never wrote what happened. He just quoted the note. Mom didn't look any different that day. Actually, she looked a little more cheerful, she was back to humming those Hebrew kid songs. She was playing with you on the kitchen floor, something I think she hadn't done in weeks. Anyway, she was alive. She hadn't done 'it.' But that was when I made my mistake. I was in such a hurry to find Mom after reading her suicide note, that I left the pages out, on top of Dad's chest of drawers. When I realized I hadn't cleaned up after myself, I rushed back into their room and there he was, reading the thing. He looked at me as soon as I walked in. He probably heard my panting. But he ignored me, just turned around, and went back to the diary. So I left. I waited all day for him to scream at me for poking through his stuff, for reading his diary. He had an explosive temper before the divorce. I'm not sure you remember. Afterwards, he changed, but before! He'd scream at me for not clearing my breakfast bowl, or leaving my homework on the dining-room table. He'd wave a spoon at me like it was a knife, threatening me. And especially while he was sleeping with Yelena. That was the only time in my life he spanked me, and he did it frequently, I think maybe three or four times. That's also when he slapped Mom. You know, I was afraid of him. I started to think of him as the real gangster, like he had it in his blood."

Yael shut her eyes tightly. Tears leaked through nevertheless. Her cute, gentle father. Her role model. The reason she became a rabbi. She opened her eyes but looked away from her brother, as if not seeing could lead to not listening. She brushed her hand along the surface of the boulder, and wondered if she could stuff pebbles or dirt in her ears. But she wiped her eyes with a tissue and kept nodding, because that was all Arthur seemed to need to keep talking. And she really did want to know.

"But he never mentioned it. Never accused me of snooping through his stuff or of reading his personal papers. Back then, I assumed he just didn't want to talk about it, so he ignored me. It didn't occur to me that he, an adult, our father, could be sloppy. Now I realize, he probably thought he left it out himself. For several years I assumed he knew I'd read it, that I knew all about this sordid episode. Now, I don't think so. The fact is, he was too absorbed in his own soap-opera life to think much about me at all. I was a character in the diary, but not a significant one. He barely mentioned me. He was much more concerned with you."

She looked up, blinking in the starlight.

"How a divorce would affect you. How it would be for you growing up in a home without two parents. I guess he figured I was already grown up. Or, I was just naturally tough because I was a boy, or his son. Or, I don't know, maybe he just chose to ignore me. But he did write about you, much more than he wrote about me."

Two-year-olds, Yael thought, are more interesting than eleven-year-old boys. Certainly cuter. As a two-year-old, she'd been learning new words, giggling and screeching, experimenting with her limbs, unfolding new emotions, while Arthur had been skulking around, sullen, rebellious and fearful. She thought of Arthur's twins, and how almost a year before, at her wedding, when she'd felt too agitated and distracted to speak even to her parents, she couldn't take her eyes off the two-year-olds, couldn't keep her hands off their chubby elbows, couldn't resist tickling their bellies, provoking giggles, snorts. If she'd kept a diary the day of her wedding, Yael probably would have left Arthur out of it entirely and focused on the girls. The ugliest two-year-old, she thought, is more charismatic, more charming than the most delightful eleven-year-old boy. Her heart ached for her brother. He found the diary – the suicide note! – at exactly the wrong time, at the height of his emotional neediness, but the nadir of his attractiveness to his parents. Yael could only imagine the long-term traumatic effect. She would discuss all this, she promised herself, with her brother, help him heal, urge him, if he still felt pangs, to seek professional help. She would find the right shrink, make the referral. This was, after all, her profession. She could help. But not right now. Now, she needed information. She needed to know the story. "Arthur, I'm trying to understand what happened to his job, and how that screwed up their marriage. Cantor Weinman…"

"The scumbag."

"Pardon me?"

"A name I made up for him. I never told anyone about it. You mentioned the smell. Is it still bad?"

Yael stared at her brother. The scumbag. He made up the name? "Yeah," she answered. "It's, uh, not pleasant. I assumed it was because of the stroke, because he can't really take care of himself. I figured he used to be a normal person."

"Hardly. He had a beautiful voice. But, honestly, he frightened me. Even worse than Dad, at Dad's worst moments. If it hadn't been for all the distractions – the affair, the scandal, the funeral – I'm sure Mom and Dad would have focused on what a creepy guy he was. But they didn't. He actually babysat for us a few times."

"Yes, he told… what do you mean, creepy?" Yael thought for a second, pondering the cantor's beautiful voice, his bulk, his odor. His madness. "Really, what do you mean by that? Why creepy?"

Arthur looked away and sighed. "Later," he said. "One story at a time. You wanted to know how it all blew up. Divorce, scandal, job loss?"

She nodded.

"Our cousin was murdered. Marco Gottlieb, just 'Marco' in the press, the famous Jewish mobster. Weinman told you this. He was a killer, and he was killed. That's what happens to criminals, right? So, someone had to do the funeral, and who else, but his cousin? The synagogue board didn't like that, but they couldn't very well fire Dad for officiating at the service of his first cousin, no matter how evil the guy had been. Every Jew deserves a Jewish funeral, right? What bothered the board, at first, was who asked him to officiate."

Uncle Flavio, she thought. Cuba's chief spy! The mastermind behind the Kennedy assassination. Peter will love this. Or maybe Castro himself?

"Yelena, Marco's wife," Arthur said. "She showed up at the synagogue the night of the murder. Dad was there for choir rehearsal. He wrote it about in the diary. She burst in, crying, babbling away in Hebrew, Spanish, and Yiddish. Dad took her to a corner of the sanctuary and they talked, in front of thirty witnesses. The members couldn't hear what they were saying, but I guess they couldn't miss the body language. At this point, Dad and Yelena had been sleeping together for two months. After the funeral, which was covered by every newspaper in the tri-state area, one of the choir members approached the synagogue president, told him about that night, the hysterical widow, the overly solicitous rabbi. I guess Dad 'fessed up right away. Mom already knew. I learned that from the diary."

A coyote howled. Arthur started, but Yael, accustomed to that high-pitched whistling wailing sound – for her it was no more threatening than the nightly cricket chirping – watched her brother's frightened face, now bathed by starlight. "It's okay," she whispered. "Just a coyote." She stared into his eyes, willing him to go on.

"They fired him in April, two weeks after the funeral. The thing is, he considered leaving Mom, leaving us. In his heart, he wanted to move in with Yelena. He didn't tell

Mom this. He promised Mom he would never see Yelena again. He begged her for forgiveness, and she forgave him. But he was lying, again. The day after he swore it was over, he slept with Yelena. He didn't tell Mom, or anyone. But he wrote it in the diary."

Yael nodded and took her brother's hand, a simple act of intimacy, but still startling because, despite their closeness, they rarely touched each other. Her father, she thought, was a liar and a cheat. She was finding this out now, and she knew it would be difficult, if not impossible, ever to assimilate it into her identity as a loyal, loving daughter. But she would survive. As a rabbi, she'd heard of worse, even of community leaders, supposedly good men – actually, not "supposedly," but genuinely good men, or good women, for that matter, who became weak, and then cruel. Yael would get over it. But what if she'd found out at age eleven? At a time when she imagined she was living in a happy home, with a father who was a role model for hundreds? What if, as a budding adolescent, she'd discovered her father was a fraud, who'd considered abandoning her for a stranger? Who'd nearly driven her mother to suicide? Would she ever have gotten over that revelation? Was her brother "over" it? She squeezed his hand, and was not surprised to see a small tear leak from his eye and drip halfway down his cheek.

"He got a new congregation in Cleveland. He and the Jersey *shul* hushed up the scandal. It wasn't in anyone's interest for others to find out. And, you know, he was good at what he did. It didn't take him long to get the Cleveland job. But even after they moved, he phoned Yelena, at least once a week. She even visited a few times. It was all in the diary. I guess Mom found out, or just got tired of living with him. I think you know the rest. They got divorced one year after the move."

She nodded, keeping her eyes on his starlit face. He'd stopped crying. Oddly, he was now smiling, as if remembering a joke. "You kept reading the diary?" she asked. "Even in Cleveland?"

"Just for another month. Just enough time to read how much he regretted staying with a bitchy wife and a sullen, spoiled adolescent. I'm quoting now, from memory. You're the only one he liked. That's what he wrote. That was the last thing I read. That's when I stopped reading – when I found out he didn't like me."

"Oh, come on, Arthur. He was just..."

"Hey, I know. I've had twenty-five years to get over this. He was venting. That's what you do with a diary. I got that, even at age eleven. Look, I didn't like him very much either back then, but we've both gotten past it. But I never told anyone. Not even Toby. I have this inhibition against making him look bad. Everyone thinks he's a saint. I don't want to burst any bubbles. But when you called, I figured you should at least hear it from me, and not from the scumbag. And in person. This isn't the type of thing you tell your sister in an e-mail. Or over the phone."

He reached for his flashlight. But Yael touched his arm. "I'm sorry, Arthur. I just have one more question."

He looked at her.

"Cantor Weinman. The scumbag. There's something else?"

132

He inhaled deeply, then pursed his lips exhaling, as if he were letting the air out through a straw. Yael felt his breath on her wrist. "Let's finish our hike," he said. "Have dinner. Then we can talk more."

But at dinner, the three of them shared two bottles of wine, and Peter and Arthur sang Hank Williams songs while Yael tried to harmonize, even though she didn't know the words and could never find the right notes. They turned in after draining the last bit of merlot, and Arthur left first thing in the morning, the next day.

Over the next two years, as Yael's relationship with her boss Rabbi Loeb flourished, as he trusted her with more and more complex and sensitive assignments, she grew indignant, alarmed, then merely irritated as Weinman ignored her and began hanging out with Judah. The two men met together once, sometimes twice a week, always smoking cigars and often drinking brandy. Guttural laughter, along with fetid cigar smoke, leaked through Judah's office door whenever the cantorbag came for a visit. When Yael attempted to warn off her senior colleague, or just ask why he wasted his time with the low-life, Judah told her that everyone was allowed one loser as a friend. Anyway, he told her, it was a reclamation project – a *tikkun*. And, really, he wasn't so bad. He was funny, smart, and he still sang beautifully, despite the stroke. Did Yael have any evidence that he was dangerous? Yael readily admitted that she did not. She did, however, begin using her brother's nickname and, somewhat against her intention, it spread to the office staff, so that even Manuel the janitor and Javier the security guard called Weinman "the scumbag," though not to his face and never in front of Judah.

That night, the night of Arthur's visit, the night of her boozy dinner with her brother, the cantor's name did come up once. Peter and Arthur were crooning Chuck Berry's "Memphis, Tennessee," with Yael accompanying on hand-claps. Arthur reached out his hand and grasped Peter's mandolin strings. "Newspaper articles," he said, sounding suddenly sober. "You said Weinman gave you newspaper articles. Anything else? Anything else in that envelope?"

Yael wanted to stay drunk. She didn't want to talk about the scumbag. So she giggled. Peter winked at her, and blew her a kiss. "Some contracts, didn't you say? Didn't he tell you there were some contracts in there, Yael? Do you want to look at them, Arthur?"

Arthur shrugged. "Maybe after the song," he said.

But after the song, they had some more wine, then fell asleep. Yael didn't return to the scumbag's manila envelope for another two-and-a-half years, five days after someone strangled Aviva Loeb to death.

Three

EPSTEIN

CHAPTER 1

It was Charlotte who told Yael the police had arrested Cantor Weinman for the murder of Mrs. Loeb. The secretary reached Yael at 7 a.m. on her cell phone as Yael was walking to work along the bike path. She'd stopped driving to the synagogue ever since she found reporters camping out in the parking lot, imploring anyone who used the front entrances – pregnant moms with their toddlers, electricians, elderly sisterhood volunteers, all synagogue staff – for interviews. Her first thought was that Charlotte always knows everything. It was Charlotte who'd told her that Aviva had been killed, Charlotte who'd kept her away from Judah the day after the murder, Charlotte who'd told her who was officiating at the funeral. During those two dreadful days after the murder, Yael wondered about Charlotte, at her suddenly passionate protection of Judah, her mysterious acquisition of all relevant information. But now, hearing her eager voice, birdlike in its high, southern, sing-song quality ("It was him all along," she sang. "The scumbag! The scumbag!"), Yael imagined Charlotte less as a shadowy figure, possibly a suspect who knew too much, and more as the neighborhood busybody.

And speaking of suspects, her second thought was, thank God he's not arresting me. He believed me. In fact, relief that Weinman was finally going to be put away mixed with a deeper satisfaction that Yael would no longer, in any way, have to defend herself against the preposterous notion that she had murdered her boss's wife.

After that first meeting in his car, the tall, skinny cop Epstein had interviewed her for three consecutive days, all in her cramped living room, surrounded by Peter's exotic stringed instruments. He started each session by plopping a brown paper bag filled with chewing gum and Diet Coke on the chipped wooden coffee table, then pointing at it, like a grandmother offering treats. Yael always shook her head at first, but by the end of each meeting, she somehow ended up with three or four empty cans next to her, and an achingly full bladder.

The first time, he opened abruptly with her alibi, or, as he put it, her lack of one. She was with her husband, she repeated, when Charlotte phoned, but before that, while Aviva was getting herself strangled, Yael was alone in her office, writing sermons. And no, not on the computer, so there wouldn't be a record there. Longhand, on a yellow legal notepad. And she couldn't recall any phone conversations or e-mails she'd written. No alibi.

Next, he segued quickly to the supposed affair she'd been having with Judah. "I followed your advice, Ms. Gold," he said, two globs of gum in his mouth, though he wasn't chewing at all. "I asked around."

She looked at him. There were only two seats in the crowded room, so they sat next to each other on the loveseat. Every other surface was taken up with instruments, sheet music, CDs, videos, and DVDs – Peter's collection of eclectic passions, ranging from every version of every *Star Trek* episode and movie, to every Orson Welles Shakespeare film, to all of Glenn Gould's recordings. When Peter fell in love with something, he collected every recorded instance of that particular thing, and then filed it somewhere in a pile in their living room. That left Yael and Epstein sitting side by side, but both scrunched as far away as possible from the other. Yael had to strain her neck to look in the cop's eyes. Unlike most tall people she'd known, he made no effort at all to bend down and meet her gaze. "You asked around," she said.

"I'd like to hear your version."

"My *version*? I was *not* having an affair with him! And, anyway, I didn't…"

"I'm sorry, Ms. Gold, but with you, we don't even need lie detector tests. Do you know what your face looks like now? Are you aware of the blushing?"

"Dammit!" she said, loudly on the first syllable, but catching herself just an instant too late, so she nearly swallowed the 'it.' "I blush – I'm blushing at the *idea*. I don't blush when I lie. I mean, I don't generally lie. I just…" She shook her head. "I was not having an affair with him."

"You were in love with him. *Are* in love with him. Even now."

God, she wanted to hate this guy, to put him in the same category as Weinman, Addison, her other tormentors. But, through the fog of her irritation, she understood what he was doing. And it wasn't as if he wasn't on to something. "I am not in love with him," she said, aware that she was still blushing but trying, nevertheless, to inject as much truth as she could into the shaky statement. After all, she was never in love with him. She'd had a crush on him. There was a difference.

"Was he having an affair with someone else?"

She shook her head. *Shul* gossip, she thought. Dark thoughts from a jealous wife, that blossomed into insubstantial, strange suspicions. What synagogue, what village, didn't have its rumors? Still, this was a murder investigation, and she really wasn't very good at shading the truth. She told him about her lunch with Deborah, and reminded him of the encounter with Aviva in her office.

"So," he said, the gum visible in his surprisingly small mouth, "the day before the murder, you heard speculation that Rabbi Loeb may have been involved with two women, both of whom happened to be pregnant?"

"But it was crazy!" she said. "I didn't *believe* it." But she wondered suddenly if that was true. Wondered, even more, what she now believed.

That was the first interview: her non-alibi, her non-affair, speculations about other non-affairs, hints that she might have had a motive. Each subsequent session followed exactly the same pattern. He started by asking about her whereabouts at the time of the murder, offering suggestions about how she could prove she really was in her office: "You didn't take a single call? Your cellphone didn't ring? No one came in to empty your trash can?" Then he worked her over about her supposed relationship with Judah, always pressing for her "version," hinting that the synagogue gossip mill had named her again and again as the senior rabbi's true love interest. By the second round, Yael readily admitted that she'd developed a crush on Judah some time during her stint on the jury, but she *never* acted on it, never would have acted on it and, anyhow, when would she have had the time? She couldn't exactly have professed her love for him the day Aviva was killed. She'd hoped her admission would get him to back off, but instead he'd argued about the meaning of the word "crush."

"So," he said, "at a sex crime trial, you developed a passion for him, something powerful and irrational?"

"No, no, that's not what crush means at all. Crush is a schoolgirl thing. A little stronger than admiration. Crush isn't passion. That's exactly the difference. You can control it. I controlled it."

"You *controlled* it? Kept it under wraps? That must have been hard. For a whole day, until his wife was killed?"

She just shook her head. He was baiting her. She should call a lawyer, maybe Ralph Markowitz, the former synagogue president who seemed to defend every state official who stumbled into gambling-related corruption. Peter had wanted to phone Ralph right away, after the first session in Epstein's car, but Yael didn't want to be the first rabbi in her class to lawyer up in a murder investigation.

In any case, Epstein always dropped the insinuations against her and quickly moved on to other women. Surely, he said at the third interview, that lunch with Deborah wasn't the first time it had occurred to her that Addison may have been sleeping with Rabbi Loeb?

"Actually, I can assure you that it was the very first time it occurred to me. I'm kind of naïve. That's where the blushing comes from. Everything makes me blush. It's because I'm innocent. I am innocent," she repeated.

He looked at her and, despite the strain on her neck, she held his eye. "Hmm," he said.

It was Peter who remembered the contracts. After the third interview, after she'd been reduced to proclaiming her innocence, apparently to no effect, she was about to give in and call Ralph. She'd filled her husband in, more or less, on the tone and content of the sessions, leaving out, of course, her crush on Judah.

"I just don't know if he believes me," she said at dinner that night. One positive outcome of the current mess: Yael and Peter were spending more time together. Epstein had told Yael not to speak to any other potential witnesses, so she'd stayed home from work the past three days. Peter, ever the loyal trooper, had cancelled his classes and his gigs so he could keep her company. "Maybe I'm really the only one without an alibi."

Peter shook his head. "But it's just obvious who the killer is."

Yael frowned. "Obvious?"

"Well, it's not you. And Addison or Tzippi? Come on! You think they could strangle someone to death? And Rabbi Loeb? What would be the motive? If he's having affairs, he could have just divorced her. That's a lot less messy. But, really, think about it. Who's the one truly dangerous, inarguably unstable character who's been hanging out at the synagogue for over two years? Who also happens to have developed some kind of obsession with Judah?"

"The scumbag," Yael said softly, tilting her head, watching her husband. Until that moment, it never occurred to her that other women might also be suspects. She never liked Addison, but to think her capable of murder? And Tzipporah? Absurd. For that matter, she hadn't spent much time in the last few days thinking about other suspects at all. She'd been too preoccupied with her own lack of any alibi.

"Of course," Peter said.

"Well, yeah, I guess I thought of that. And I'm sure it must have occurred to Epstein. But then why is he harassing me? It's been three straight days!"

Peter shrugged. "I guess they don't have all the evidence they need yet. So he's trying to get a fuller picture. And he probably thinks you're lying about something. It's the blushing problem."

She looked at him, feeling the blush, hot, red. "I'm not lying about anything. You know that, don't you?"

"I'm sure you wouldn't lie to a police officer," he said.

Not to a police officer, she thought. To him? She decided not to pursue it. Instead she made a joke. "Maybe it was Uncle Flavio."

"Contracts!" Peter responded immediately.

"Peter."

He reminded her. They'd never looked at the contracts in the scumbag's envelope. They'd intended to, over two years ago, but had forgotten all about them. Ten minutes later, after retrieving the manila envelope, they were on the phone with Detective Epstein. An hour later, he came by to retrieve them. They were contracts for murder, arrangements between various gangsters and Marco Gottlieb –

criminal, mob boss, hired killer, gangster, Yael's cousin. None of them, of course, contained the name Edgar Weinman. But how had the scumbag come to own them? Why would he possess these relics of murder?

Peter didn't know, Yael didn't know. But they both thought it was relevant to this particular murder investigation. Detective Epstein didn't comment when he took the envelope, just thanked them grimly, reaching down to shake Peter's hand. But he must have agreed with their assessment because he stopped scheduling interviews with Yael, e-mailing her that it was fine for her to return to work. Three days later, the tall detective arrested the scumbag for the murder of Aviva Loeb.

Yael saw Judah as she walked quickly through the back entrance of the synagogue. He was leaning against the wall, watching the door, as if waiting for her to appear. He'd grown a short, reddish-brown beard, a sign of mourning. But he was otherwise well groomed, his hair blow-dried, his white shirt and brown cotton pants wrinkle-free. Leaning against the wall, he gave the initial impression of fatigue, but his eyes were wide open and he was smiling brightly. On second glance, Yael interpreted his slouching as simply a relaxed pose, a picture of confidence and strength. As if he was holding the building up, and not the other way around. Yael had wondered how she would feel on seeing him after the murder, the interrogations, the gossipy revelations. She wasn't surprised, though she was disappointed, that her feelings seemed not to have changed at all. His warmth, his relaxed vitality, his sexiness, *something* about him floated down the hallway and hit her like a physical force. She smiled at him.

"It's good to see you," he said, his voice slightly raspy, as if he were getting over a cold or, Yael considered, he'd been weeping and wailing.

"It's good to be back." She was about to embrace him – lightly, she thought, just a kiss on the cheek, a greeting for an old friend – when she saw Addison emerge from his office. Yael looked at the two of them and then waved weakly at Addison, who stood still, smiling, her belly jutting forward, blocking half the hallway. The pregnant woman ignored Yael entirely; she just stood there grinning.

"Staff meeting at ten," Judah said. "Okay, Yael? Addison and I have to go through some budget numbers, and then we all have to get together. Ten o'clock okay?"

"Uh, of course. Should I come by a few minutes early, go over the agenda?" That had always been the practice before staff meetings. In fact, usually Yael and Judah went out to lunch before the meetings and planned the agenda together. And that, she thought ruefully, was before he'd designated her his "partner," before the reorganization that was supposedly "about her."

"Not necessary, Yael," he replied quickly. "This won't be an ordinary meeting. You understand."

She nodded and glanced again at Addison, who ignored her and stared adoringly at Judah. "Not an ordinary meeting," she repeated, but by the end of that four word sentence, Judah and Addison had already retreated to his office.

It was, in fact, an exceedingly unordinary meeting. They sat around the huge oak conference table in the boardroom, a full-time staff of thirty-five – teachers, administrators, youth workers, social workers, assistants, janitors, their security guard, and Yael, the one other rabbi. Yael found a spot next to Tzippi, who was munching on Doritos, a full-size bag open in front of her. Yael touched her hand. Tzippi smiled weakly and then, to Yael's surprise, averted her eyes. She doesn't want to look at me, Yael thought. She thinks I – what *does* she think? "How *are* you?" Yael whispered. Tzipporah shook her head. "Have to keep eating," she said.

Have to keep eating? That's how she responds to: How *are* you? And what about, How are *you*? "Tzippi," she said, "is there something wrong?"

She shook her head again, this time vigorously. "Later," she whispered, as Judah walked in the door. Followed – another surprise – by Addison, who, placing both hands on her belly as if she were holding it up, shuffled to a corner while Judah made his way to the head of the table. Normally, no one who didn't work at Anshei Emet attended staff meetings. Judah insisted on it. Just professional staff, no volunteers. But Addison stood there, looking vaguely nauseous but also smirking, as if she were sick, and proud of it.

"Thank you all for being here this morning," Judah began. He smiled. His beneficent leader smile, Yael thought, the warm glow his face radiated whenever bestowing compliments on staff or non-leadership congregants. The twinkling blue-eyed look that somehow reached every individual in a room, no matter how crowded, and made you think he was talking to everyone but was *especially* proud of you, and you alone. "Any news to report?"

They laughed out loud – genuine laughter, breaking through several fatty layers of tension. Tzippi, her mouth still filled with Doritos, cracked up loudest. "Well," he said, "I guess there hasn't been a shortage of news. We'll take a break from the news." He paused, looked down, pursed his lips, and touched his left index finger to his temple, scratching lightly at his silver hair. The sermonic look, Yael noted. He's gathering his thoughts, or, better, *playing* someone who's gathering his thoughts, because he knows exactly what he's going to say. "A few moments before I heard about Aviva's murder, I happened to be studying Psalm 30. You may recall the last few lines: 'You've transformed my mourning into dancing. You've opened up my mourning clothes, and adorned me with joy.'" He looked up, his finger still idly probing his sideburns. "I wonder if that will ever happen to me. Not grieving, but dancing? A sudden miraculous transformation, wearing party clothes instead of the dark rags of mourning?" He shook his head. "Right now, I don't see it. I'm closed to it. I've closed myself up, like Aaron, after he lost his sons. I'm dumbfounded. God's turned his face away from mine, and I'm astonished."

You could hear a pin drop in the room. Not because of the words themselves, though Yael appreciated the imagery, mourning as a kind of shutting down, healing a reopening. But Judah had the gift; the tone of his voice perfectly matched the shiny silver of his hair, the pale glimmer of his face. You listened out of esthetic obligation. Also, Yael had no idea where he was going with this.

"Help me open up," he continued. "I expect that from you, my colleagues. My friends. Don't let me curl into a ball, like a turtle retreating to his shell. Open me up. That's what I need. That's what you can do. I loved her. No one should doubt that. But also, be patient. You'll need to be patient. Tolerant, even. Forgiving." Yael could swear he was looking directly at her, boring into her with his blue eyes, though she was also sure that everyone else in the room felt the same way. His finger still scratching just above his ear, he looked like he was about to say more, which meant, in Yael's experience, that he would say more, that he would now, in fact, get to the point, astonish his audience with an utterly fresh and meaningful insight. Tears filled his eyes. He half smiled, then walked quickly out of the room, followed, as if attached, by Addison. His last word – "forgiving" – hung in the air. For what? Yael wondered. After a few moments, everyone turned to look at her, as though expecting an answer to that or other questions.

But Yael wasn't ready to assert any but the most informal leadership. She shrugged. "We've all got work to do," she said firmly, looking at the table so she wouldn't hold anyone's gaze. She wasn't Judah, she wasn't going to move anyone with a look. And she certainly wasn't going to give a sermon, or a pep talk. She pushed down with her thumbs and stood up quickly. The room emptied. Everyone had work to do.

Eight hours later – eight non-stop hours of returning phone calls, e-mails, preparing for classes, writing sermons, a two-hour stint visiting various hospitals, fighting traffic, and circling construction-pocked parking lots hoping for a space – eight hours of typical frenetic rabbinic work, offered to congregants, as Judah had taught her, as if she had all the time in the world, as if she'd built her day around the phone call to Bertha wishing her a happy eightieth birthday; or the visit with eight-year-old Josh, recovering from heart surgery, handing him an official Anshei Emet healing teddy bear; or the call to the chair of the ritual committee, arranging for him to pick up the Torah ornaments so they could be polished – after eight hours of feigned and real joy, of fake and genuine heartbreak, of exhilaration, but also frustration and boredom, she knocked lightly on Judah's door.

No answer, but she heard voices, faint, not whispering, male and female. It was a thin door; Judah was inside talking to a woman. Addison? She tapped again next to the mezuzah. Again no response, but still two soft voices, Judah and, well, *not* Addison, someone else, a voice Yael recognized but couldn't quite place. Holding her breath, trying not to feel guilty – was she a partner or not? – Yael leaned on the door, turning the knob.

Judah and Tzippi stood facing each other, neither's body touching the other in any limb or extremity, but standing as close as one body can to another without actually touching; twelve inches separated their necks, but the tiniest space kept their chins and noses apart. They were standing in the far left corner of the office, bookshelves on two sides, a good ten feet away from Judah's desk. His back was to the books, as if Tzippi had literally cornered him. As Yael pushed through the entrance, Tzippi glanced up, then moved away slowly, staring at the floor. Judah beamed at Yael, a shockingly serene look in his eyes, as if he'd been meditating, or just woken up from a quick, refreshing nap.

"Sorry," Yael quickly mumbled, without moving away from the door. "I thought you were alone."

Judah smiled beneficently. No worries. All was right with the world. Tzipporah would not meet her eye.

"I'll come back," Yael offered.

"No," Judah said quickly. Tzippi shook her head. No one moved.

No? Yael thought. As in, no, don't come back? Or no, please don't go; please stay. She did neither, holding on to the door, straddling the thin line of carpeting separating the office from the hallway. Paralysis, she thought. It was as if someone had sprayed the office with a paralyzing drug.

Finally, Tzippi sighed softly – or maybe it was gas; she *was* pregnant – and walked swiftly out of the room. Judah watched her go, then, with equal serenity – the same grin, same bright-eyed joy – turned to face Yael.

She stepped in, letting the door slowly swing shut. She tried to remember the last time they'd been truly alone together. Ten minutes, on the day before the murder, when he'd told her that it was about her, that she was his partner now, the day she'd finally convinced the jury to convict. It seemed like years ago, like she'd finished adolescence and was only now grown up. Before that? Three weeks ago, she calculated, the day before the trial took over her life. They'd spent a good two hours together, putting the finishing touches on the reorganization. That's when it happened, she realized. That's when she fell in love him, when a switch toggled from no to yes, or more like from resistance to acceptance. But that was a long time ago, one murder ago, several grueling rounds with Detective Epstein ago, a week of suspicions, of rumors, of panic.

She smelled perfume, probably Addison's, but maybe Tzippi's, though she didn't recognize the scent and she worked with Tzipporah every day. She studied Judah, the mourning widower, smiling like a Buddha. She had a lot to say right now to this man, her mentor, her teacher, her boss: questions, questions, questions, comments, questions.

"How are you?" she asked.

He laughed. Many, Yael thought, would call it a gleeful laugh, but she caught the bitter edge. At least she thought she did. "I'm hanging in there," he said. "It's good to have friends."

He hadn't moved from the corner, nor had he asked Yael to sit. So they stood, the bulk of Judah's large office, his couches, chairs, conference table, coffee table, and a good twenty feet separating them. Yael felt like they were in separate rooms. "How are you, Yael?"

"The police questioned me," she said.

"I know."

"You know?" she said.

"I mean, I assumed. They questioned everyone. Everyone who – well, almost all of my friends. I apologize. I'm sorry you had to go through that."

"No, no," she said. "There's no need to apologize. I just – I, it was kind of a shock. They asked me for an alibi. It seemed like I was a suspect."

He nodded.

"I mean, I feel like I have to say something totally absurd – like, I didn't do it. Do I have to say that to you?"

"Of course not. I would never believe that, Yael. Anyway, we know who did it."

"Cantor Weinman?"

"You were right about him, Yael," he said evenly. "I should have listened to you two years ago. If I had, Aviva would probably be alive today." Amazingly, he was still grinning, though his eyes turned soft, and Yael noticed deeply engraved wrinkles above his brows. She'd never seen them before. It was as if they'd just opened up on his face.

"I don't – you can't think that way, Judah. He's, he's like a dybbuk. He draws you in, and then attaches himself to you…" She shook her head. "Look, even I would never have pegged him as a killer."

His tilted his chin, another of his sermonic looks. "We try to help people, don't we, Yael? Wounded souls. We gather them in. Isn't that our vocation? Isn't that why we do this work? But to think that this sacred mission of mine might have led to Aviva's death. That's…" He shook his head. "That's hard to take."

Then why, she thought, are you still smiling? Why the homiletic voice, as if he were addressing a congregation, or teaching a practical rabbinics course? She should go to him, she thought, grasp his hand, comfort him, be a *pastor* to this man who had just lost his wife to a brutal murder. But when she looked at her boss, she still saw Tzippi's profile, as if her guardian angel, still vaguely visible, had never left the room. "Is there anything I can do?" she asked, standing still, her arms at her sides.

"Oh, I'm sure there's a lot you can do. But, as it happens, our Detective Epstein needs to see me now. Jewish, I suppose?"

Yael nodded.

"Hmm. I guess that's good," Judah said. "Ever see him at *shul*?"

"Uh, no, I don't think so".

He shrugged and kept his eyes on her, still smiling. "I'm meeting him at the house." He looked at his watch. "I'm already late."

"Can I – should I drive you?"

"Oh, I'm still a pretty good driver, Yael."

"Of course. I didn't mean…"

He laughed. "Relax. Look, the worst is over. Next week, we start getting back to normal. You and I – just the two of us – we'll meet, figure out where to go from here."

The worst is over? she thought. Over? What did that mean? That Aviva's dead? That they caught the killer, and now everyone's *over* it? "Call me if you need me," she said, and left without another word.

She'd taken one step out the back door, heading quickly toward the bike path, when she felt her Black-Berry vibrate. She looked at the incoming number and frowned; she didn't recognize it. She thought about punching "ignore," but she'd been away from the office for several days, and it could easily be someone who'd been trying to reach her. She pressed the green phone icon and answered.

"Baby Doll!" a voice responded, all too familiar, musical, now demonic.

She gasped. Her knees weakened, as if someone had swung a bat at them. She stumbled back and landed on a boulder, on her rear end.

"You think I'm taking the fall for this all by myself? You don't think I'm taking others down with me? Your husband? You? What do you think?"

"How can you be calling me?"

"You think you give the cops some old papers, you solved the case? Your *tsuris* is just beginning, Rabbi. I ain't sitting in here *confessing*, like some *baal teshuvah*. This ain't Yom Kippur, not for me! I'm naming names! Names that go far back; and you *know* what I'm talking about, Baby Doll."

"How can you be *calling* me!" she screamed into the phone.

"Rabbis and gangsters! Rabbis and women! Sex and violence. I got a story to tell, Baby Doll, *your* story, and now I got me an audience. I got lieutenants taking notes, I got FBI opening up old files, asking *me* about unsolved crimes. And I am goddamn naming names! So *don't* think you put me away, that the worst is over!"

A demon, she thought. From another world. Her hand trembled against her ear. Did God send him? Was this her punishment for wicked thoughts, wicked deeds? His voice was like an electric current coursing through her Black-Berry, up her arm, into her ear, to her brain. She couldn't stop shaking, couldn't even remove the phone from the side of her head.

"I think you remember now, Baby Doll. You remember who I really am! As if you ever forgot! You *know* that I will bring you down. You'll end up in here, hopefully in my cell, with me! Like old times, huh, Baby Doll!"

With an extraordinary, exhausting effort, she lifted her thumb and pressed the red hang-up icon. Then she dropped the BlackBerry into the dirt and rifled through her purse, tossing out her keys, lipstick, tissues, and billfold, looking for a business card. She found it – Epstein's – at the very bottom. She fell to her knees, grabbed the BlackBerry, and punched in the number.

"Epstein."

"He called me! How could he call me?"

"Ms. Gold?"

"The scumbag! I mean, I mean Weinman! Weinman called me, just now. How could he call me?!"

"Please, calm down."

"He's in jail! Didn't you put him in jail? *How can I be hearing his voice?*"

"Listen, it happens. They get to make phone calls. Or someone smuggles in a cellphone and he pays them off. It doesn't take demonic powers. But we better get together. I'll need you to tell me everything he said."

"What if he calls again?"

"Bring me your phone. I'll show you how to block the number."

"I know how to block... It's my phone! I know how to use it! I just – he's supposed to be in jail. *I shouldn't have to hear his voice!*" Yael suddenly heard panting. She whipped her head around, looking for a coyote or a black bear. But she realized it was her own mad breaths, her own choking gasps; she was hyperventilating. Fear, she thought, on this level. It was an utterly novel sensation. She not only didn't recognize it; she didn't recognize herself, sweating through her clothes, desperately holding in her pee, shaking, screaming, panting like a wild animal.

"When can I see you?" she asked, amazed that she was now pleading for a meeting with this man who'd tormented her for days, who'd *suspected* her. But she would beg to see the devil if he could prevent that voice from coming through her cellphone.

"I'm with Loeb right now. How about tomorrow afternoon? There's a few other things I need to ask you, anyway. A few new developments. I'll need your take on things. Tomorrow."

Loeb, she thought. Judah. His last name tossed out as if he were an ordinary guy. "Tomorrow?" she asked, trying to still the quiver in her voice. "But what if. . ?"

"Just don't answer any number you don't recognize until then. Simple enough?"

She held her breath, the only way she could think to keep from panting. "Simple enough," she croaked, then hung up. Tomorrow afternoon, she thought.

But by then, she'd have even bigger problems.

CHAPTER 2

"Rabbi Loeb wants you at the meeting."

It was Charlotte, waking her up at six-thirty in the morning. She'd slept exactly two hours.

At first, Peter hadn't allowed her to unplug all their phones, pointing out that caller ID would rescue them from the scumbag's demonic voice. But that night she hopped out of the tub with a splash the first time the phone rang, wrapping herself quickly in a towel, and eyeing the corners of the room, the cabinets, the closet, as if looking for a place to hide. It was Peter's mother. The second time, she twisted her ankle as she leapt off the living-room rocking chair. It was Peter's agent. But even with the phones unplugged, she couldn't sleep. She couldn't get past the admittedly lunatic notion that Weinman's breath in her ear meant that he'd escaped, that he'd traveled through the invisible cell lines and now resided somewhere in her brain, and was only biding his time, waiting to emerge, in the flesh, in her room. At four in the morning, she took one of Peter's Ambiens.

The phone sounded like a dynamite blast. She bounced awake and stared at her husband. "I plugged it back in at six," he said, apologetically. "Listen, we need the phone."

She turned to check the ID. Congregation Anshei Emet. She snatched it up. "Rabbi Loeb wants you at the meeting."

"Charlotte."

"The meeting, Yael. Rabbi Loeb decided you should be there."

"The meeting."

"Executive committee. Today, at 9 a.m."

"But I didn't know…"

"Of course not. How could you? It was a secret. But now Judah, I mean Rabbi Loeb, wants you there. Yael, are you alright? Am I not making sense?"

"A secret? A secret meeting?"

"Nine a.m., Yael. Rabbi Loeb would like you to be there."

Peter watched her hang up the phone. "A secret meeting?" he asked.

"Not so secret anymore," she said, shaking her head, wondering how long an Ambien lasted if you've never taken one before. "I mean, they asked *me* to come."

Thirty minutes later, Peter touched her elbow at the door. "Did you want to say goodbye?" he asked

Irritation, or something hotter, flashed through Yael's heart. Peter didn't seem to get it. She was *scared*. And deeply confused. In her current confounded state, she wouldn't always remember to peck her child-husband's cheek before leaving. And anyway…

"Just remember that you're strong," he said. "You're the strongest person I know."

She looked at him. Had he shaved? His beard looked neater, like a real beard, not some afterthought from a guy who never remembered to shave. And his eyes were strangely narrow, not wide, not childlike. "You're strong," he repeated.

She exhaled. She'd been holding her breath. "Thank you," she said.

Same room as the staff meeting; same set-up. Baskets of bagels and muffins from Bialystock's decorated the shiny oak conference table like centerpieces, along with pitchers of coffee and bottles of water. But a decidedly different cast of characters sat around the table. Anshei Emet's executive committee members – the president, two vice-presidents, treasurer and secretary – were all rich, successful, and connected to the gaming industry, the region's only real source of fabulous wealth. Deborah, the president, was the managing partner in a law firm that represented five of the Strip's eight mega-casinos. Bill, the treasurer, owned two of those casinos. Mark, the first vice-president, was CEO of the architectural firm that built Bill's casino, as well as the latest additions to the hospital and the university. Jerold, the second vice-president, ran the venture capital firm that lent Bill much of the money to open his second casino. Then there was Addison, the secretary, who'd been Bill's CFO for ten years before marrying her husband, Manny, a plastic surgeon and professor at the medical school. But she wasn't in the room.

Deborah, Bill, Mark, and Jerold were dressed for work. For the men, that meant specially tailored, two-breasted European suits in different shades of blue, and thick, multicolored ties; for Deborah, it meant a gray Armani business suit, with canary-yellow shoes. Apart from Judah and Yael, the synagogue staff, from teachers and youth workers to maintenance, generally comported with an almost aggressive casualness – jeans and T-shirts most days, with barely a minute or so spent in front of the mirror each morning. Yael, who tried to look professional but, nevertheless, slouched more towards her co-workers than her bosses, couldn't decide who better represented the "real world" – the poorly dressed professionals or the perfectly coiffed laity.

Yael's hand shook, but just a little, as she poured herself a cup of coffee. She looked at the sugars and cream, and decided, for the first time in her life, to try her coffee black. She took a sip, winced, took another, and decided that, yes, black was better. At least for now. She sat in a corner, away from the officers. She slowly removed her BlackBerry and placed it on the table. If he called, she thought, maybe she could get someone else to answer.

Deborah welcomed everyone. "And thank you for coming, Yael." Yael started at hearing her name, but then smiled weakly and looked at her coffee. Deborah turned to Judah, who sat next to her at the front of the table. "Well, Rabbi Loeb, you asked for this meeting. Why don't you go ahead?"

Yael lifted her head slowly, as if peeking at something she really wasn't meant to see. Same Buddha-like grin. But his eyes were bloodshot red, and the crevices in his face – the word "wrinkles" would no longer do – looked like they'd doubled in size overnight. Judah must have gotten even less sleep than her.

"Thank you, Deborah. I guess I'll start with the most difficult admission. This will become public soon, but I want you, my dear friends, to hear it first. It's about my marriage.

For many years now, Aviva and I have had an open marriage."

He stopped to take a long sip from his water bottle. He was still smiling.

Deborah stared at him, her chin scraping her neck. Yael had never seen a chin fallen so low, or a mouth more wide open. Judah could fit his entire thick fist into Deborah's O-shaped mouth. "I'm sorry, Judah," Deborah said, pulling herself together, "but you'll have to explain a little. What do you mean by an open marriage?"

He laughed lightly. *Laughed*! "I would have thought it was obvious. We were free to see other people. We would stay together for companionship, because we shared essential values. But we had no sexual relationship. When it came to – uh, that – we were both free to sleep with—"

"Okay," Deborah interrupted. "You don't have to go into details."

"Well, Deborah, I think I'd better explain some things. You see, our intimate life – our sexual life – failed a long time ago. But must sexual intimacy define every important relationship? Aviva was my soulmate, my closest friend. But she and I couldn't – well, we couldn't. We couldn't do that. So, we agreed to an open marriage. She was free, and I was free to, uh, seek—"

"What the *hell* are you talking about?" Yael had pushed her seat out from under her and was standing, pointing her index finger at Judah. A black fury, like a sleek bullet, punctured her gut, sending poison through her bloodstream. She felt herself go beet red, felt the heat fly off her cheeks.

"Yael," Deborah said. "I really think you should—"

"*She* was free? *She?* Aviva? Who did she sleep with, Judah?"

"Really, Yael," Deborah said, now also on her feet. "I must insist. Control yourself!"

Judah cocked his head at Yael. He was still smiling, though now less serene than curious. What was this mad creature going to say next?

"And who exactly are we talking about with you, Rabbi Loeb? Congregants? Pregnant women? Who exactly did you invite into this open marriage?"

"Rabbi Gold!" Deborah said. "That is enough!"

Yael shook her head violently, as if she were trying to shake herself awake. Her neck hurt, her shoulders ached. She was still standing, her accusing finger still pointed at her boss. She looked at Deborah. The president's mouth again yawned open wide enough for a fist, her chin again sunk low against her neck. Yael watched the men, red-faced, probably angry, but hard to read.

She fled the room. She tried to slam the door but could not muster the strength.

In the hallway, the sight of Tzippi stopped her in her tracks. She glared at the education director, the individual charged with inspiring their Jewish teenagers, looking first at her eyes, then lower, toward her slightly bulging belly. She imagined her gaze as a super-charged CT scan, able to see past skin and bone and deceptions into Tzippi's innards, able to discern the life growing in her womb as well as the intricate web of lies she'd spun in the dark parts of her brain. Tzippi looked at Yael beseechingly, her brown eyes close to tears. "Yael," she muttered, and that was all she could manage. Yael held her friend's sad gaze for slightly longer than a second. Then she shook her head, disgusted, nauseous, and walked away.

"Yael," a voice from behind her called. Not Tzippi, she realized. Deborah.

"Yael!" Deborah yelled. "Why are *you* running away? Stop!"

But she kept walking, out the back door, into the desert hills, toward home.

CHAPTER 3

"Dad," she said, her mouth six inches from his ear.

He responded, as usual, by turning his bald head slowly in her direction, reacting not to her voice in particular, not to the sound of his daughter, nor the hint of supplication in her weary tone, but simply to a voice, not his own, echoing in the void. It could have been a bird singing. It could have been glass breaking and shattering into a thousand pieces. It could have been anything. He turned.

Deborah had urged Yael to take a week off before assuming all of Judah's duties. Judah was on a leave of absence until the board decided what to do with him and his revelations. "Spend some time alone with your husband," Deborah had told her, "before... well, you know. Before." Yael thought about a rafting trip through the Grand Canyon, or catching the bluegrass festival in Telluride – Peter's first choice. But she decided to leave Peter in Desert County and visit her father in Cleveland, specifically The Jacob Stone Taylor Road Home for the Aged, a venerable Jewish nursing home, now, thanks ironically to her father's own fundraising talents, home to one of the most advanced Alzheimer's units in the United States.

Her father, Rabbi Abraham Gold, recognized no person, not Yael, not his son or grandchildren, nor any of the private nurses the family paid to surround and care for him. His eyes greeted everyone the same, blankly, zombie-like. His face was devoid of curiosity, let alone emotion. Yet, in every sense but cognitive, he remained acutely aware of his surroundings. He turned his head to face any noise; shrunk back at the slightest touch, ate his favorite foods – veal cutlets, cooked broccoli, fish soup – with relish, always using knives, forks, spoons, always folding his napkin onto his lap. One of the nurses told Yael that he brushed his teeth himself every morning, and washed his face (though they didn't let him shave), but automatically, with the exact same motions, at exactly the same times, as if he were a machine programmed to maintain itself.

"Dad," Yael repeated, and he turned his head again. Like a fruit fly, Yael thought, flying to the light. A voice attracted his attention but only for a few seconds. Then he reverted to the most comfortable position for his neck – staring straight ahead. "Why did you do it?"

It? She meant, she supposed, the affair with the gangster's wife, but more broadly, why disgrace his position as rabbi, why embrace hypocrisy over truth; why not control his appetites, his emotions? Why nearly drive his wife to suicide? "You were a rabbi," she whispered, this time too softly for him to hear. She didn't want him turning around again.

She'd rented a car and drove straight from the airport, informing neither her brother nor her mother. She thought she'd probably call one or the other after seeing her father, but maybe not, maybe she'd stay at the Ramada Inn next door, spy out her father's room, wait until it was free of guests, and then sneak in, making sure, at least for a week, that he was never apart from a loved one. That way she could ask her questions to him and him alone, and not be distracted by answers.

She was surprised by his appearance, but not because he looked worse than he'd been six months before, the last time she'd seen him. She was surprised at how *good* he looked. He walked every day, ate well, groomed himself properly. He dressed himself every day in pressed jeans and a golf shirt, like a golden-age retiree. If anything, his outward appearance improved, even as he'd lost his mind altogether.

"Why did you do it, Dad?" she repeated, once again drawing his gaze, if only for a moment. She remembered the time she'd told him she was applying to rabbinical school. He'd asked the same question, using the same bewildered, judgmental tone. "Why?" he'd asked, as if she'd committed some odd utterly uncharacteristic offense, like embezzling, or cheating at craps. "Because I believe in God," she'd answered. "I believe in the Jewish people." Because of you, she'd thought, but didn't say it. He shook his head, as if these were interesting responses but to a different question altogether. "Why?" he'd repeated.

Now, nearly ten years later, she touched his face with two long fingernails, and he quickly turned away. "Why?" she said again.

"Why what?"

Yael jerked around. "Mom!" she said, blushing.

"Were you going to scratch him?"

"What are you doing here?" She watched as her mother marched to her father's bed, and kissed his smooth cheek.

She was astonished that, rather than jerk away as he did whenever Yael touched him on any part of his body, he sat impassively, accepting the peck. He might even have leaned into it. Yael continued to stare in amazement as her mother took her cheating ex-husband's hand and sat next to him on the bed. Rabbi Gold did not turn to look at his ex-wife, but he did let loose a low growl that sounded to Yael like a purr of contentment. Her mother and father holding hands sweetly, like lovers: this was a sight Yael had never seen.

"What am I doing here? I should ask you the same thing. I live here." She stroked her ex-husband's palm with her finger.

Yael studied her mother's face. Unchanged would no longer be accurate – the face had changed considerably in the last five years, with new wrinkles around the eyes, and a slight sagging of the cheekbones. From the time Yael was old enough to be conscious of the details of her mother's appearance, she'd noted almost no changes in Beth Gold from ages forty to fifty-five. The day Yael turned eighteen, her mother forty-eight, they'd gone together to get their picture taken. Everyone remarked that they looked more like sisters than mother and daughter, with the same long, dark hair, same smooth face, same green eyes, same high cheekbones, same graceful, athletic legs. This wasn't entirely a matter of genetics; Yael always thought of her mother as the most physically attractive person she knew, so she modeled her own appearance, her makeup, hairstyle, pedicure, even walk, on her mother. Now, looking at the two lovebirds, Yael noticed clearly the signs of age, but was still struck at how youthful her sixty-year-old mother appeared, especially next to her bald, seventy-year-old father, a man who, even since Yael could remember, looked older than his years.

"I came to see Dad," Yael said. "It's been a while."

"Sounds like you came for some answers. His Alzheimer's is rather advanced. You would get better responses from a pet turtle. You may have noticed."

"Of course, I just…"

"Were you going to call me? Or Arthur?"

Yael sighed. As a girl, she'd often wondered why her mother couldn't be like other mothers, like *real* mothers, and the thought again surfaced. For example, a real mother might have kissed, even embraced *her*, rather than rush over to her ex-husband and kiss him, especially when, to him, a kiss was no more consequential than someone spitting at him. Her mother had always been unapologetically unaffectionate to both her and Arthur, even ending the custom of goodnight kisses on Yael's fifth birthday. Interrogation – usually generously flavored with sarcasm – was her favorite mode of communication with her children. Yael, of course, loved her mother, respected her mother, was grateful to her mother for teaching her about Martin Buber, and Billie Jean King, and eye makeup, Rembrandt, Botticelli, and Bruce Springsteen; for raising her alone, with little help from her father, and only surly resistance from her brother. But she *liked* her father better, preferring his kisses, his warm embraces, his pipe-smell, his kosher Chinese take-out dinners, his *laissez-faire* attitude towards phone calls and bedtimes. Yael recognized the hero in the family, knew it was her cold mother and not her warm father who contributed most to her well-being. But oh, so often, she did long for a normal mother, one who at least would kiss her hello, or say goodbye before putting down the phone.

"Of course I was going to call you," Yael said, blushing, lying. "I just stopped here first."

"Sometimes daughters call before they fly across the country for a visit. In Cleveland, that's still considered polite. To let your mother know when you're showing up. I might have gone grocery shopping for you. Buy your favorite foods."

"Mom."

"Yael." She tightened her grip on her ex-husband's palm. He grimaced slightly, though Yael could not deny that it might also have been the beginnings of a smile.

"You get through to him, Mom. It's amazing. You visit often?"

She shrugged, tilting her head so it seemed as if she was searching the horizon. "He was my one true love. I suppose that never goes away." Then, as if in answer to a prayer, she rose from the bed and pecked Yael lightly on the cheek. Then she quickly resumed her old position, as if sharing a bed with Rabbi Gold, a man she'd divorced almost thirty years ago and, as far as Yael knew, hadn't spoken to since her children left home, was the most natural situation for her in the world. "Arthur came to see you, almost three years ago," she said, talking to Yael but looking at her ex-husband's hand. "As I recall, he booked a flight five minutes after speaking with you on the phone. I don't imagine it was a sudden itch to play blackjack or roulette. He shared some family secrets. Well, that was between you and your brother. He was eleven years old when those events occurred, a boy, but you felt he had some answers for you. None of my business. But now, here you are, asking your father about those same events, when you know very well you'd get just as much out of the lamp, or his toothbrush, which, did you know, he uses every day, by himself? Yael, did you forget that there was someone else who was there? Not a child back then, and not currently a tooth-brushing vegetable? I'm the one who really knows what happened. Why didn't you ask me? Why don't you ask me now?"

Yael hesitated a moment, hoping her mother wouldn't look her in the eye. "I thought it would be too painful for you," she said. "I didn't want to open up old wounds."

"Ah, you were concerned for my feelings. How touching."

Yael laughed and shook her head. Her mother, she thought. A cold fish, an ironist, annoying as hell, but she could always tell when Yael was stretching the truth. "Honestly? I didn't think you'd tell me the truth."

Beth raised an eyebrow, her Vulcan look. Arthur used to joke that the creators of *Star Trek* had based Mr. Spock on their mother. Except Spock's half-human, had always been Yael's reply.

"Arthur didn't," Yael added. "He didn't tell me the truth."

"Oh? What lies did he tell?"

"He didn't lie. But he left something out."

"Yes? What did he leave out?"

"I'm not sure."

"Yael." She took Rabbi Gold's hand and placed it on her lap. "Something's wrong. You don't have to be a mother to see that. And of course I know exactly what you're thinking, and you're right. I should be a *good* mother. I should take you in my arms, beg you to tell mommy all your problems. But you know I won't do that. So, tell me, I assume this has something to do with Aviva's murder?"

Yael nodded. She'd told Arthur and her mother the barest details about the crime, leaving out that she'd been a suspect, and Judah's revelations about his marriage. She also didn't say anything about Cantor Weinman's arrest, but that had been covered in several newspapers, so Yael assumed they knew.

"Okay. When you're ready, you'll tell me more. But now. You have questions about my charmed life with your father?"

Yael sighed. Her mother would force her to say the words.

"Dad had an affair? With his cousin's wife?"

Beth studied her daughter, her ex-husband's hand still planted on her lap. "He did. Wife, then widow."

"Why? Why did he do it?"

"You're asking me? You're asking me why *he* did it?"

"Mom. Just now, you practically begged me to ask you."

"I thought you'd want to know how *I* felt," she snapped. She threw Rabbi Gold's hand onto the bed and stood up. He looked at her momentarily, then turned away and studied his hand.

"Sorry," Yael said quickly. "Of course it was awful for you. It's just that right now, I'm interested in—"

"Him. You're interested in him."

"He was a rabbi, Mom."

"He was a husband. He was a father."

"Of course. I'm sorry."

"Why should you be? You were only two years old. Anyway, you shouldn't be so hard on him."

"Really?"

"I wasn't exactly a picnic in those days. I wasn't the lighthearted, loving spouse you see before you today." She resumed her seat on the bed. Without prompting, Yael's father placed his hand in her lap. She stroked it absently, as if she were petting a cat. "The fact is — oh, what do you care? It was a long time ago! You were a baby!"

"Mom."

"I know, I know, I begged you to ask. But I don't have any explanations. I – I was me, which, I guess, wasn't what he wanted. What else can I say? I probably should have been more – I don't know. *Her!*"

"You excuse him?"

"Never!" she said quickly, still petting the hand. He was back to staring straight ahead, at the midpoint between Yael and the doorknob. Beth watched him breathe. "It was a scandal," she said softly, almost a whisper. "He humiliated me. I don't excuse! But," she said, speaking to Yael, facing her ex-husband, "I forgive."

Yael shook her head. "Mom. I'm sorry, but I still have a hard time understanding—"

"Of course you don't! Of course you don't *understand*. That's my point, exactly. You can *never* understand. Because it didn't happen to you."

"What are you talking about? Of course it happened to me. It changed my life. It destroyed my family."

"Oh, Yael. That's not what destroyed your family."

"What?"

"The marriage was over, Yael. We couldn't stand each other. He didn't love me; I sure didn't love him. It was just a matter of time."

"But, Arthur told me—"

"Eleven-year-old Arthur. The expert on his parents' emotional life."

"He found Dad's diary! He saw your suicide note!"

"My – he saw my…? What on earth are you talking about? What diary?"

Yael watched her mother slowly turn red, noting how the anger on her face made her look younger, more beautiful. Her eyes lit up and her skin glowed with righteousness. Yael had inherited the blushing from her mother, but while Yael blushed all too easily from embarrassment, it was rage that provoked her mother's shift in cheek color. She was both furious and flabbergasted. Yael remembered Arthur telling her he was sure their mother knew about his snooping around in his father's drawers, peeking in his diary. But maybe not.

"You didn't know that Arthur read Dad's diary?"

"Yael, believe me, I have no idea what you're talking about. What diary?"

Vulcans never lie. Arthur often reminded her of that whenever she doubted something her mother said. Her mother didn't seem to know how to lie, at least not in answer to a direct question. So, not only did she not know that Arthur had read his father's diary, she wasn't even aware of the diary's existence. Yael wondered if it was still around, if she could read it one day.

"I'm going to let Arthur tell you that story," Yael said. "When he wants to. When you ask him. But, well, did you try to commit suicide?"

"I – I didn't. I wrote a note. That was all. I wrote a note."

Yael nodded. "Okay. But Mom, that's a pretty dramatic thing to do. If, as you say, the marriage was already over. You wrote a note. You were, well, you have to admit, you were contemplating the idea. But, why? If you couldn't stand him, even before the affair?"

"The scandal," she said softly, the red draining from her face. "It was the scandal. Hard to take."

Yael nodded. Scandals, she knew about.

She slept that night at her mother's house in Cleveland Heights, in her old bedroom, still decorated with posters of Cleveland Indians manager Mike Hargrove, and Browns quarterback Bernie Kosar, and Bruce Springsteen. The next morning, Arthur came by to take her and her mother to breakfast at Corky and Lenny's, her favorite diner as a teenager. As she poked around her matzo brei, biting and chewing approximately every third forkful she brought to her mouth, Yael waited for her mother to bring up the diary, the suicide note, the scandal, the Kennedy assassination, rabbis, gangsters, something about her past with her father. Instead, her mother spoke animatedly of her new job: marketing director for the Jacob Stone Taylor Road Home for the Jewish Aged, and its new state-of-the-art Alzheimer's wing.

"So that's why you visit every day!" Yael said. "You didn't tell me."

"You didn't ask. You never ask. Anyway, my office is in a different wing entirely. It's at least a ten-minute walk to your father's room. It's good exercise. I usually walk up the stairs, instead of taking the elevator."

"Do you hold his hand for the exercise, Mom?" Arthur asked.

"As a matter of fact, I do. For him. It's good exercise for him. So his finger muscles don't atrophy, and he can keep brushing his teeth every day."

"They arrested Cantor Weinman for the murder," Yael said. Someone has to talk about this, she thought.

"What!" Arthur exclaimed. Beth looked at her plate of lox and eggs.

"It was in the news," Yael said. "But I wasn't sure you saw."

"Well, thank God," Arthur said. "Thank God they finally put that creep away."

"Mom," Yael said. "Any comment about Cantor Weinman? Are you happy they put that creep away?"

Beth Gold brought her coffee mug to her lips, then changed her mind and set it down. She studied her daughter, while pink splotches, like roses, bloomed quickly in her cheeks. Uh, oh, Yael thought. "Is there something you want to ask me, Yael?" Beth asked softly, a tight whisper, snake-like in its hissing quality.

"I'm just wondering what you think of Cantor Weinman."

"Did you think I wasn't aware he'd been arrested? Do you think I haven't been following the case? Just because you choose not to tell me anything about your life, at any time, do you think I'm not interested at all?"

"Why are you angry at me? You obviously know what I've been going through. Why am I the villain?" Strangely, Yael wasn't mad at all. In fact, if anything, she felt a little guilty, though she didn't understand why. She was also quite curious about how her mother would answer. Why *was* she so angry?

"You want to know the past. You want to know your story. You summon your brother to Desert County, who tells you about sneaking around my room as a child. You ask your father who does *not* know who you are. I'm sorry, but he doesn't. But you don't ask me. I *lived* through it. And, not to mention, I am your mother. Some daughters talk to their mothers."

So that was it, Yael thought. It takes a murder and a scandal to bring out twenty years of burning resentments. Yael preferred her philandering father to her righteous mother. That was the problem. Or, Yael considered, was her righteous but also crafty mother just changing the subject? After all, she was asking her now, just not the questions she wanted.

"I am asking you questions. I asked you about Cantor Weinman. Was he—"

"Jesus!" It was Arthur. Yael and Beth turned to look. His face was now red. A family genetically programmed to wear grievances on the face. "What is it with you and Cantor Weinman?" he said. "Obviously, he's a killer! What more do you need to know?"

Just what you're not telling me, Yael thought. She looked at her brother, then turned to her mother. What they're both not telling me. What she needed to know, but couldn't, for the life of her, ask.

"I think he may have killed JFK," Yael answered.

When they wouldn't laugh, when they only stared at her in utter incomprehension, she giggled, and after a few awkward seconds they joined in.

Four

CHARLOTTE

CHAPTER 1

Yael bent down to examine a flower, a Desert Lavender. It was late March, the middle of wildflower season, four weeks after the murder, two since Judah's revolting revelation about his supposedly open marriage. She resisted the impulse to pluck the flower and carry it with her to work – illegal, but, more importantly, somehow profoundly *wrong*, as if, like a desert pirate, she'd be plundering treasures that belonged to someone else. Instead, she examined the color: not the deepest blue she'd ever seen, but certainly the loveliest, prettier than a robin's egg, sadder than the sky. She thought of the blue of *tchelet,* the ancient dye Hebrews had used to color their ritual shawls, a blue that was supposed to match the blue of Heaven. This particular flower, along with its four neighbors, the first Desert Lavenders of the season to pop up along the bike path, included several yellow buds in the center, sparkling like gold coins. No scent, Yael noted, but, my God, so extraordinarily lovely. Yael would be the first person to admit that she was not a flower person. Not, she told herself, someone to stop and smell the roses, or look at the Desert Lavenders. Ordinarily, that was Peter. But something about the flower matched her mood, and not in the banal sense of feeling blue over her new responsibilities, over her dreadful disappointment in Judah. Somehow, the blue and gold tugged at her, the melancholy and the regal, depression and potential. It made her stop. And think.

Suddenly, she heard a mandolin; someone was plucking the opening notes to "If You've Got the Money, I've Got the Time." Why, she thought, certainly not for the first time, did she allow Peter to program her BlackBerry tones? She looked at the incoming number.

"Charlotte," she said.

"Yael!"

Oh, no, not again. Charlotte's voice, ringing like an out-of-tune mandolin, heavy with urgency. How many more revelations could she stand? How many more could there be? In fact, only one that she could think of. She sat down on a boulder.

"Charlotte."

"They arrested him! Yael – I'm sorry, I know I should say Rabbi Gold, it's just so hard to get used to, and, you know I'm trying, but I'm *so* upset. Yael! They arrested him!"

Yael shut her eyes. Blue, she thought, and blue was all she saw in the darkness. "Who, Charlotte? Who did they arrest?" Please, she whispered to herself.

"Judah. They arrested him for murder! For murdering his *wife*," Charlotte added, as if Yael had forgotten who the victim was, or had imagined that Judah might have killed someone else.

This isn't happening, Yael told herself, realizing, as she thought the words, that they carried the least amount of conviction since she'd first adopted the phrase as a silent mantra weeks ago. It *is* happening, she thought, and it's not the least bit surprising. Her last three discussions with

Epstein – they were "discussions" now, not interrogations; he'd clearly stopped suspecting that she had anything to do with Aviva's death – had focused on Judah: his relationships with other women, his cigar-smoking, brandy-swilling sessions behind closed doors with the scumbag, Aviva's frightened look when she mentioned his name the day before the murder. The truth is, Yael had been awaiting exactly this news for several days.

"Charlotte," she said, about to give the secretary instructions on how to proceed. But a thought occurred to her. "How do you know?"

"What do you mean, how do I know?" she exploded. "How do I *know*? He called me! Judah called me! I already called his lawyer. What do you think I'm doing up and in the office at seven-thirty in the morning? I'm calling everyone who—"

"Charlotte. Please listen to me." She heard gasping breaths, Charlotte's this time, not her own. She opened her eyes, saw the sun bounce off her boulder. "Please *do not* make any calls, or do any errands for him. You do not work for him."

"What do you mean? I'm his *secretary!*"

"Charlotte, you work for Anshei Emet. I'm your supervisor. I'm telling you, do not do anything for him. Not on your own time, not at all. I recommend you not speak to him."

"Yael, you know I can't just abandon him!" Yael heard a violent blowing of the nose, and then choking, sobbing sounds. Charlotte, Yael knew, was a tough lady, a thirty-five-year-old widow, raising two children on her own. Yael had never seen her cry, even on the anniversary of her husband's death.

"Charlotte, I'm instructing you to have nothing to do with him." Yael labored to put steel into her voice. "I don't want you to lose your job."

The secretary was now sobbing uncontrollably. Through the cellphone's tiny speaker it sounded like a wailing cat whose tail had just been stepped on. "Charlotte, the synagogue needs you now. The community. Right now. I need you to call everyone on the board."

Charlotte whimpered twice, response enough for Yael. She instructed the secretary to call a board meeting for that morning. And not by e-mail. "Call everyone," she said coldly. "And pull yourself together. He's not worth it."

She'd taken two steps away from the flowers, toward work, when her phone rang again. Charlotte, she thought, or, more likely, Deborah, who would have heard the news through the legal grapevine. But she didn't recognize the number on the screen. Tentatively, she pressed the green phone button with her thumb.

"Baby Doll! Boy, they fucked up now."

Hang up, she told herself. But the voice held her. She couldn't move.

"They think Judah did this? That Judah hired me? Jesus, these are Keystone Kops. They must have been talking to your husband. Haven't they ever heard of motive? You need to talk to your boyfriend, Epstein. Didn't you tell him about all the women? Surely Judah's told you by now? Boy, that must have been a shock to you, huh, after your dad and all."

She hung up. It was the mention of her father. Otherwise, the scumbag's evil voice, darkly seductive, beautifully malignant, would have held her as long as he wanted to talk, which might have been hours. With shaking hands, she scrolled through her address book until she found the name, and pressed the button.

"Ms. Gold," he answered, all business, seven-thirty in the morning, as if he'd waited up all night, expecting her call.

"He called me again!" she shouted, and was astonished to hear her panicked voice echo all around her. It's a canyon, she reminded herself. "He called me again," she whispered tightly into the phone, trying to project her soggy breath right into his ear. "You told me you'd make sure that didn't happen again."

He sighed. Yael imagined his long, lanky frame, hunched over a desk. Or maybe he was eating breakfast, sipping coffee while he talked, bringing a steaming mug to his thin mouth. In her mind, she saw the sharp angle of his closely shaved chin. Rescue me! she thought. I need someone to rescue me.

"When did he call?"

"I just hung up on him." She tried, but could not keep the tremor from her voice. A slight breeze hit her bare arms, and she trembled. Why, she wondered, hadn't she worn a jacket? Because, she realized, it was eighty degrees. It was the desert. It might reach ninety-five today. Still, she shivered with cold.

"I'll check it out."

"You arrested Judah."

"Are you surprised?"

"Weinman says Judah didn't do it. He says you're all messed up. He called you a Keystone Kop."

"He's playing with your head, Rabbi Gold. He's been doing it to you for years. Try to stay calm. He's in prison. He's not going anywhere. He can't hurt you with a cellphone."

Yael, in fact, did calm down, though it was more the force of Epstein's voice than any genuine reassurance. Yes, the scumbag couldn't hurt her physically with a cellphone. But he *was* hurting her, even now, as she talked to the tall cop. The voice in her head hurt her. The memory of the splotches on his otherwise deathly pale face. It hurt. "Will I have to testify?" she asked.

"You asked me that already. I'm not the prosecutor. But I assume you will be called. You've got important information."

"I *don't*," she said. But she did. She knew she did.

"I'll call the prison right away; get them to find out how he keeps getting a cellphone. He'll go back to solitary. Please don't worry."

She laughed. Don't worry. It was the funniest thing she'd heard all day. Of course, it was just past seven-thirty in the morning. She replaced the BlackBerry on her hip, and walked four steps along the bike path. The sun now hit her full on the back. Beads of sweat rolled down her neck. Still, she trembled slightly and wondered if she was coming down with something. She took out the phone and called her husband. No answer. Must be in the shower, she thought, or still sleeping. She heard his high, nasal voice, accompanied by an Andy Statman *freilich*, ask her to leave a message. "They arrested Judah," she said, surprised to feel tears running down her cheeks. "Please call," she added, and hung up quickly before her voice dissolved altogether into sobs. She was the strongest person he knew. That's what her husband had told her before the last awful meeting. But what did that mean? How many strong people did he really know? She sat down on a boulder and cried for ten minutes, her head in her hands, tears leaking through her fingers, splattering her stone seat. Then she got up, shivered, shook herself, and walked to work.

Normally, board meetings started at least ten minutes late, as the last of the busy, successful men and women rushed in, fresh from appointments with the governor's office, or the gaming board, or with judges, the mayor, the city council, or with their kid's teachers, coaches, or with their masseuses, stockbrokers, tennis coaches or personal trainers, or caterers, contractors, or landscape architects. These were busy folk, undeniably committed to the synagogue, but with a range of obligations, and Anshei Emet rarely came out on top. But today, a weekday working morning, not a Sunday, not an evening, everyone was there by 9:45, fifteen minutes *before* the meeting.

Deborah sat in her usual place at the head of the table, next to Yael, now the "acting senior rabbi." Glancing around the table at the fit, tanned, expensively dressed crowd, Yael saw red eyes and damp, tear-stained cheeks. The men, she noticed, had been crying as hard as the women. She wondered if they'd been weeping for Judah or Anshei Emet, a community forever shamed, no matter what happened at the trial. She decided it was for both, because for these wealthy men and women there was no distinction. Judah was Anshei Emet, and Anshei Emet was Judah. He'd brought them all, without exception, on to the board. They served the synagogue, but they served it by serving him. Yael was mildly surprised to see Addison sitting in the back sobbing quietly, away from the table but still in the room, part of the group. Her stomach bulged out in what Yael considered a grotesque fashion, though she knew it was normal for the eighth month of a pregnancy. What was grotesque was that Addison showed up at all. What was grotesque, she thought, was most likely the pregnancy itself. She thought briefly about Tzipporah. Would she have to fire her, her friend? How did all this happen? And what on earth was she supposed to do?

"Might as well get started," Deborah said, clearly and calmly. Her cheeks, at least, were white and dry, no tears in the president's eyes. "Thank you all for coming." She breathed in deeply, and looked around the table as she exhaled. One of Judah's tricks, Yael thought. Look everyone in the room in the eye before delivering an inspirational message. Deborah's hoping to inspire the room with her words. Good, she thought. God knows, someone needs to. She sat back in her chair, and waited.

"Rabbi Gold. You called this meeting. You have something to tell us. Please."

She'd almost forgotten. She had called the meeting. This was her job. Still, she was momentarily startled. Something to tell them? What could she tell them that they didn't already know? What could she say to them that would be of any use?

But she nodded her head and took a sip from her water bottle. Everyone in the room looked directly at her, probably for the first time in her career. "Well," she said. "I can see you've already all heard the news. Rabbi Loeb." She fought to keep her voice steady. She would not cry, not for him. "Our rabbi has been arrested for murdering his wife. Now, first thing: he's innocent until proven guilty."

"Damn right," someone whispered. It was a male voice, but Yael couldn't see who said it.

"Yes, that's right," she said, nodding. "That's our system. Innocent until proven guilty. It's also, by the way, the philosophy of Jewish law. So that should be our attitude, as a community. Nevertheless, Rabbi Loeb has shared with us some of the evidence against him, which he admitted is true. These things he admitted, they were immoral. They were sinful. He let us down. We should acknowledge that." She looked down, at her water bottle so she wouldn't, even accidentally, look at Addison. But she sensed others in the room staring at the pregnant woman. "Now," she continued, turning her head slowly, trying to imitate Judah and catch every eye in the room, but giving up after the first three pairs of eyes turned away, "what do we do now? We're still a synagogue. A community. A *faith* community."

A hand went up. It was Bob Wilson, an entertainment lawyer whose firm represented some of the biggest acts playing on the Strip. Bob offered her tickets nearly every month to some big name – last time it had been Elton John.

Peter, she recalled, had just giggled through his nose when she suggested that this time maybe they could go. Yael didn't appreciate the interruption, but she nodded at him because she knew that even if she didn't, he would speak anyway. Like most members of the board, important people, accustomed to holding a room's attention, Bob was used to having the floor whenever he wanted. "Yael," he said. "I'm looking through my mind for some kind of Jewish teaching. Some spiritual guidance. Something, you'll forgive me... that Judah might say. And all I can think of is one word: forgiveness. *Solucha*, right? Forgive. Isn't that the point, right now?"

"No," Yael answered quickly. "I'm sorry, Bob, but that's not what's relevant now. For one thing, we don't know if Rabbi Loeb's guilty or not guilty of killing his wife. So, how can we forgive? And, as for the other... stuff... we don't know everything yet, we don't know the extent of it. And, mostly, he hasn't asked for our forgiveness. So, it's a good teaching, Bob, but it's not the right time."

"But, Yael—" he said.

"Excuse me," Deborah interrupted. "I would very much appreciate it if we all started saying Rabbi Gold and not Yael. Rabbi Gold is our rabbi now, our senior rabbi. Our only rabbi."

Thank you, Yael thought, as she tried to remember what she was going to say before Bob had interrupted her. The room was no longer quiet. Whispers echoed off the wall. She wasn't holding them. Addison stared at her from the back of the room, smirking.

"Rabbi Gold!"

She looked to her right. It was Eric Arnson, a former president, CEO of Arnson Gaming, owner of three mega-casinos. "You say it's not forgiveness. Now's not the time. Then tell us, please. What is the teaching? What does Judaism instruct us to do, in times like these? I'm sorry to put you on the spot, but this is what we expect of you now."

Times like these? What does Judaism teach us for these times? When the rabbi screws a board member, a youth director, probably others; when he murders his wife? These times, the times of Jews in the desert, making their living off gambling? Judaism doesn't give easy answers to traumatic events, Yael thought to say, but didn't. Anyway, if they would just stop interrupting her. But then a teaching popped into her mind. "*Harchek mi shakhen ra,*" she said. Bruce Bowen, the ritual vice-president, the only board member fluent in both Hebrew and rabbinic literature, gasped. "'Stay away from an evil neighbor,'" Yael translated. The whispers turned to grumbling. So Yael raised her voice. "I'm sorry, but you asked for an appropriate teaching. If he's guilty of murder, well, he's committed an obscenely evil act. But we don't know that, we don't know if he killed Aviva. But, even so, he admitted to doing evil. He sat in this room, and told some of us. My advice – my *teaching* – is stay away. Don't contact him. Don't entangle our synagogue any more with him. I'm sorry, that's all the Jewish teachings I can think of, sitting here, at the spur of the moment, in my position. It may come to repentance, forgiveness. It may come to all that. But right now, we have to consider our membership, our children. We have to protect what's left of our reputation. It's not a time to forgive. Frankly, it's a time to judge.

Harshly. And draw conclusions. I told Charlotte today that she was not to help him in any way. I threatened to fire her if she did. Let's face it, I can't order anyone in this room to do anything. But, you're looking for teachings, this is what I'm teaching. Keep your distance from evil."

Now they were paying attention. Some were gaping at her, open-mouthed. She doubted that Judah had ever held the room with such command. Of course, Judah had never had the opportunity to refer to an Anshei Emet rabbi – a rabbi who everyone in the room either loved outright, or held in higher esteem than anyone they knew outside of their own families – Judah had never had the opportunity to call such a rabbi an evildoer, and insist that no one speak to that person. Judah, in other words, had never lost his mind in front of the group. But Yael, despite a fiery blush, held their stares. After a while, a few board members – mostly the younger ones, Doug Best, Emily Potter – shook their heads.

Then Deborah took over. She and she alone, she emphasized, spoke for the *shul* to the media. And her statements would always consist of two words: no comment. She, for one, was following Rabbi Gold's sage advice. She was keeping her distance, saying nothing. As Rabbi Gold had so wisely noted, no one could force anyone in the room to do anything. But, for the sake of the *synagogue* – she drew out the word as if she were praying – she hoped everyone would follow her lead, even as individuals, and limit themselves to no comment. After all, they didn't know what had happened, didn't know what was to come. Really, what was there to say?

Apparently nothing, since the room stayed quiet. Board members glanced at each other, everyone looking as if they were about to strike up a conversation. A few twitched their hands, itching to propel them in the air, so Deborah or Yael, or someone, would recognize them, and they could take their natural leadership positions and offer incisive opinions. But Deborah's warnings and Yael's teachings hung in the air.

After dismissing the group, Deborah asked to speak with Yael alone. They moved past Charlotte's desk – the secretary kept her eyes focused tightly on her paper-strewn desktop – into Yael's office. Without a word, they headed automatically to the corner love seats, where they plopped down, each on their own separate sofa. Their sighs came out almost in unison, identical in length, tone, and depth of feeling. After a brief chuckle, Deborah brushed a loose hair out of her eyes.

"Excuse me, Yael, but are you out of your damn mind?"

"Deborah?"

"You called him *evil*. A month ago, if you'd asked everyone in that room to define the word 'saint,' they would have answered 'Rabbi Judah Loeb.' And I suspect you might have answered the same way."

Yael nodded. "I know," she said. "It just popped out. I'm not sure why. I'm just so…"

"You were supposed to *comfort* them. We need it, Yael. Listen, I know I can be frank with you. I can see the way you look at most of us. The way you look at me. You think we're a bunch of rich, self-important snobs. And you're absolutely right. We are. But that doesn't matter. We're also human beings. Every single person in that room – well, maybe except for one, and that's a whole different story – is like a child who lost a father. You have to step in now. You're the stepmom, in fact. Whether you like it or not. Whether you like *us* or not."

"Yes, you're absolutely right, Deborah. I'm sorry. And I do like you. All of you. It's just that I…"

"But that's not the worst of it, Yael." She brushed another loose hair away, then smiled sadly. Her tone of voice during this rebuke had been firm, but not unkind. The words were harsh, but Yael also felt affection. The women looked at each other.

"You're pissed off at him," Deborah said.

"Yes."

"Well, of course. That's natural. We all are. But let me tell you what worries me. I've known Judah for fifteen years. I wasn't Aviva's best friend – I don't think she could be best friends with a congregant – but we were friendly. I guess you could say we were friends. Obviously, there's a lot she never told me, but I never doubted that *she was my friend*. Yael, Michael and I vacationed with Judah and Aviva for *eight straight* winter vacations – eight skiing trips, seven days each. We had Passover and Thanksgiving together the last six years in a row. I was a part of their lives, as much as any congregant can be. And I don't *know* what happened, but let's assume the very worst. Just between you and me, let's assume he did it. He killed my friend Aviva. And Yael, let's be honest, she wasn't your friend."

"No," Yael whispered. The fact is, she barely knew Aviva. Neither had made much of an effort to get to know the other, and now Yael sort of understood why.

"But you're still more pissed off at him than I am. That's what I heard in there, in that horrific meeting. Your anger. Yael, you're enraged, you're furious at him. Like it's personal. And that worries me. Because it makes me wonder why."

Yael shook her head, startled. "Deborah, I swear to you, I never—"

She put up her hand. "Please. You don't have to say it. One thing you and I need to keep in mind is that we will almost certainly be witnesses. So we should be careful what we admit to each other. But I appreciate what you just tried to say." She reached across the coffee table and touched Yael's wrist. "And I believe you. But it's almost beside the point, right now. Because I can see how you feel."

I will *not* cry, Yael told herself, and, in fact, she was pretty good at holding back tears, even if her face and voice gave up all sorts of secrets. Deborah tightened her grip on Yael's wrist.

"I wish I could be your friend right now, Yael. I think you need one. But I can't. My only priority now is to keep the synagogue together. Because, no matter what you think, we're not just a bunch of spoiled, narcissistic, amoral casino operators. Without Anshei Emet, there wouldn't be Jewish schools in Desert County, there wouldn't be a Jewish future; there wouldn't be *Judaism*. And you know that more and more Jewish families move here every year. The rest of the Jewish community in America is shrinking, but we're growing. The doctors and lawyers and accountants and agents and, yes, gaming executives – these are Jewish jobs in Desert County. But without our synagogue, there wouldn't be a *community*. And now, we could go either way. You know, we could be exactly one week away from collapsing totally. I can't let that happen. There's too much at stake. So I can't be your friend, even though a child can see how much pain you're feeling. I need to be your boss. And, frankly, I need you to shape up. No more sermons about our evil rabbi, okay? If people want to forgive or forget, or ignore or visit him in jail, let them. It's not the point, right now. Right now, the congregants need *you* to *comfort* them. Think of us as a huge bereaved family."

Yael nodded, taking shallow breaths, keeping the tears at bay.

"Neither of us asked for this," Deborah continued. "The situation doesn't play to either of our strengths. But, you know, here we are. Desert County. You play the hand you're dealt."

"I don't know, Deborah," Yael said, her voice finally under control. "You seem to doing fine." And, so that wouldn't be interpreted as an insult, though she sort of meant it that way, she added, "Thank you."

Deborah released Yael's wrist. Like exhausted boxers, they both fell away from each other, leaning back on their respective sofas. "There's one more thing," Deborah said. "Michael has a message for you. From Judah."

"Michael? Michael's defending Judah? Deborah, I'm not sure…"

"Calm down. Not any more he's not. *I* told him. It's a huge conflict of interest. Anyway, Michael's never done a murder trial. But, of course, Judah called Michael the day after the murder, when he first realized he might be a suspect. Michael found him another lawyer – Bart Grim, not a member, thank God, not even Jewish. But, a great lawyer. Michael still has visiting privileges. Apparently he's not so well-versed in your Jewish teachings. He's not keeping his distance. Even though, by the way, *I* told him to keep away, without even mentioning our sacred rabbis. Anyway, here's the message."

"Deborah, are you sure this is proper? You even said: we're witnesses, we have to be careful."

"It's not at *all* proper. But what the hell, it's nothing secret. I don't enjoy passing along this message, and I do so without any recommendations. But it's pretty simple. He just wants to see you."

"Michael?"

"No, no. Judah. He wants you to *visit*. The exact word he used was 'implore.' He *implores* you. He wants you to come and see him. In prison."

CHAPTER 2

"You're going? You're actually going to see him? In prison?"

Peter and Yael had just polished off a large pizza, with anchovies and onions. She'd told him about the board meeting and her conversation with Deborah; he'd shared with her a dispute he'd been having with another faculty member about whose turn it was to chair the committee to hire the visiting artist. He also told her that he and Bruno, his songwriting partner in the Desert Cryers, had finally solved that thorny composition issue that had been holding up their latest piece. They'd decided to switch to waltz time, and also to try a minor key. Worked like a charm. A typical how-was-your-day marital conversation. My day? My boss, the rabbi, was arrested for killing his wife, and the hit man my boss supposedly hired called me from jail, and the president of the synagogue accused me of having an affair with that rabbi, and now the rabbi has summoned me to his prison cell. And how was your day?

"I don't *want* to visit him," Yael said. "But Deborah made it pretty clear that everyone still loves him. The congregants probably expect me to be his pastor. At least for now. Until after the trial, and the verdict."

"You mean until he's convicted."

She sighed. "We don't know that will happen, do we? But that reminds me. Something Weinman said…"

"Yael, please tell me the truth. Do you want to visit him?"

"I just told you, I don't. I just think I should. Deborah told me—"

"Deborah instructed you to visit him? The man accused of killing her friend?"

"No, but she passed along the message. And she implied—"

"You understand why I'm asking?"

She looked at him. There was a hurt in his eyes she hadn't seen in several years. This, in fact, was a conversation they hadn't had in some time, since before they were married. "I think so," she said softly. "There's nothing, Peter. And there wasn't."

"Okay," he said quickly.

"Nothing at all."

"I believe you. Totally."

But Yael wondered. Did he believe her? "You're right that it's not that Deborah asked me to go, or that anyone expects me to go. I don't want to see him. But I do need to ask him some questions."

"Like, did he kill Aviva?"

She nodded. "I probably will ask him that. At least give him a chance to deny it. But I also need to know about the women. Mostly about Tzippi."

"You'll ask him to name names?"

She nodded. "I'm the rabbi now. His behavior damaged the community. I need to know the extent of the damage."

He closed his eyes and hummed a tune – klezmer, minor key – tapping out time on the tabletop. "I suppose you do," he said. "Want me to drive you? When should we go?"

She smiled. My loyal, puppy-dog husband. "I think it can wait until morning," she answered.

The prison sat on top of a desert ridge, surrounded by brush, mesquite, and prairie-dog holes. A chain fence topped by barbed wire encircled the complex. Peter parked their Toyota in the visitor lot. He'd brought along the latest Emmylou Harris box set, along with Keith Richard's new memoir, so he was prepared to wait for hours in the car.

Yael locked her purse, watch, bracelets, rings, and BlackBerry – anything that might get stolen, or set off an alarm – in a courtesy rental locker before entering what turned out to be the first of three metal detectors. A yelping whoop blared out after her first step. It was her belt, which she removed and added to the locker. At the second metal detector, her shoes triggered the alarm. Thankfully the guard, glancing at her clergy name tag, allowed her to keep them on her feet, as long as she promised not to give them to anyone who might use the short heels as weapons.

Judah was waiting for her in a lawyer room, a cramped, glass-enclosed cubicle holding two wooden, elementary-school-style, single-person desks. He was dressed in a bright orange prison jumpsuit, but Yael was relieved to find him clean-shaven and, she could guess from his soapy smell, freshly showered. For some reason she had expected to find him shackled, but he was free of handcuffs or other impediments to his movements. Evidently, despite the charge, he was not considered dangerous. As usual, the first thing she noticed were his blue eyes, which seemed to plead all on their own.

"I didn't do this, Yael," he said, even before she'd finished folding herself into the kid's desk. "I didn't kill Aviva. I want to say that right away."

She looked at him, taking in his entire visage, his down-turned mouth, the lines on his brow. As was often the case, he gave the impression of being an actor. Now he was play-ing the role of an unjustly accused, innocent man, but he wasn't the innocent man himself. He was a good actor, but still an actor. His hands, she noticed, were rock-steady, much steadier than her own.

"Okay," she answered.

"I mean, think for a second. Why would I kill her? If I wanted out, I'd just ask for a divorce. And if I was afraid of a scandal, I mean, wouldn't I realize that the same scandal would certainly erupt during a murder investigation, with the police nosing around?"

"Okay."

He tilted his head, and smiled. "Well, okay. And thank you for coming. I also wanted to say that right away."

"Okay," she repeated. Maybe that's all she would say the entire visit. Everything's okay. What could be wrong? As if in response, she tried to look him clearly in the eyes, maybe even smile, but she couldn't hold his gaze even for a second. She looked, instead, at the cigarette-burned desk, the dried chewing gum on the floor, her fingernails, her watch-free wrist. He, on the other hand, kept his eyes clearly on her, as if she were the guilty one and he the accuser, or confessor.

"Yael," he said. "I didn't kill her."

"You said that," Yael answered.

"You don't believe me?"

She shrugged. "What difference does it make?"

"You think I'm lying. That I'm a liar?"

She looked up sharply, watching his eyes. "You lived a lie," she said.

He shook his head. "Not true. I always told Aviva."

"Oh, please," she said and got up, nearly knocking over the desk. She looked around the room. Was she locked in? How was she supposed to call the guard?

"Yael."

"You son of a bitch," she said, breathing hard. Then she sat down.

"Yes, I deserve that."

"Oh, God. You don't know. You don't know what you deserve. And you can't imagine how much I despise you. Why am I here?"

"Yael."

"Just tell me!" she snapped, and the words echoed in the small space. She looked through the clear glass wall, expecting a guard to intervene.

"Maybe I just want someone to talk to. A rabbi. A pastor."

"Oh, for God's sake. Ask for the chaplain."

"Yael."

"Judah, I'm not your *pastor*. I'm not your rabbi. I looked up to *you*; it was never the other way around. And we were never friends, so please don't say that."

"Really?"

Now she looked at him, squarely, fully, his goddamn blue eyes, the deep creases on his forehead, his ghastly orange uniform, his hair, freshly trimmed. Friends. Were they ever friends? They spoke easily to each other. He taught her sacred texts and she listened, and shared her ideas about God, community, Torah. She confided in him on several intimate issues, including conflicts with her husband, problems with her mother. She'd thought he confided in her occasionally, about his spiritual yearnings, his aspiration to love everyone as much as he loved God, his occasional doubts. But clearly he was keeping some big things from her. Still, they worked well together, laughed while they toiled. Was that friendship? Maybe it was, she conceded. "Why am I here?" she asked softly. "Why did you want to see me, Judah?"

"Because I'm innocent."

"Okay, okay. You're innocent. Please stop saying that. It doesn't do any good. I'm not the prosecutor. I'm not the jury. You want to practice saying it, please practice on someone else."

"You can help me."

Now, suddenly, she couldn't keep her eyes off of him. He absolutely *fascinated* her. He looked so calm, somehow more self-assured now, behind bars, than when he was the most popular Jew in town, speaking before thousands, reveling in the adoration. Was this the face of a killer? She shook her head. "I don't understand. You mean with my testimony?"

"No, no," he said quickly. "I want you to tell the truth. I'm innocent, Yael, so the truth can only help me."

She kept staring. Who was this man? Is this a species I know?

"Edgar thinks you're the key."

She shot up, searching for a guard. Why the *hell* did she come here?

"Yael! Yael, please just listen. I didn't want – please just listen. You owe me that."

She sat down. A jack-in-the-box, she thought. I pop up and I pop down. But she heard it finally in his voice: vulnerability, fear, tenderness. You owe me that, he'd said. And she did, she supposed.

"Edgar," she said, practically vomiting the name. "The scumbag. He says *I'm* the key. My God, Judah."

"He's rather obsessed with you, Yael."

"No kidding. I'll never understand why you spent so much time with him. Don't you see, Judah, that was how you—"

"You're right," he said, putting up his hand, like a traffic cop, stopping her in her tracks. "You're absolutely right. But now is not the time. Yael, listen. You must know the prosecutor's theory. Epstein's theory. They think I hired Edgar to kill Aviva. They discovered that Edgar at one time had been a hired killer. They even found my briefcase, with five thousand dollars cash in his apartment. Someone set me up. The prosecutor will argue that as soon as I found out what Weinman was, I got the bright idea to use him to kill my wife, because she – well, you already know why."

Yael's anger surged. It danced, shimmied through her bloodstream. She knew why! Oh, yes. Because Judah was sleeping with married women, and Aviva was in the way, or, better, Aviva was about to tell someone and get Judah fired. Of course she knew why. Again, she felt the urge to bolt, but she was done leaping out of her seat only to be talked back down. She'd come all this way. She'd hear him out.

"There's only one problem," Judah continued. "*I didn't do it*. I didn't hire Edgar."

"Did Edgar tell the police you'd hired him? Is that why they arrested you?"

He shook his head and laughed bitterly. "Edgar's playing games. *You* know him. Reveling in the attention. All he'll tell me is that you're the key to this. That I should ask you. "

"Wait a minute, he talks to you? In this prison. Here? He's here?" She looked around, afraid he would burst in.

"Of course he's here. Calm down. I need you, Yael, to get a hold of yourself. He's segregated. So am I. But, yes, we've managed to communicate a few times. It's not easy, but we manage. And as to your question, I think so, yes. I think he told the prosecutor that I paid for him to do it. He probably arranged for them to find the briefcase. But I also think he says whatever he feels like, whenever he feels like it. I think he'd change his story. But first, I have to speak with you. That's what he said. Because you're the key."

"Judah, I just don't know what to say to you. He's crazy and evil. I've known that for a while. I tried to tell you. My only question now: is that true of you, too? Are you evil, and also crazy? Because I *do not know what you're talking about*. I'm the key? What can that possibly mean?"

"Can I tell you what I think it means?"

She looked, waiting. She would limit her words, as much as possible.

"I didn't hire him. But I'm fairly certain he killed Aviva. They've got some good evidence. And, the fact is, the few times I've seen him, he doesn't deny it. Which means that someone else hired him. I think Edgar suspects you might know who that is."

"Me? I *know* who killed Aviva? I'm sorry, Judah, you couldn't be more wrong."

"No, no, Yael. Please listen. Not that you know for sure. But that you have your suspicions. A strong sense. And your strong sense is probably right. That's what Edgar has led me to believe. That you know who did it, even if you're not quite aware yet that you know."

Insanity. Fantasyland. I know, but don't know I know? She threw up her hands. "Judah, how could that be true? I mean, let's be honest. Who else would it be, if not you?"

"Well," he said, suddenly lowering his voice so Yael had to lean in to hear him. "It's not as if I was the only one with a motive. There are others who might have wanted Aviva to disappear."

Yael stared at her former boss. She'd loved this guy, she thought. A schoolgirl crush, call it what you want, but she'd *loved* him. No more. "I don't believe this," she said tightly. "Addison. You mean Addison. Or Tzippi. And you want me to – to what, Judah? Ask them? Ask them if they killed Aviva?"

"I can't tell you what to do, Yael," he said quickly.

That's for damn sure, she thought. She got up, and looked at him one last time. She was shocked to see a tear on his cheek. When had he been crying? She banged on the glass and a guard appeared right away. Her intention was to leave without saying goodbye, without another word. But his voice called her back. She turned around.

"I think you should also speak with Charlotte," he said.

She opened her mouth to respond, but changed her mind quickly. She nodded at the guard, who touched her elbow and led her away. She felt like a prisoner, being escorted to her own cell. She imagined the guard slapping on the cuffs, throwing her in some damp dungeon, slamming the steel door shut. Instead, he released her at the metal detector. She sailed through it, then through the second and third ones without setting off alarms. She didn't realize she'd been holding her breath until she stepped into the parking lot and saw Peter waiting for her in the car. She exhaled.

"So, how was it?" Peter asked, pulling out of the driveway, heading down the hill.

How to answer that one? Totally and utterly devastating? The worst moments of my life? Too surreal for words, in the worst possible way? Torture, torture, torture? "I don't think I can talk about it right now, Peter," she said.

"Uh, okay. That's okay. Anyway, there's something I'd like you to listen to." He fiddled with the car CD player, punching a button, turning a knob. The sound of a steel pick clanging violently against steel strings filled the air. "Listen to this banjo solo," he said. "Tell me if you've ever heard anything like it."

She shut her eyes, pretending to listen. She suddenly remembered that she'd never asked what she came to ask. She'd never demanded that Judah name the names of every congregant he slept with.

"Never," she said softly.

"Nothing like it in the world," Peter agreed.

CHAPTER 3

Yael didn't sleep at all the night after visiting Judah in prison. Partly, it was disgust over her former boss' brazen request that she investigate his wife's murder, that she look into his former girlfriends, though of course he wouldn't say their names out loud. It smacked of cowardice, the idea that Yael should check out the women, as if Judah was willing not only to sleep with them, but, when the going got rough, implicate them in the murder of his wife.

But mostly she couldn't sleep because she realized he wasn't guilty. And it wasn't right for him to be in jail for a crime he didn't commit. She had no evidence of his innocence, but she could hear it in his voice, see it in his face. A poor liar herself, Yael was, nevertheless, pretty good at sensing lies in others, and she sensed truth from Judah, at least when he denied killing Aviva. She supposed that she could have been fooling herself. Maybe she was still in love with the bastard, and her heart was lying to her brain. The police, after all, wouldn't have arrested him without reason. But, beyond the sincerity in his voice, the way his gaze never faltered, how his hands remained rock-steady while he professed innocence, she believed his argument over motive. Why kill his wife, when he could more easily move out, or get a divorce? Yes, divorce might generate unpleasant gossip, maybe even a scandal if Aviva talked, but a murder investigation would blow up into a disaster of sordid revelations even if Judah wasn't arrested, even if he wasn't a suspect. Judah was many things, but he was not stupid, and he would certainly realize that if he killed her, even if he hired Weinman to murder her, he would become the first suspect, and all his illicit affairs would see the light of day. So, really, he had no motive to kill her, and every motive not to, every reason to keep the status quo: stay married, and fool around in secret. For some reason, the prosecutor and the police didn't see it that way, but Yael knew human frailty; she knew the prosecutor could be wrong. In any case, she was sure.

Presumption of innocence. She pondered the concept at three in the morning, as her eccentric husband snored beside her, no doubt dreaming of Vivaldi, Alberto Mizrahi, and banjo runs. She understood it intellectually, nodded agreeably as the judge explained it when she'd served on that awful jury. In our system, he'd explained, we offer the accused the benefit of the doubt, we assume they are innocent. Only *after* we evaluate the evidence – not even during, when we listen, but *after* – can we pronounce one way or the other. And only then, when the prosecution has proved guilt beyond a reasonable doubt. Okay, she got it. The problem was, Yael had a habit – and she wouldn't call it a bad habit – of sizing people up right away, and allowing presumptions to pop up in her brain, like weeds, or wildflowers. For instance, she took one look at that accused child molester, with his plump, pale face and despicable, toothy grin, his torn jeans, his thin wool tie, and presumed one thing: guilty. Yet, as the trial progressed, she put aside her presumption. She listened to the evidence. If it had convinced her otherwise, she would have voted not guilty, she was certain of that. Even if she didn't change her presumption, she would have followed the law. Her head would have talked her heart into it; she was sure.

Reasonable doubt. Yael wasn't very good at that, either. When it came to guilt or innocence, she didn't harbor doubts. The guy either did it, or he didn't. With the child molester, frankly, she never entertained the tiniest smidgen of a doubt. He grabbed that girl and... but, even now, three weeks later, she couldn't form the words in her thoughts. He did what he did.

She'd presumed/believed, at first, that Judah was just as guilty. But she changed her mind. Again, not because of any evidence. She'd presumed him guilty before she spoke with him. But seeing him, hearing him, contemplating, for hours on a sleepless night, the role he'd played in her life – all that finally flicked a switch. She grew a new presumption, and she had no doubt this time that she was correct.

And that was exactly her dilemma. If she knew he was innocent, how could she not help out? Didn't she owe him that? He'd hired her, mentored her, befriended her, trusted her. This was what tormented Yael that night, after practically spitting in his face in prison, and all but excommunicating him at the board meeting. He'd been good to her. And she'd turned on him, not, she realized, because she'd presumed he'd killed his wife – though she did believe it at the time – but because he'd slept around. But sleeping around, as much as it violated the Ten Commandments, was not a crime in American law. If he didn't kill Aviva, he

shouldn't be in prison. And Yael should help out. Because…
because she was his friend.

She figured Addison was a good place to start. It seemed
obvious now, since Judah's confession, that she was one of
the women. Her enormous belly jutted out like a rotund
scarlet letter. It fended people off as much with its sheer
size as what it clearly represented: adultery. The next day
Yael phoned her and, without waiting for a response, said
she'd be right over. Yael told herself she wasn't coming to
solve Aviva's murder, she was just trying to clarify the extent
of Judah's adultery. If it came to accusations, she would
stick to the seventh commandment, not the sixth. But she
also weirdly imagined herself as a rabbinic Perry Mason,
breaking Addison down, tricking her into confessing.

That ambition evaporated immediately when Addison
opened the door, and Yael realized she hadn't the slightest
idea what she was going to say. The two women stared at
each other on the front porch of Addison's sizable home,
wordless, until Addison invited her in.

"You don't like me, do you, Yael? I don't think you ever
liked me."

Addison was mammoth. Her belly protruded onto the
coffee table, taking up half the space. It brushed up against
the framed photo of Manny feeding wedding cake to
Addison. Addison was only in her eighth month, but Yael
didn't think it was physically possible for her to get any bigger. Surely the taut skin would simply snap.

"Of course I like you," Yael lied, and blushed.

"Oh, you're such a liar," Addison said and laughed
lightly, warmly, as if sharing a joke. Her immense belly

shook up and down as she chuckled, jiggling the coffee table and shaking the photo. It was as if a mild earthquake had hit Addison's living room.

Her housekeeper served strawberries, whole wheat crackers, brie cheese, and herbal tea. "The only foods I can keep down," Addison apologized. "And I'll probably throw all this stuff up anyway. After I'm done talking with you," she added, giving Yael the impression that it was the conversation more than the eating which would lead to the vomiting. Yael took a strawberry with a finger and a thumb, and held it.

"You want to know about me and Judah?" Addison said.

Yael tilted her head. "Why would you say that?" she asked, truly wondering how the other woman could read her mind so clearly.

"Well, no one's asked me. I know what you all *think*. I assumed someone would follow up on the rumors. I figured it would be Deborah, but I think she hates me even more than you do."

"Deborah doesn't hate you, Addison," Yael lied.

"He's not the father," Addison said, as if in reply.

Yael turned the strawberry and examined it from the bottom. Like all the strawberries on the plate, it was big and juicy, oversized, like an expectant mother. "Okay," she said. 'Okay' had become her favorite word, the very best way to respond to protestations of innocence.

"Judah is *not* the father of my child."

"Okay," Yael repeated. She popped the entire mammoth strawberry into her mouth, a good excuse not to speak.

"How dare you accuse me. How dare you accuse *him*!"

Yael chewed slowly and swallowed, admiring the strawberries, wondering where Addison had purchased them, how much they cost, wondering, in general, why wealthy people invariably served extraordinarily plump and delicious strawberries. Of course she hadn't accused Addison of anything, but she was willing to concede the point. A look, or a turning away in disgust, can be as sharp as an actual accusation, and anyway, Yael had certainly believed that Judah was the father of Addison's growing fetus. "Okay," she said with a full mouth, thoughts racing, fitting Addison's denial into a rapidly shifting version of reality, trying to form exactly the right words. She studied the plate of strawberries, keeping Addison's pregnant-plump face in the corner of her eye. "So you and Judah never…?"

Addison blinked. "We didn't have an affair."

"Okay." They sized each other up, as if seeing each other for the first time. "But Addison, that's not exactly what I asked. I'm sorry, I just need to know exactly…"

"Once," Addison said softly, almost a whisper.

"Ah."

"But it was my idea. I was already six weeks' pregnant, that's how I know… well, you know. I don't have a good marriage. I don't – didn't – want the baby. I came to see Judah. How much of this do you want to know?"

I don't *want* to know any of it, Yael thought. How much do I *need* to know? Am I here as pastor? Confessor? Police investigator? Attorney for the defense? Official representative of Congregation Anshei Emet? "Whatever you want to tell me, Addison," she said.

Addison nodded, and told her the story. First, her marriage. Her husband Manny was bisexual. Well, more gay, it seems, than bi. Addison was his first serious female relationship since high school. He'd been honest from the start, sharing the secrets of his sexual past – he'd never come out of the closet – but also assuring her that he valued fidelity and monogamy, and if they married, he was certain his sex drive would remain focused on her. He probably meant it at the time. But three years into the marriage, he began yearning for men. At first he satisfied himself with male pornography or phone sex with on-line hookers. But around the time he impregnated Addison one drunken night after an argument, he began an affair with a male art history professor.

He told Addison about the relationship, just as he'd shared everything about his sex life with her in the past. The pregnancy shocked him; it shocked both of them. They didn't know what to do. Addison considered an abortion, but she hated the idea, mostly on religious grounds. Manny wanted to give the marriage another try. He was willing to give up the art historian, pledge fidelity to Addison; become a good father. But they both knew he would break his pledge. His inner yearnings were too powerful, and eventually they would win out.

So she made an appointment with Judah, to ask his advice.

"And he *slept* with you?" Yael asked. Rage, again, filling her bones. How could she ever live with it?

"It's not that simple," Addison answered. "You see, I'd fallen in love with him. I hadn't told anyone, not Manny, not

Judah. I barely admitted it to myself. But we'd worked so closely for so many months. I was the one who drafted the reorganization, you know; I did the projections, *all* the spreadsheets. He was great with the spreadsheets. He caught on so quickly with the numbers. And he was also so wise and, you know, so witty, and, well, you know how he looks, and all the rest. I just . . I think you know what can happen."

The spreadsheets? Yael thought. He was great with the spreadsheets? But, the truth was, she *did* know exactly what Addison was talking about. There was no point denying it. For Yael, it was Judah's spiritual mentorship, his pastoral guidance. For Addison, it was his facility with spreadsheets. And all the rest. She got it.

"You came on to him?" Yael asked.

"Absolutely," she answered. "I guess that's really why I made the appointment that day. I went there to seduce him. I know it doesn't make any sense, but I think my idea was if I could attract a man I loved, a man I desired; if I could make a man desire me, then I could have enough confidence to give my marriage another try, and to become a mother. I needed to feel like a real woman, to know that I was a real sexual person, before I could go back to Manny."

Yael shook her head. The logic escaped her. She needed to sleep with another man so she could stay with her husband? But it didn't matter. She didn't have to understand.

"I know you don't get it, Yael. How could you? It's not something *you* would ever understand. Not in a million years. But the point is, Judah's *not* a sexual predator. When he shared his marital arrangement with me – just to teach me that sexless marriages can work – I saw an opening. We did it right there in the office. But just that once. And it worked. It was... therapeutic."

Yael felt nauseous. Bloated, after one strawberry. Therapeutic! "Addison," she said, her voice quivering slightly, "you came to him for counseling. You shared intimate details of your life. It doesn't matter how you felt about him. He took advantage of you. In his own office – in the synagogue! It's desperately wrong, what he did, Addison."

"It was two consenting adults, Yael."

"You were married! *He* was married."

"But you're missing the point. Even you should be able to see it, Yael. These weren't real marriages, not the way you define the word. Anyway, I came on to him. I told you. I practically tackled him. Frankly, the sex wasn't all that great. I don't think either of us thought it was worth it. Do you really want to hear the details? "

"No. No, I don't." What she wanted, desperately, was to leave this place. But, again, was that her role right now? Wasn't Addison a congregant, still in trouble, someone who needed her support? Shouldn't she put her own feelings of revulsion to the side, and offer pastoral guidance to this sad, misguided woman, victim of a predatory clergy?

"I'm sorry, Yael, I'm going to have to ask you to leave."

"Okay."

"Nothing personal," she said. "Manny's coming home in ten minutes. He's taking me to the OB."

"Of course."

"I don't want him to see us talking. The only way we'll survive as a couple is if we can take some time away from

Anshei Emet, away from all the accusations. For months, that's all he and I talked about. After the last board meeting, when you told us all that Judah was guilty, I promised Manny I'd stay away, at least until after the trial."

"Okay. Yes. Uh, but, Addison, I didn't say that Judah was guilty. I just wanted to…"

Addison stood up, a complicated operation. She shifted her knees to the left, then pushed down on the coffee table, creating another earthquake-like rumble, while she pushed her large rear end into the air, and then, with a loud exhale, snapped her upper body into a standing position. She smiled at Yael, not in friendship, but more inviting her to join in celebrating the accomplishment of rising to her feet. "It doesn't matter, Yael. Look, I don't really know if the man is guilty or not. The fact is, I don't know him all that well. You probably know him much better than I do."

"I suppose I do," Yael said. She remained seated. Suddenly, standing up seemed like a daunting operation.

"Do you mind, sweetie?" Addison asked, tilting her head toward the door.

"Oh, of course."

Addison walked her to the entrance. Yael found herself studying the large pool. Oddly, it sat in the front yard, as if inviting guests to ritually bathe before entering the house. "Come for a swim sometime," Addison said. "Bring Peter. Manny adores Peter. Says he's the most brilliant artist on the faculty. Not that that's saying much. You know, they do spend a lot of time together, our husbands. We should really all get together some time."

Yael looked at Addison. Talk about not knowing another person. Was she trying to tell her something? Or was this an offer of friendship? Or just small talk? "Can I ask you one more thing?"

Addison looked at her watch.

"Just take a second," Yael said. "Back at our lunch, right before the murder. We were talking about my trial. When I was on the jury. How did you know? How did you know I was the hold out? That I'd convinced the jury to convict?"

Addison chuckled warmly, two old girlfriends, sharing a laugh. "Thought I was all-knowing, huh? Sweetie, it's a small town. Belinda Dumanis and I went to law school together. She told me. She tells me a lot."

Belinda, Yael thought. The prosecutor. "Hmm."

"Goodbye, Yael," Addison said, kissing the rabbi on the cheek, her belly rubbing up against Yael's chest. "Thanks for stopping over."

Yael called Tzipporah from the car, telling her she was dropping by right now, not allowing for a refusal. Might as well get this over with, she thought, though she didn't see how she'd be able to sit through another session of confessions and denials, of tawdry revelations and indignant rationalizations. Addison's story left her stunned, relieved, and appalled. Relieved, because it wasn't as bad as she thought; this was no heated affair, no motive for murder, not for Judah or Addison. If this was all the police had, she wondered how they could have arrested him. Appalled, because sleeping with a troubled congregant – even once – was still the rankest violation of professional ethics. It was a sin, plain and simple. For Yael, it was just as corrupt, just as morally bankrupt, as a passionate, adulterous fling. And hearing Addison describe it so matter-of-factly – it was therapeutic! I came on to him! – only heightened her disgust. This was a deeply troubled woman, someone who used sex to confirm her adequacy as a mother. She needed genuine help, but Judah screwed her, literally. He belongs in jail. But not for murder, she quickly reminded herself.

It was not quite eleven in the morning when Tzipporah let Yael into her two-bedroom condominium, but Yael smelled garlic and tomato sauce, and saw the kitchen table set for two.

"I made brunch," Tzipporah said, kissing Yael on the cheek. "Spaghetti with meat sauce and garlic bread. Sorry. Lately, I have to eat all day or I get the dry heaves. Dr. Moss says it should go away any day, but for now I keep snacks everywhere – in my car, in the office. And on my day off, I just cook all day and eat. Cook and eat, that's my day. Come on. There's enough for two, I think."

All Yael had ingested since the night before were two of Addison's humongous strawberries, so she was actually hungry. She accepted a bowl of spaghetti and meatballs, and a large hunk of garlic bread. But she fiddled with her fork while Tzipporah shoveled in mouthful after mouthful.

"Hmm," she sighed. "I got the recipe from Manny, of all people. Addison's husband, your favorite board member. He loves to cook."

"Okay," Yael said.

Tzipporah stopped eating and looked up. "Okay?"

"I mean, good. It's good." She tasted a forkful. It was okay.

Tzipporah chewed loudly, grunting, teeth grinding, lips smacking. Chewing for two, Yael thought, studying her friend. Tzipporah's rosy cheeks radiated joy, contentment. She's happy, Yael thought. Or maybe she's just really hungry.

"Why are you here, Yael?" Tzipporah asked.

"I think you really do know, don't you Tzippi? Do I have to ask? I mean, why have we been avoiding each other for two weeks?"

"Judah. You want to know about me and Judah?"

His first name, Yael noted. Judah, not Rabbi Loeb. No one on the staff, in conversation with each other, ever referred to him by his first name. Tzipporah had all but confessed. Yael waited for more. But Tzipporah, her wrists and jaw moving in perfect tandem, just shoveled spaghetti and meatballs into her mouth, chewing, grunting, groaning.

"Tzippi?" Yael prompted.

But, like a well-trained ditch digger, she shoveled rhythmically, a mouthful every two seconds. After four shovelfuls, she put down her fork. "Ask."

"Did you have an affair with Rabbi Loeb?"

Tzipporah chuckled. "No beating around the bush, huh? A straight question? Well, my answer to that is, no. I did not."

"Okay."

"Okay? Hey, that's a great word. So we're okay? Want more spaghetti?"

"Tzipporah."

"What are you accusing me of, Yael?" she asked, her cheeks still rosy, but her voice fierce, as if she took great, healthy joy in lashing out. "You performed my marriage ceremony. Who do you think I am?"

"Tzippi. I just need to know the truth. I don't accuse. I... I just need to know about him. About Rabbi Loeb. For all sorts of reasons."

"You don't think we hear rumors? My God! That Judah's the father of my baby? Deborah asked me flat out! Is that what you're asking me? Did you think Judah was there on my wedding night? Is that the type of person you think I am?"

"Why do you keep calling him Judah? We never use his first name. Tzippi, really, I'm not judging you. But you must understand that I need to know. We can call this a pastoral visit. Confidential. Legally, I won't be able to tell anyone. But, please. Was there anything?"

Tzipporah studied her plate. She seemed surprised to find it empty. She swished her fork around, as if searching for hidden morsels. "Just once," she said. "It happened just once. That was it. And then it stopped, but we stayed friends."

"Once," Yael repeated. Was that the pattern? Did Judah have sex with every woman in Desert County except for her, but just once?

"I had a crush on him," Tzipporah said softly, speaking to her plate. "Just like you."

"I did not..."

"Oh, come on. Yael. Believe me there isn't anyone at that synagogue who doesn't know. But it's nothing to be ashamed of."

"Doesn't know *what*?"

"That you have a crush on Judah! Or, *had* a crush. I presume it's in the past tense."

"Okay," Yael said. "I mean, yes. I guess. I had a crush on him. And that's all. But so what?"

"Exactly. So what?"

Yael nodded. She took a moment to remind herself of her innocence. Despite the muddy feelings of guilt she'd been carrying the last several weeks, she'd never even told Judah, much less acted on it. "But you, Tzippi? It was more than a crush?"

"God, we're like two sorority sisters! Crushes. It's like high school. Yes. It was more than a crush. One time." She touched her fork to her plate. "Will you tell Tony?"

"Of course not. But, didn't the police ask you? Epstein, the investigator?"

She looked up, alarmed. "The police? I never spoke to the police. Who's Epstein? Why would the police care?"

"Tzippi, Rabbi Loeb's accused of killing his wife. I assume his other relationships would be relevant."

"Yes, but, my God! It was only once." She laughed suddenly. "You weren't thinking that Judah killed Aviva because of me? So he could run away with me? Is that what you were thinking?"

"Of course not," Yael answered, trying to chuckle but coughing instead. Actually, she'd been playing with the idea that Tzippi had killed Aviva so *she* could run away with Judah. Now, both ideas seemed equally absurd. But the idea that Addison murdered Aviva, after one "not all that great" time with Judah, or that Judah killed Aviva to be with

Addison – it also made no sense. So, why did Judah tell her to find the women? A new feeling crept up on Yael, not anger, or passion, or anxiety, but simple, pained curiosity. Who killed this poor woman? And why? She looked across the table at her friend. Her breasts were beginning to swell; there was a slight, concave curve to her normally flat belly. Soon she would grow as enormous as Addison. "Just one time?" she asked.

Tzipporah nodded. "I was becoming serious with Tony. Actually, it was right after that outdoor Purim concert. Peter's band, the Klezmelodics? Klezomatics? Klezma – whatever he called them? Remember, he presented that whole Purim song cycle?"

"Of course." How could she forget? Peter hummed the melodies for months leading up to the concert: in the shower, while washing dishes, once or twice in the middle of making love.

"I was helping Javier clean up, picking up trash off the lawn, putting away the pizza, the. *hamentashen*. Judah walked by and decided to help out."

"Okay," Yael said.

Tzipporah shrugged. "Not much else to say."

Not much else to say? Did they do it right there, on the grass, among the dirty paper plates, the pizza boxes? Did Javier watch? Join in? "Okay," she said.

Tzipporah hesitated. "I told him… I told him that I was afraid of getting in too deep with Tony. That I wasn't sure if I really liked him, but that I could easily see myself compromising, staying with him because I couldn't be sure if there would ever be anyone as sweet, and kind, and… normal."

Yael nodded. Normal was good, she thought. And so was sweet and kind.

"He offered to go upstairs, to his office, where we could speak privately. Comfortably." She looked at Yael.

"Tzippi."

"Just wait. When we got there... you know, it was really my idea. I came on to him."

"Oh, God."

"And it was sort of therapeutic. It was like he was allowing me one quick fling, so I wouldn't go through life wondering what I was missing. My last naughty act before growing up. And it worked. When I walked out of that office, I knew I would stay with Tony for as long as he wanted me. You know what's funny?"

"Funny?"

"The sex wasn't all that good. But, you know, maybe that was the point. Maybe he wanted to show me that sex disappoints. Or, that crushes don't mean as much as we might think. It was like he was counseling me, using his, well, using sex."

Yael stood up. "I have to go," she said, balling her fists, too angry to sit still, too angry to breathe. How do I control this, she thought, this raw naked fury? How can I stand it?

"Yael. Sit."

"No. I'm sorry. I can't. Tzippi, he was *married*. You didn't think about that?"

Tzipporah pondered the question. She looked to the ceiling, as if trying to remember. "Yes," she said slowly. "I did think about it. But, you know, he told me. He told me about his marriage."

"He told you it was an open marriage?"

"That's what he said."

"You believed him?"

She shrugged. "I guess I did."

"So you slept with him? Your boss. Spiritual leader of your community."

"Just once." Tzipporah said. She touched a finger to her lips, seemed to consider carefully what she was about to say. "But, wouldn't you have, Yael? If he told you about his marriage? You had a crush on him, too. Wouldn't you have done it? Just once?"

"No," she snapped, relieved that she meant it. Nevertheless, she blushed.

"Well, okay then," Tzipporah answered.

Yael fled, shaking too hard even to slam the door shut behind her.

On the bike path, behind the synagogue building, Yael's thumb hovered over her BlackBerry. This is foolish. I've become a fool, she marveled. I barge in demanding answers when I haven't even formed the questions. I'm going to call that tall cop, but I don't even know what I'm going to say. Something's wrong. Something's missing. Someone's not telling me something. I'm feeling something, but I don't know what. Someone needs to help me, but who? She pressed the button.

"Epstein," he answered.

What a great way to answer the phone, Yael thought. "He didn't do it," she said.

"Ms. Gold?"

"Something's wrong. Something's missing."

"I'm not understanding you."

"I've been speaking to... some people. It doesn't make sense. Something doesn't add up. There's something you're not telling me." A fool! Yael thought. Me! When did this happen? When did I become a blithering idiot? "What's the motive? Doesn't there need to be a motive? From what I can tell, he had a few quickies in his office. Do you all really think he would kill his wife over those?"

"Ms. Gold, am I hearing you correctly? You're investigating this murder? Pardon me, but I didn't take you for a fool."

"Yes, well, I'm surprising myself. But, listen; there are some things I need to *know*. I'm the rabbi of the congregation now, and it's important I understand who exactly Rabbi Loeb damaged, and the extent of the damage. But what I'm telling you is, I don't see all that much damage. Some misguided women came on to him, and he slept with them. It's not *evil*. It's not murder."

"Yes. You understand that he's not in jail for sleeping with anyone."

"But that's my point. He told me to check out the women. Well, I have, and I don't see..."

"He? *He* told you? Rabbi Loeb?"

"Hmm," she said. She shouldn't have told him that. He'll tell the prosecutor; she'll probably have to testify about the conversation. Foolish. Time to get to the point. "You arrested the scumbag – I mean Edgar Weinman – right after speaking with my husband."

"Ms. Gold, I don't..."

"Twenty-year-old contracts. Pieces of paper. He showed them to you. What could they really mean after twenty years? They could have been forgeries. Anyway, I've been thinking. Is that really how it's done? You want someone killed, you *write* out a contract? I'm no expert here, but isn't the word 'contract' just an abstraction? What do they do, get them notarized? But that's when you arrested the scumbag. When he showed you those papers. There must be more to it than that. What aren't you telling me?"

"Ms. Gold, I don't even know what to say. I'm not a marriage counselor. But shouldn't you speak to your husband?"

Excellent idea, she thought. One problem. Peter doesn't speak with her about the murder. Every time she broaches the subject, she finds herself listening to a discourse on Mahler's Jewish influences, or on why the mandolin should now replace the electric guitar as the driving force in rock music.

"He hasn't called you again, has he? Weinman?"

"Not yet," she answered.

"Call me if he does," he said, not needing to add the obvious: *don't* call unless he does.

"I will. But, please, can you…"

"I'm sorry, Ms. Loeb. You're not a victim; you're not family. I can't speak with you about the investigation. But you cooperated with me, and I'm grateful. So I can tell you this. The 'damage,' as you call it, is more severe than you imagined. And I think you should speak to your husband."

He clicked off. Almost simultaneously, the BlackBerry's red light began flashing; it was another call. Unlisted, her screen flashed.

"Gold," she answered. "I mean, hello."

"The women" a voice hissed in her ear.

She shivered violently. *"How are you calling me?"* She tried shouting into the phone, but her voice shook and it sounded more like pleading.

"You're not done. There are a whole lot more than you think, Baby Doll. And deep down, you know it. Find the women."

"Fuck you!" she screamed, and threw the BlackBerry against a rock. She panted, shivered, gagged. She felt bile shoot up from the bottom of her stomach, through her esophagus, into her throat. She focused all her vanishing willpower on stopping herself from retching. She hugged herself in the 90-degree heat, waiting for the chills to subside. Then she bent down to pick up her BlackBerry. Not broken, she saw, not even scratched. She raised it high, and imagined herself smashing it with all her might against the rock. Instead, she replaced it in her purse.

In her office, she phoned Epstein. "He *called* me!" He sighed loudly, and said he'd check it out right away.

CHAPTER 4

Five minutes after Judah's arrest, Yael had received a call from Ari Weiss, a reporter for the *Desert City Journal*. Shaken, she refused comment. Over the next half hour, her BlackBerry had vibrated non-stop – reporters calling from Los Angeles, Washington, Phoenix, and all the New York tabloids. Then the networks called – ABC, CBS, NBC, Fox, CNN, MTV, VH1, the Christian Network, Shalom TV. Also, the news magazines – *Time*, *Newsweek*, *U.S. News and World Report*, and the blogs and online journals. Yael spoke with no one. She stopped using the front entrance to the campus in order to avoid television crews. She began using the bike path as her office, writing e-mails and placing calls, even meeting with bar mitzvah students, while sitting on her favorite boulder and inhaling the desert odors: wild flowers, mint, coyote dung. Her graduation photo from rabbinical school appeared on TV, and in several blogs and newspapers. Yael winced at the goofy smile, her beaming eyes, her too-long hair. Was I really that happy three years ago, she thought, lingering over the picture in *Gawker*. And so young? Interestingly, she was barely mentioned in the articles; she was, after all, a bit player in the drama. Nevertheless, her photo appeared all over the place, sometimes without a caption, as if she were the murdered wife, or maybe the killer. A woman rabbi, Yael thought, a young one (and good looking,

Yael had to admit). Still news, more than twenty-five years after women won the right to become rabbis. Her mother thoughtfully clipped and sent her articles from the *Cleveland Plain Dealer*, as well as the *Los Angeles Times* and *Boston Globe*. But she needn't have bothered. For the first week, Yael obsessively read everything she could find on the murder.

But three weeks later, the reporters had moved on. Yael's BlackBerry stopped buzzing; the camera crews disappeared from the synagogue parking lot, even as Yael continued to hide out behind the building. By early spring, even the *Journal* lost interest. The local baseball team won ten straight; temperatures reached over 100 degrees Fahrenheit six days in a row, a record for April, and the Gaming Commission opened up yet another investigation into the scandalous link, at the mid-size casinos, between prostitution and gambling.

Yael figured they'd escaped the media horde until Homicide TV, a new station headquartered in Phoenix, announced it would launch its "groundbreaking" network by televising the infamous "Rebbetzin Murder" trial in Desert County. Suddenly, anyone in the United States could watch Judah stand trial. Cantor Weinman, who'd cut a deal with the prosecutor, would be the star witness.

But Yael couldn't watch, even if she wanted to. Epstein himself called to tell her that witnesses were not allowed to read newspaper articles on the murder or watch Homicide TV until after their testimony. He would be sending an officer by to unhook Yael and Peter's cable.

"Isn't that a little drastic? Can't I just promise not to watch?"

"Please be there exactly at noon, Ms. Gold. To let in the officer."

But it wasn't just any officer. It was Epstein. "My goodness," Yael said, opening the door, tilting her head up so she could look the tall cop in the eye, "you really do everything. Investigate murders, sex crimes, repair TV sets. Or, in this case, break them."

"The cable guy's outside," he said. Without being asked, he moved past her, and folded his large frame onto the living room sofa. "I wanted to talk to you."

"Should I call my lawyer?" she said, forcing a smile. She stood by the entrance, her hand still gripping the doorknob.

He didn't smile back. "Did you speak with your husband?"

I thought you weren't a marriage counselor, she wanted to answer. Instead, she shrugged. "It's not so easy," she said.

He watched her. "Are you going to offer me something? Coffee? Are you going to sit down?"

She shook her head. "I don't think so."

"You told me that someone's not telling you something. Care to be more specific?"

She felt a familiar pull, but resisted it with surprising ease. This was a handsome cop. But why was he here? "Why are you asking?"

"Because I feel the same way. And I don't like it. I don't like the way this case is working out. I don't think it's going to end well. Someone's not telling *me* something."

She nodded, her hand still on the door. There were specific questions she could ask, pointed suspicions she could share, but she wasn't sure she wanted the answers just now, not from him. "I will talk to him," she said. "My husband, that is."

He nodded, then turned to the blank screen on the TV. He looked as if he was immersed in a show. "Then you'll talk to me," he said. "After you speak with your husband?"

She didn't answer. He watched the blank TV.

Finally, he got up. "Well, you know how to find me," he said. He touched her hand lightly as he left, his pant leg brushing against her hip. Yael watched as he strapped his lengthy body into his car. Then she sat on the sofa, picked up the remote, pointed, clicked. Static. She surfed from station to station. Nothing but static.

She decided to cheat. If, she told herself, they'd asked her to sign an affidavit swearing not to watch the trial on TV – like they did with the newspaper articles – she would have signed, and complied. Probably. Instead, they broke her TV, zapping all the channels, not just the cable. Not that she watched all that often. In the past few months, she'd only clicked on news stations, looking for pictures of herself. But that wasn't the point. The point was, they'd broken her set when they simply could have asked her, politely or rudely, lightly or insistently, not to watch. So, really, she hadn't agreed to anything. And there was a TV in the synagogue youth lounge equipped with basic cable coverage. It was easy for Yael to check the youth schedule, sneak into the lounge when no one was using it, click on the wide-screen, high-definition TV, and not feel the least bit guilty.

That's what she told herself, but the guilt was there, just slightly buried beneath the surface. Otherwise, why would she have locked the door behind her; why close all the blinds; why leave all the lights off; why flinch every time she heard Javier whistle while walking down the hallway; why jump out of her seat in a panic when a coyote howled in the distance? Fear and guilt over breaking the rules wrestled with stronger forces – curiosity and a desire not to make a fool of herself with her testimony – and it was no contest. Plain, morbid curiosity won out. The first moment the lounge was free, Yael rushed over.

It was two o'clock, the second day of the trial. With trembling hands, she lifted the remote and surfed the channels. She gasped out loud when Epstein's round face and bald head filled the screen. For a bizarre instant she wondered if he was spying on her, before she came to her senses and realized he was the first witness. She tilted her head and watched the bald cop with intent interest, as if every twitch of his facial muscles, every freckle, every line on his white, clean-shaven cheeks revealed incalculably valuable secrets. Yael was so caught up in his face that it took her several seconds to remember to listen.

"A piece of rope," he was saying. "Fourteen inches long. Probably cut from a jump rope."

The rope. Yael closed her eyes, then opened them. Suddenly, as if he'd kept it up his sleeve as part of a magic trick, Epstein was handling the rope. Yael realized that the DA must have handed it to him while her eyes were shut, but the experience of seeing it appear out of thin air – not to mention seeing it *at all* – the thing that killed Aviva – filled her with awe and dread.

"Where did you find it?" a female voice asked, youthful-sounding, nasal, annoying, like an out-of-tune fiddle. Belinda Dumanis, Yael realized, the prosecutor, also the prosecutor in Yael's child molestation case. Yael had met the woman several times. She'd sat in on two of the Epstein interrogations, both times without saying a word. And she'd asked all the questions at Yael's three-hour-long deposition. To the extent that Yael thought about her at all, she despised the short blond assistant DA, but for no reason other than her displeasing, whiny voice, and complete lack of a sense of humor. Maybe also, Yael admitted, because she was out to convict Judah.

"In the kitchen trash," Epstein answered. "The killer left it there."

"And you're certain it was the murder weapon?"

"Absolutely."

"How can you be sure?"

"Blood stains. Hair. Skin tissue. All in a line. All belonging to the victim."

Yael shut her eyes as tears leaked out. The victim. Aviva. *Her* hair, *her* blood, *her* skin tissue, clinging to an assassin's rope like a signature, like a trademark. She'd known how Aviva died, that the killer had strangled her. But to hear it on TV, from the mouth of the cop, to hear him discuss blood and tissue stains with a shrug in his voice, as if they were nothing but evidence, not the life blood of a confused woman – she'd been *alive*, desperate and teary, trembling in Yael's office just a day before her murder – it nauseated Yael.

Oddly, the smell of the scumbag seemed to fill her nostrils until, gasping for breath, sucking in air, she opened her eyes and watched Epstein listen to the next question.

"So she was strangled from behind?"

"Yes, from behind."

Yael heard a noise from behind, a scratching, a squeak, and then footsteps. She jumped up.

"Whoa, relax!" It was Tzipporah, holding her keys. Yael grabbed the remote; the wide-screen went blank. The two friends stared at each other. Yael brandished the remote like a weapon.

"You're not supposed to be watching that, are you?" Tzipporah said, curious, not accusing.

"What are you doing here?" Yael asked. The question was so absurd – it was Tzipporah's work space – neither had any choice but to laugh, first lightly, with giggles, then loudly, rudely with great guffaws, until they both bent over and Yael worried about Tzipporah's baby.

"Turn it on," Tzipporah urged.

They watched Epstein talk about collecting blood and tissue samples. Yael was grateful that the rope was gone, thankful they'd stop talking about the killer sneaking up from behind. Mostly, she was grateful that the testimony was dull, focused on the details of blood preservation and the chain of evidence. Maybe she could find the strength to turn away. She looked at Tzipporah, whose tilted head and wide-open eyes suggested total fascination.

"I'm going home," Yael said.

Tzipporah jerked her head. She seemed surprised that Yael was still in the room. "The lounge is free tomorrow night," she said. "I think the rebroadcast starts at seven. See you then?"

Yael nodded. "See you then," she said. Tzipporah turned back to the TV.

By the time she arrived the following evening, Tzipporah was sitting on the ugly green velour sofa eating popcorn a fistful at a time from a huge metal mixing bowl. Without taking her eyes from the TV, without interrupting her wide-jawed chewing, Tzipporah motioned to Yael to join her on the hideous couch.

The familiar voice startled Yael even before she saw the face that filled up the screen. It was Deborah, the synagogue president. The vivid, shockingly detailed, wide-screen image – the traces of yellow on her front teeth, the three gray hairs across her forehead, the pores under her eyes – gave Deborah a frighteningly lifelike look, as if she were the real person, watching Yael and Tzipporah on TV.

A disembodied, high nasal voice came from the TV's speakers. Belinda Dumanis, the annoying assistant DA with the pimply voice. "How did you respond," the prosecutor asked, "when Rabbi Loeb told the group about the open marriage?"

"The meeting," Yael whispered. "She's asking about that awful meeting. Oh my God, she's going to ask me about it too. What am I going to say?"

"Shh!" Tzipporah hissed.

They watched Deborah take a deep breath and then frown. "You know the expression 'her face fell?' I never understood it until Judah – until Rabbi Loeb – told us about his marriage. My face collapsed. You could have picked my jaw up off the floor."

"You were surprised."

Deborah scrunched her brow, reared back her head, and stared into the camera. Yael understood that Deborah was looking at Belinda – the camera obviously was placed behind her. But still, it felt like Deborah was studying Yael, her eyes wide with astonished disappointment, wondering how anyone could be so stupid. Yael shifted in her seat, trying to avoid the synagogue president's gaze.

"I was *beyond* surprised," Deborah said.

"Of course. Now, let's go back to the night of the murder. February 28th. You saw Rabbi Loeb that night, did you not?"

Deborah sighed. Yael could tell this was not a question Deborah wanted to answer, and she knew why. This would be extremely damaging to Judah.

"I did," she said. "At the synagogue."

"It was choir rehearsal, correct?"

"Yes."

"Was it Rabbi Loeb's custom in the past to attend choir rehearsal?"

"No, it wasn't."

"And how do you know that?"

"I was in the choir for fifteen years."

"And in all your fifteen years, how many choir rehearsals did Rabbi Loeb attend?"

Deborah paused, as if to count. "None," she said.

A thought occurred to Yael. "Ask her what *she* was doing there," she said.

"Yael?" Tzipporah looked at her, her mouth filled with popcorn. Like a toddler, she spoke with her mouth full. "Are you talking to the TV?"

"Of course not," Yael said. "It just, you know, it looks so real."

The DA continued. "In fifteen years, he had never attended a single choir rehearsal. But he was there that night."

"He was," Deborah responded.

"Did anyone besides you see him?"

"Of course."

"Who, specifically?"

"Well, everyone in the choir. I think you have the list. Marcus, the choir director. Probably Javier, our security guard. Manuel, our janitor. And there was me. And Charlotte was there, Rabbi Loeb's secretary."

Yael slowly raised herself up from the couch, still staring at Deborah's lined face. "Goodnight, Tzipporah," she said.

"You're leaving?"

"We're, uh, Peter and I are, uh, I have to call and see if, I have to check something."

"Gosh, you are a *terrible* liar. You switch lies in mid-sentence."

"Yeah, well, thank God. That's why I stopped being a suspect. Epstein could always tell when I was lying."

"See you tomorrow?"

"You'll see me." She nodded at the screen. "I'll be up there."

"Tomorrow? Already?"

"Epstein's sending a car."

Tzipporah nodded. They both watched Deborah slowly leave the stand. A commercial for a new *Desperate House-wives*-themed casino filled the screen. "Good luck, Yael," Tzipporah said.

"Okay."

Yael waited until she reached her favorite boulder on the bike path before removing the BlackBerry from her purse, and then waited another thirty minutes, staring at the stars. She punched in Deborah's home number. No answer. She tried her cell, still no answer. She studied the sky. Another clear, perfect night, still warm, the pre-dawn chill hours away. She noted Orion, the Big Dipper; spotted Mars glowing red and bright. She thought of angels, celestial choirs. She thought of her husband, and reluctantly left her boulder and headed home.

"How was the meeting?" he asked, as soon as she walked in the door. He was sitting cross-legged on the couch, the banjo-cello thing balanced on his lap. He looked, to Yael, like a skinny guru, channeling deep thoughts through exotic, eleven-tone music.

The meeting. She remembered. She'd left him a note. *Gone to a meeting.* She could lie fairly easily in written form. "Actually, I was watching the trial. On Homicide TV. We get cable in the youth lounge. They replay the trial every evening."

"Oh?" he said, plucking a string. Yael noticed him tightening his grip on the ugly instrument.

"I watched yesterday, also. In the youth lounge. I saw Epstein testify. Today it was Deborah."

He nodded slowly, his hand still moving up and down the board. "Do you want to tell me about it? Or would you rather hear this tune I'm playing with? I'm thinking of using it as the main theme in the new work."

It occasionally occurred to Yael that her husband, in addition to being undeniably weird, was also supremely artful at handling her. He used his eccentricities to project guilelessness; he was just a simple musician, what did he know about the brutalities, the corruptions, the mendacity that characterized the material world? True, he was an avid observer of certain corruptions – take his fascination with the Kennedy assassination, for example, or his obsessive delving into Yael's family skeletons, her background of rabbis and gangsters. But that was exactly the point. He was an *observer*, not a participant, an amateur anthropologist, studying human folly in his spare time, the way some of his colleagues kept bees or took up carpentry. But the world of human conflict was really Yael's world; she was the pastor who helped others navigate their messy human relationships, and she could do it well because she'd navigated a few messy ones herself. He was willing to hear about Yael's world – the world outside of music, the world of murder and deceit. After all, hadn't he just offered to listen? But he also offered an alternative. A new theme! Compositions! He wasn't changing the subject. He had nothing to hide, no reason to avoid discussing Aviva's murder. He was simply elevating their conversation.

For the last three weeks, as the trial neared, as Yael wrestled with her theories about how and why Aviva was killed, Peter's deft attempts at distractions succeeded, or, more accurately, Yael allowed them to succeed. She wasn't ready to confront anyone, much less Peter, with the shards of anomalous facts which didn't add up to anything other than a vague suspicion that something wasn't right, that someone (who?) wasn't telling her something (what?). She was about to tell Peter yes, definitely; play the new theme. His music, even when she didn't understand it – and she understood nothing that emerged from this bizarre, new instrument – really did transport her. And God knows, she needed distraction from her upcoming testimony, which she dreaded more than she'd dreaded anything in her life, more than standing outside her father's room knowing that when she walked through she'd encounter a zombie, a walking dead man, not her father. But Yael understood that the time for truth was approaching. Whether she was ready or not.

"Who do you think killed Aviva?" she asked. She still stood at the entryway, watching her husband's scruffy beard, his bare, pale, skinny legs, the infernal instrument that covered his boxer shorts.

He plucked two notes. "I should think that's obvious," he said softly

"Weinman?"

"Well, yes, I think he admitted it, didn't he? But the question is, who put him up to it? And that seems obvious to me."

"Judah? You're convinced it was Judah?"

He looked straight at her, didn't answer. Instead, he ran his long fingers along the fretless board, playing what Yael had to admit was a haunting melody, vaguely klezmer, but with a touch of Appalachian bluegrass. Somehow Peter, with his quick, graceful fingers, could make that bizarre contraption sound like an oud, a banjo, and a mandolin all at once. Yael was about to give up, listen for a few minutes, then go to bed, when Peter stopped playing. "Motive and opportunity," he said.

"Well, yes," Yael said, not moving from her place at the door. "That's what I hear from Epstein, and from the DA. But motive doesn't really work for me. He wants to avoid a scandal, so he hires a totally unstable person to murder his wife?"

Peter shrugged, plucked a few chords, and closed his eyes. What did he really *know* about such things? Human motives. What fools these mortals be. "Can't argue with opportunity, though, can you?" He played six more notes, slowly, moving the tip of his left index finger along the board with each pluck, producing a lovely whine, as if a baby was crying, but softly, politely, just communicating an innocent sadness, but not wanting to cause a fuss.

"You mean because Judah and Weinman spent so much time together? But how much time does it take to hire a killer? I mean, I spent *time* with the guy. So did everyone on the staff."

He nodded. "Okay," he said.

She watched him play. He closed his eyes, lost in his whiny composition. She wanted to grab the banjo-cello and smash it against the window. She wanted to smash it over his head.

He opened his eyes, as if reading her thoughts. "Didn't Weinman finger Judah? Isn't that why they arrested him?"

"Well, that's what Judah told me, during that charming visit. But, anyway, the scumbag wouldn't *lie*? He strikes you as an honest man? I'm sure he made a deal. He turns in Judah; he saves his life."

"Okay," Peter said, and kept playing.

Yael was aware of the weakness in her argument. Yes, of course, the scumbag was a liar, and the jury would recognize that right away. But he being a liar didn't disprove this particular statement. In fact, Yael knew Epstein and the DA well enough to know they never would have picked up Judah, never would have authorized a deal to save the scumbag's life, merely on his scummy word. Of course there was the briefcase, the money. But there would have to be other evidence, probably something she hadn't heard yet. And even without other evidence, Judah was the most logical suspect. He had cheated on his wife, serially, and, despite her misgivings about his supposed motive, the fact is, he had a lot to lose if the board discovered his fooling around. So, yes, he seemed guilty. The problem was, Yael *knew* he was innocent. She just couldn't say how she knew. At least not yet.

And what about Peter? Why did Epstein keep asking her to speak with him? Why had Weinman himself said that arresting Judah must have been her husband's idea? And why did Epstein arrest the scumbag right after talking to Peter? These facts were shards, pieces of something. But they were sharp, jagged, dangerous to touch. She was afraid to pick them up, even to go near them, at least until she put them all together. So she let Peter play on, as he did every night and day, play his mournful Jewish or country and western melodies, write sad songs, while Yael muddled through her music-free days as interim senior rabbi, dread dripping into her heart hour by hour, as she waited to testify against her friend and mentor.

"It's beautiful, Peter," she said, with genuine admiration.

He smiled, like a child.

CHAPTER 5

It was the same courtroom. After Epstein walked her through the metal detectors, she almost turned left, toward the jury room. He had to grab her elbow, steer her toward the foyer where witnesses waited. During jury duty she'd emerged from the cramped, airless room every day nauseous, exhausted, with a splitting headache and the sense that something in her soul was fraying to the point of ripping away. Yet today she positively yearned for that experience, if it would save her from the witness stand. She would embrace a dentist's chair, exploratory surgery, a ten-hour board meeting, if she could avoid testifying.

As she walked through the courtroom toward the elevated witness seat, the jury to her left, she wondered if all witnesses felt this way: guilty, her guilt displayed to the entire room; with the cameras, to the entire world. Yet this, she knew, was absurd. She hadn't committed a crime (other than watching the trial on TV). Still, her voice shook as she swore to tell the truth. And when Judah caught her eye, she had to pause and shake her head slightly to avoid choking up.

Belinda Dumanis smiled widely, probably to calm Yael's nerves, but the blond woman's squint, the sharp wrinkles under her eyes that accompanied the grin, made the smile look like a grimace, or the fearful look of a chimp confronting an enemy. It looked like a skeleton's smile.

"How long have you known the defendant?"

Yael blushed. Christ. Was she going to blush before answering *every* question, even the most innocuous? She remembered as a juror how closely she examined the facial expressions of every witness, trying to search for truth in the eyes, or shifts in color. They'll think I'm lying the whole time, Yael worried, as she answered the question. "Four years," she said, then shook her head and exhaled. "I mean three."

She saw Judah laugh softly. The only one here who really knows me, she thought. She smiled, suddenly calmer. "Three years," she said, "and seven months."

For the next ten minutes, she explained her role at Anshei Emet, focusing on her daily interactions with Judah. The DA stuck to boring questions – explain the staff organization chart; tell us who did what, who answered to whom – and slowly Yael's voice steadied. Maybe, she thought, that's all they need from her: a dull look at Anshei Emet's organizational structure. She could explain that as well and as boringly as anyone.

But, as she knew would happen, because both Belinda and Epstein had told her many times, they got to the heart of her testimony. That awful day, the morning Judah explained the true nature of his marriage to Aviva. Yael knew that the jury had already heard the story from Deborah, so she was surprised to see them lean forward to hear her describe the same incident, as if something would change in her telling.

She told the story – the call from Charlotte, the gathering in the boardroom, Judah's announcement. Yael remembered her fury that day, but tried very hard to hide it from the jury. What would be the point?

"And how did you feel?"

Yael stared at Belinda. She hadn't told her she was going to ask that question. And, anyway, how could that be relevant? She looked at Judah's attorney, Bart Grim, who was ignoring her, scribbling on his pad. Judah, on the other hand, studied her intently, his head tilted back, his eyes shiny with anticipation, as though Yael were about to deliver life-saving wisdom.

"How did I feel?" Yael repeated. "I'm – I'm not sure I can explain…"

"Were you angry?"

"Objection!" Grim's voice shot out well before Yael could begin to formulate an answer.

"Sustained," the judge said quickly.

"Okay, then, let me ask what you did. What did you do when Rabbi Loeb admitted to sleeping with other women in the course of his marriage?"

"What did I do? I – uh…" Incredibly, she drew a blank. She stared stupidly at the young DA. "I don't remember." Why were they asking her this? What did it matter?

Belinda smiled; another death's-head grin. Yael thought of witch doctors, of horror-novel clowns. Then she remembered. "I was angry," she said softly, as much to herself as to the jurors, remembering as she spoke. She saw Judah nod. "I yelled at him. I lost control." She felt herself blush. "It was inappropriate, but I…" She shrugged and shook her head. "Then I ran out of there. I couldn't – I couldn't stand to be in the same room with him."

Belinda nodded, first at Yael, then at the jury, the grin replaced by a sour frown, as if empathizing with Yael, as if she too couldn't stand to be in the same courtroom with this philanderer, and would love nothing better than to run out. "Thank you, Rabbi Gold," she said with her high school debater's voice. "No more questions."

Before Yael could reach for her water bottle, Grim, a silver-haired, slim, tall man, with the long, wiry arms of a retired tennis pro, was standing less than three feet away. Yael could smell his aftershave. "Why were you so angry?" he demanded. He seemed angry himself. Suddenly everyone's angry.

"Well, I…"

"You had feelings for Rabbi Loeb, isn't that right?"

"Of course. I've admired him for—"

"You were jealous?"

"Objection!"

"Sustained!"

Yael stared at Judah's lawyer. The question, objection, and judge's response came so quickly, they were virtually indistinguishable. And left Yael confused. What was she supposed to do? She turned to the judge, but he was ignoring her, looking sternly at the defense attorney.

"Next question," Grim said. "Who introduced Cantor Weinman to Rabbi Loeb?"

"Cantor Weinman?" Yael asked, genuinely puzzled.

"Cantor Weinman."

She remembered. The scumbag. His real name. They wouldn't call him the scumbag here, would they? "I'm really not sure," she said coolly. She felt her face tingle, but was fairly sure it didn't progress as far as a blush. Anyway, she'd been blushing since she'd climbed up into the witness chair.

"It wasn't you?"

"No, it wasn't me."

"No more questions," he snapped, and turned around. "For now," he added, facing the jury, his back to Yael.

"What was that about?" Yael asked. Epstein had followed her out of the courtroom. They were sitting outside, on the benches, next to the statue of Errol Alexander, the first and only State Supreme Court Justice from Desert County. Yael sipped a black coffee, Epstein smoked. "Was I *jealous*? What was he getting at?"

Epstein laughed. "Oh, he was trying to make you a suspect."

"What!"

"Don't worry. They do that all the time. Remember, he has access to all my notes. He knows that we thought of you ourselves, before we figured it out. But he was just throwing mud up against the wall and seeing if something would stick. You notice he backed off right away."

Yael nodded. Oddly, Epstein's confirming that she had been a suspect early on didn't particularly bother her. He was only doing his job. She watched him flick his ashes onto the lawn. He had surprisingly slender fingers, considering his beefy palms.

"But I was interested in your answer to his last question," he said. "Or, I should say, your lie."

"It wasn't a lie," she said quickly. "I didn't introduce Judah to the scumbag."

"I know you didn't," Epstein said. "But you do know who did, don't you? I don't think he's keeping it a secret. He told me."

"Peter," she whispered.

Epstein took a deep drag on his cigarette, then flicked the ash and tossed the butt at the statue. "Maybe you should talk to him," he said.

Technically, the ban was lifted. Now that she'd testified – and despite the defense attorney's grumbling threat, she wasn't on his witness list – Yael could watch Homicide TV just like every other resident of Desert County. Epstein had sent the cable guy back over that morning. But she liked the wide-screen, HDTV in the youth lounge, enjoyed the smell of stale popcorn, the comfy mess of torn upholstery, the broken foosball game, ping-pong balls littering the sticky floor. Plus, watching in the youth lounge meant she didn't have to watch with her husband. She found the remote buried under a ripped throw pillow. She was about to click on the TV when she heard a key move in the lock; the door swung open. It was Tzipporah. The education director smiled widely, then took her place on the sofa, scrunched up against the end. Yael noticed the bulge pushing up from Tzipporah's shirt. It looked oddly angular, as if the fetus were poking its elbow through its mom's belly. Yael thought of the movie *Alien*. She turned on the television.

Both women gasped simultaneously. It was the scumbag, filling the screen, the high definition accentuating the red blotches on his forehead, his wide nostrils, the crevasses lining his cheeks, the white pimples on his nose, drops of sweat trickling down his face. Yael could have sworn she smelled stale aftershave, as if the odor of his personal scum escaped the TV and filled the synagogue youth lounge.

"How did you meet Rabbi Loeb?" a voice asked – nasal, youthful, female, disembodied. It was the prosecutor.

The scumbag seemed to know the exact location of the camera because he stared right into it, which meant that, from Yael's perspective, his eyes bored in on her. She gripped the side of the couch to stop her hands from shaking.

"Oh, well, that was Rabbi Baby Doll. I'm sorry, I mean Rabbi Gold. Yael Gold. Baby Doll was a nickname I learned from her father. I still call her that sometimes."

"She introduced you?"

"Yes," he said to the camera.

"What the hell," Yael whispered. She didn't know whether to be furious or simply puzzled. He was lying; she had never – would never have – introduced him to Judah. But what was the point of his lie? She noticed Tzipporah staring at the screen, open-mouthed. The scumbag was chuckling, a truly frightening sight.

"I wouldn't actually say 'introduced,'" the scumbag continued. "More like she forced me on him. She had marched me over to his office, sat me on his couch, and shut the door. The excuse was I needed counseling that she wasn't qualified to give, but I think she was sick of me. Can't say I blame her. I would have been sick of me, too."

There was a pause. Weinman winked at the camera. He winked! Yael was 100 percent positive that the gesture was meant for her. He knew she was watching; he was tailoring his answers for her benefit.

"Why?" the nasal voice said slowly. To Yael, it sounded like Belinda was reluctant to pursue the subject. She remembered how easy it was to get sucked into the scumbag's conversation. Even as a witness in a murder trial, he seemed to control the dialogue. "Why was Rabbi Gold sick of you?"

"Oh, I'd been a pain in the ass. Sorry, I mean pain in the neck. I kept taking her down memory lane, telling her stories about her old man, a great old guy, finest rabbi I ever knew. No wonder she got sick of me. Who wants to hear it? Especially when I told her about all the affairs, all the times he screwed around. See, I don't think she *knew*, or if she knew, she didn't realize the extent of it. You see, besides the scandal that got him fired, he'd been *shtupping*—"

"Enough." It was the judge. Yael recognized his deep bass voice, which, at that moment, she loved more than any voice she'd ever heard. Enough is right, she thought.

Another pause, another wink from the scumbag. Yael could hear whispering, then a voice-over – a Homicide TV anchor – explaining that the attorneys were all gathered at the judge's bench for a conference. Yael wondered if Homicide TV would ever shell out for another camera. She would donate the money herself, she thought, if she could look at something on the screen for one second other than the scumbag's leering, pockmarked face.

"Yael, are you okay?" It was Tzipporah. With great effort, Yael tore her eyes away from the screen and looked at her friend. Tzipporah's eyes yawned open with alarm. "You're breathing really hard, Yael," she said. "And your fists – you've got to open them up. You're hurting yourself!"

Yael looked at her hands, both tightly curled. Her fingernails, she noticed – saw more than felt – dug deeply into the palms of both hands. It stung, though if Tzipporah hadn't said anything, Yael might not have noticed. She uncurled her fingers and slowed her breathing. "Maybe you shouldn't watch," Tzipporah said.

Yael shook her head. "I have to."

"Alright," The DA's voice came from the TV. "Rabbi Gold introduced you to Rabbi Loeb. For counseling. Now, let me ask this straight out before we get into details. Did Rabbi Loeb hire you to kill his wife?"

"Yes. Yes, he did." And now he spoke with conviction. No playful tone, no smarmy chattiness. But something in his expression changed. He scrunched up his forehead and pursed his lips, looking almost pensive. Or... repentant? Apologetic. As if the admission troubled his conscience. It's a good act, Yael thought, who knew the scumbag was no more capable of guilt than he was of compassion. But then she wondered, why? Why play at feeling guilty now, when he was owning up to the crime, helping the court, testifying against a guilty man?

"Tell us how he spoke about his wife."

"Oh, he was petrified of her. See, he was screwing around as much as Baby Doll's father. Maybe even more, if you can imagine. You see, that meeting when he told his board that he had an 'open marriage.' That was a bunch of shit – I mean, I apologize, I meant to say a bunch of crap. That is to say, it wasn't. He was screwing every woman he could put his pecker in, but she—"

"Please, counsel." It was the judge. Weinman stared thoughtfully into the camera, lips pursed, while the soft, male voice-over informed the audience that the attorneys were all gathered again in front of the judge's bench. "He's shaking his finger at prosecutor Dumanis," the voice told the TV audience in a whisper, as if sharing a confidence. "I've never seen him so agitated."

In the meantime, Yael stared at Weinman. The scumbag. Why had they come up with that awful name? What really did it signify? Why couldn't she get it out of her head? She noted the ghostly pale skin, the red blotches, the iny, sunburned bald scalp. If you needed an illustration for the word "ugly," she thought, that would do. He was the ugliest thing she could imagine. But there was something new in his expression, something she'd never seen from him. There was no hint of a sneer. No sneaky intelligence behind the eyes, no sense that he was in charge of the conversation, that he was reading your mind. What was she seeing now, in his high-definition face, more real seeming than real life? Honesty? Was that it? He looked like he was honestly appraising the questions and responding simply, in his own scumbag way, with the truth. That's not possible, she thought. He's acting. He's lying.

"No more swearing," the judge snapped. "Do you understand?"

Weinman looked around, startled, as if wondering who the judge was instructing.

"Do you understand, Mr. Weinman? Any more swearing and I'll end your testimony, and you will bear the responsibility. Do you understand?"

"Swearing?"

"Mr. Weinman."

"I understand, Your Honor." Still looking straight at the camera, he smiled, showing each of his yellow teeth, plus the various empty spaces along his gums where teeth used to be. It was, Yael thought, simply a hideous sight.

"He was afraid of his wife?" The prosecutor continued her whiny examination.

"Yes, yes, he was terrified of her. He was afraid she would tell the congregation about his – uh – his fornications, his – uh – fornicating around with, uh, with other men's wives. And, if she told, he would be totally – that is, uh – he would be totally dismissed from his position."

"He'd be fired."

"Yes, that was his deepest fear."

"So, he hired you to kill her."

"Yes, he did. He told me to kill the – uh – to kill the lady. To kill her. He would pay me."

"It was his idea?"

"What?"

"To kill her. He thought of it? Not you? You didn't volunteer to kill her?"

"Why would I do that?"

257

"Please just answer the question."

"It was his idea. He gave me money. A lot of money."

"How much?"

"Five large, before. Another ten, after."

"Large?"

"Thousand. Sorry. Five thousand, then ten. He paid me fifteen thousand dollars to kill his wife. Most I ever got."

"The most *ever*? You've done this before? You've killed people for hire?"

"Oh, yes, many times. It was my job, for years. I was a hit man. I worked for Rabbi Gold's uncle."

"Objection!"

Silence. Not even a voice-over to instruct the viewers. Yael watched the scumbag's bovine face. Evil, she thought. I'm looking into the face of evil, on a widescreen TV, in high definition. In the youth lounge.

"Strike that answer!" the judge growled.

"Yes, let's move on," Belinda said. "How did he pay you? Cash?"

"Cash, yes, cash. I don't take credit cards. Hundred-dollar bills. He put it in his briefcase, and handed it to me. Just like the movies. Said I could keep the briefcase."

"What happened to the briefcase?"

"You guys took it. When you searched my house. Two days after the murder."

Two days, Yael thought. At that point, she was a suspect; at least that was the impression Epstein gave. But they'd already found the money.

"Tell us about the night of the murder."

He shrugged. "I told him to get lost. To leave the door open for me."

"Him? Please say who you mean by him."

"Rabbi Loeb. Judah Loeb. That guy, over there."

"Okay. Did you tell him where to go? How to get lost?"

"Yeah. I said he should go to some place where he'd be seen. Like the *shul*. So he'd have an alibi. I suggested choir practice. I knew they were rehearsing that night. I told him to go check it out. I'd heard them a few times myself. They're not half bad."

"So it was your idea that he appear at the synagogue that night?"

"Yeah, as a matter of fact. I told him to go check out the choir. They're not half bad. That's what I told him."

"And while he was checking out the choir, you broke into his house, and murdered his wife?"

"Didn't need to break in. He left the door open for me. Anyway, she knew me. I'd been to the house many times. She wasn't the slightest bit scared when she saw me. Not until she saw the rope."

"The rope? You mean the murder weapon?"

"Yeah, I used a piece of a kid's jump rope. Works pretty well. I've used it before. All you gotta do is, see, jump behind the person, maybe distract them first with a bump, or a scream, then sneak up real quick behind 'em, loop the rope around the neck and pull with all your might. It's over pretty quickly. You'd be surprised. With Mrs. Loeb, all I needed to do—"

The TV clicked off. Silence, deafening, like a scream.

"Yael! Yael! You're shaking! You're moaning. *Yael!*"

Yael jerked her arms toward Tzipporah, her fists aimed forward, like loaded pistols. She held her breath, not sure she remembered how to breathe. Her entire body – fingertips, toes, neck, crotch – was damp. Had she wet herself, or was it all sweat?

"Yael!"

She exhaled sharply through shut lips, then took in another deep breath and held it. The shaking resumed, uncontrollable. Her fists clattered against each other, in a mad parody of applause.

"Breathe out! Now!"

She did it. She exhaled. And inhaled, and exhaled. She breathed, in and out, normally. The shaking stopped. She looked at the remote, still in Tzipporah's hands, then looked at her friend's face.

"Yael, you can't watch any more of this. You lost control. Are you aware of that? You looked like you were having an epileptic fit. You were groaning, like someone was torturing you. You couldn't stop shaking. And look at you! You look like you're about to attack me."

Yael glanced at her fists, then quickly unfolded her hands and laid them on her lap. The breaths still didn't come easily. And she still trembled, if not violently. She was cold, wet.

"Yael, I'm going to drive you home."

"No!"

"Yael."

"No, no, I just need a second." She closed her eyes, brought her knees to her forehead, and sucked in air through her nose, smelling the sickly sweet sweat. Then she looked up, and tried to smile. "I'm all right. I can make it on my own. I walked here. I'll walk home. I need the air."

"Yael, I was going to call 911. I can't let you just walk home. At least let me walk with you."

"No, no, I'm fine. It's just that I *knew* him. I knew him when he – well, a long time ago. He's always scared me. And just to hear him, to watch him describe…" She shook her head, and balled her fists tightly to stop the trembling.

"I understand. Totally. But I still think…"

"I need to be alone, Tzippi. That's how I can process the experience. I need to walk, alone. It's just a ten-minute walk. I've got my BlackBerry. I swear I'll call you if the trembling starts again. But the air will help. And Peter's home. I won't be alone."

Tzipporah nodded, but she tilted her face, clearly unconvinced. "Maybe I should call Peter, have him come over here. You can walk home together."

"No! Well, that's not a bad idea. But I'll call him. If you call, he'll panic. But that's a great idea. I'll call him right now, from my office, have him meet me there." She jumped off the sofa, and reached for the door.

"But, Yael, why don't you—"

"I'll call you when I get home," she said. "Thanks!"

She hurried across the empty synagogue campus to her office. She flicked on the light. The couch caught her eye immediately, like an unwanted visitor. She remembered the last day of Aviva's life. How Judah's wife, not long for this world, had sat there, waiting for Yael, smoking, lipstick askew, looking panicked, looking like she needed something from Yael but had no idea what. Yael shook the image out of her head and reached for her office phone. She punched in some numbers, not her own, not Peter's cell. It was Deborah's number. She had some questions for the synagogue president.

CHAPTER 6

They met at Yael's favorite boulder, on the bike path. Two coyotes exchanged whiny howls. The moon was three-quarters full, the sky, as usual, filled with stars. The two women sat alongside each other, as if sharing a park bench. Deborah asked Yael if she minded if she smoked.

"I didn't know you smoked," Yael said. She thought of Aviva. Then of Epstein. Suddenly, everyone smoked.

"Just in college. Twenty-five years ago. I started up again about two months ago. I needed calming down. You can probably imagine why." She lit a cigarette, inhaled, then exhaled smoke through her nostrils. The moonlight bathed Deborah's face, giving Yael a high-definition look at each line, crevasse, and splotch, as if it were broad daylight, or Yael were watching her on the wide-screen TV. Most of Yael's trembling had passed, though she still felt an occasional spasm in her hands, forcing her to clench them into fists.

"Why were you at choir practice that night?" Yael asked.

Deborah smiled weakly, flicking ash on the dirt path. "Getting right to the point, eh?"

"You're not in the choir. You haven't joined the choir in years. You don't even like this choir."

"They interrupt! We try to sing along, and they interrupt with those imbecilic folk melodies. Who's that guy who

263

wrote those la-la-las? Shlomo Carlebach. That's all they do! I can't stand it. It's not just me. No one likes them! No one I know, anyway. If it were up to me, I would have disbanded them years ago. You don't really like them, do you, Yael?" She flicked another ash. So far, she'd only puffed once from her cigarette. Apparently she was more interested in holding the burning stick than putting it in her mouth.

"Is that why you were there?" Yael asked. "To ask the choir to disband?"

Deborah stared at her. "Yael, I'm sorry if I ever gave you the impression that I trust you. I don't, you know."

Yael shook her head. "Deborah, I'm not sure—"

"Are you wearing a wire? Did Epstein tell you to meet me out here, with the coyotes, in the middle of the night?"

"Deborah, I think—"

"You were so pissed off when Judah told us about his supposed open marriage. And then you decided to crucify him in front of the whole board."

"Yes, I know. We discussed that, Deborah. I apologized."

"You slept with Judah, didn't you? Please, Yael, just tell me the truth. I just want the truth from *someone*. Tell me the truth, and I'll tell you the truth."

"I did *not!*" Yael said. Her hands spasmed; she clenched them into fists, just to stop the trembling, but she was angry enough to use them. She shut her eyes tightly, then opened them. Deborah flicked another ash on the dirt. "I didn't." Yael repeated. "I guess I wanted to," she said, saying the words out loud for the first time. "I might have, if he'd asked, if he'd come on to me. I don't know. I think I was in love with him. But I seemed to have been the one woman in Desert County he didn't seduce. He didn't even try."

Deborah nodded. "He tried with me. Eight years ago. He even fed me that same crap about the open marriage. Jesus. I should have gotten him fired back then. But I didn't want a scandal. And he is a good rabbi. He *understands* us, unlike, well, unlike others. He takes the time; he's gotten to *know* us. And, you know, he's accomplished so much. And maybe I was in love with him, too, at least a little." She looked at Yael, who tried, unsuccessfully, to uncurl her fists. "I guess I believe you, though. Why would you lie? It does explain your anger. You weren't so much mad that he fooled around, you were mad that he hadn't fooled around with *you* – that he seemed to fool around with everyone *but* you."

"Yes," Yael whispered. She wondered if it was loud enough for Deborah to hear. She didn't care. She wasn't really speaking to Deborah. She was admitting something to herself, something desperately hard to swallow. The fact was, she'd spent weeks now denying a charge – adultery, a serious charge, in her mind, a deadly serious charge – that she'd *wanted* to be true, but was actually false. She was innocent, but didn't want to be, *hadn't* wanted to be. Partly to change the subject, but also because she wanted to know, needed to know, she asked again, "Why did you come to choir practice that night?"

"That is the difference, you know, between you and him. You're a talented teacher, Yael. Good singer, great administrator. You're nice looking. You speak well. You see the big picture. You're not as talented as him in any of those things, but you're young, you'll get better. Anyway, he's a phony, and a liar, and a narcissist, and I don't think you're any of those things, though, really, how should I know? But he *understands* us. He knows how hard we try to bring something decent, I could even say holy, into our lives. He knows that we spend most of our time making more and more money for a corrupt industry. He knows we can't help ourselves because even though we're not fools – we understand that nothing we do matters in the long run; in fact, our industry does a lot of damage – we can't help it, because we have to buy that next Beemer, or Jaguar, or Versace dress, or take that French vacation, or give a million dollars to Israel, or build a tuberculosis wing at the hospital. We need the dirty money we earn, so we can spend it, or give it away, or just count it. We can't help it. But we're still basically okay people. And the synagogue helps us stay decent. Judah understands all that. He loves us for it, he loves us because we strive so hard to transcend the muck of our rich, spoiled lives; he loves our pathetic efforts to transcend the corruption. You don't love us, Yael. You don't understand us. You've never taken the time. You don't have the inclination. The truth is, you despise us, you always have; you hold us in contempt. You don't know your congregation, you don't love your congregants; you don't understand us. That's why he's a better rabbi sitting in jail for killing his wife than you are sitting here free, wishing you'd slept with him before it was too late."

Deborah's soliloquy took Yael's breath away. She literally stopped breathing as she watched the older woman flick cigarette ash on to the dirt. Then she gasped quietly, sucked in air, held her breath again, shaking her head several times before breathing normally. The logic, she thought, shaking her head. The fucking mad, bizarro logic. Judah slept around, maybe even murdered his wife, but *he* was the better rabbi because he *understood* his poor, rich congregants. Deborah was absolutely right, of course. Every insight, every charge. But she was also *so* wrong. "What were you doing at choir rehearsal?" Yael asked.

"I didn't know it was choir rehearsal," Deborah answered matter-of-factly, as if she'd been chatting about that evening all along. She smiled warmly at Yael. "Judah picked the night. But, you see, that's what I mean. That you would have to ask. That you didn't know what was really going on that night." She brought the cigarette to her lips, but kept it there, staring thoughtfully at Yael, looking like she was sucking on a pen.

"Charlotte," Yael said. That was the missing evidence. The real affair, not a one-night stand. The motive. "Charlotte was there, too."

Deborah nodded. "Charlotte. A woman you see every day. I asked her to come. I needed to speak with her and Judah. Together."

"Charlotte was the other woman," Yael said. "The real other woman. The affair. Not Addison. Not Tzipporah."

"And not you. And not me."

"How long? How long were they...?"

"God, I don't know. Two years? Maybe more."

"Charlotte's children?"

"Oh, I doubt it. But you'd have to ask her."

Charlotte and Judah. The feisty, worn, though not unattractive redhead; poor, intelligent, uneducated, not Jewish, shrewd, sad. And Judah, the rabbi, the boss, the star. For years. *Years.* Had Yael known all along? In fact, she hadn't. She figured it out an instant before Deborah told her. The fact is, she didn't know Charlotte, didn't like her, didn't dislike her; never tried to get to know her. A thought hit her, then another, with greater force.

"The police know about Charlotte? You told Epstein? Dumanis?"

"I answered all their questions truthfully."

"Deborah, please."

"Yes, yes, they know. From me, but I assume from others. I regaled Epstein and Dumanis with all my theories, including the possibility – remote, but real, at least in my mind – that you had done it. For awhile that seemed to be their working theory also. I only gave it up completely when you told the board to screw Judah. That's not something the killer would do. It would be too obvious."

So Epstein knew. "But what about Charlotte? Did Charlotte kill Aviva? Did she hire Weinman?"

"How should I know, Yael? Remember, not that long ago, I thought maybe *you* did it. A week ago, I still figured Judah did it. Why else would they arrest him? I'm not an investigator, Yael. I'm a tax attorney for casinos. You're a rabbi. Our rabbi. Remember that. It's not our job to solve this crime."

"But Judah!" she said. "He's... He's..." He's what? An adulterer? A good rabbi? A friend? A fraud? A villain? "He's innocent," Yael said.

"Could be," Deborah said, finally snuffing out the cigarette, tossing the butt into the cacti. "Maybe you should speak with Charlotte. God knows, she needs to speak with someone. But let me give you a tip. I'm no pastor. I've never taken any counseling courses. But I suggest you don't begin the conversation by accusing her of murder."

Yael nodded. Both women stood up and faced each other awkwardly. Yael felt a strange compulsion to hug the older woman; odd, considering how Deborah had ripped into her and, two weeks earlier, had suggested to the cops that perhaps Yael was a killer. Still, she felt they'd traveled some rocky path together, endured a trauma, and prevailed. She also wanted to acknowledge that she'd heard the synagogue president's complaint about her coldness. She wanted to show her that she could change, that she could understand, that she could sympathize, she could love. But embrace the woman who had turned the police on her? She stuck out her hand. Deborah ignored it and gathered Yael into her arms, hugging her tightly. Yael smelled the cigarette smoke on her breath. She fought back tears.

"You'll call Charlotte?" Deborah said, after letting Yael go.

"Tomorrow," she answered. Tonight, she was going home to sleep with her husband. She'd speak with Charlotte at work, first thing in the morning.

But Charlotte called first, waking Yael up from a sound slumber. Yael groped on the floor for her BlackBerry.

"Yael!" the familiar, Southern-fried voice cried out.

A herald, Yael thought. Bearer of news, good and bad.

"Yael! Did you *hear*?"

Yael glanced at the clock. 9:30 a.m. She'd overslept, first time she'd slept past 6 a.m. since the murder. "Charlotte. I, uh, just woke up. What?"

"Judah! I mean, Rabbi Loeb! They're letting him go! The judge dismissed the case. Yael! Isn't it wonderful! Yael!"

CHAPTER 7

"Yael! He's free! He's coming *here*. He'll be here in an hour!"

Charlotte vaulted over the front desk, a task that, to Yael, looked too difficult for an Olympic athlete. The two women embraced. Yael realized she'd never been this physically close to the secretary, never felt her bony back, never inhaled her perfume.

"Oh, it's so wonderful!" Charlotte exclaimed, still holding tight with her thin arms, speaking right into Yael's ear. "Isn't it wonderful, Yael?"

Yael had called Epstein on the walk over. Yes, it was true. First thing in the morning, the judge had released Judah because of lack of evidence. He was already out of jail, probably on his way home. Weinman had changed his story. He'd strangled Aviva entirely of his own accord. No one had hired him.

"But why?" Yael had asked him, fear grabbing her by the throat so that she could barely get the words out.

"Who the hell knows?" answered the cop. "Ask him next time he calls you."

"Yael!" Charlotte was now sobbing, singing out Yael's name, hugging her, wetting Yael's blouse with her tears.

"Charlotte," Yael said, pushing her gently away. "Let's go to my office."

Charlotte shot a glance at the front desk. "But, I should be here. So many people will call. I have to tell them the news! And, well, *he* might call. He might need me."

Yael nodded. In fact, she had a hard time imagining Charlotte away from the front desk for any length of time. Yael's sole image of the secretary was her sitting behind the wooden barrier, posted like a sentry, phone and computer to her right, visible only from the breasts up. Yael had to admit that she saw Charlotte more as a valuable piece of equipment than as part of the synagogue professional staff.

"It's okay, Charlotte. We'll have plenty of time to answer the phones, to let people know. I just need to talk to you."

Yael put her arm around the secretary, and guided her to her office. She pointed to the couch. Charlotte sat, but on the edge, facing the door, poised to leap up, and flee back to her rightful place. She clasped her hands and knocked her thumbs together.

"Charlotte."

"Yael!" Charlotte said, and smiled widely. "Back to normal, huh! Thank God!"

"Normal?" Yael said. "Aviva's still dead. Rabbi Loeb lost his wife; she was murdered. Normal?"

"Well, I just meant... I meant him finally getting out of that horrible jail. I'm just so happy. For Judah. I mean, Rabbi Loeb."

Yael stared at Charlotte. There were wrinkles under her eyes, as if she'd had trouble sleeping. She also looked skinnier, truly bony. Yael tried to *understand*. To sympathize. "Charlotte, please understand me. I'm not judging you. I just need to know."

"Yael?"

"Come on, you know. Please. Don't make me say it out loud. You. And Judah."

Charlotte immediately blushed, her facial skin taking on the color of her hair. It was if she became an all-red being, a Martian, distinctly human-like, but still a different species. Scarlet. "She told me she wouldn't tell *anyone* until we worked it out. She promised me!"

"Charlotte, there was a murder. Deborah couldn't very well keep it secret. I mean, the police must have talked to you."

"Of course he talked to me, that tall guy. And I told him the truth! I talked to the woman, too, with the baby face, the district attorney. But she told me she wouldn't call me unless she needed to. And now, with Judah free, I figured... well, you know."

"That your secret was safe."

Charlotte blew out a breath. Her face still pined for the door. But the color had drained from her cheeks, and Yael noticed a single tear dripping from her right eye. "I never saw my name in the papers. I guess I was naïve. I thought God saved me. Like he saved Judah."

By arranging for Aviva to be murdered? But Yael let that one go. "How long, Charlotte? How long has this been going on?"

"Three years," she answered.

Since I started here, Yael thought. How long had Charlotte been widowed? Yael was embarrassed to admit – to herself, at least – that she didn't know. She knew about Charlotte's kids, a boy and a girl, four and seven. She'd seen the photos on the front desk, heard Charlotte cooing to one or the other of them over the years, remembered her complaints about child care, about do-nothing teachers and babysitters. But her husband? Boyfriends? Yael didn't know a thing. Three years. Yael thought of Addison, of Tzippi. Judah had slept with them while immersed in a heated affair with his secretary. What a guy.

"We started up about six months after my husband passed away," Charlotte added.

"Ah," Yael said.

"Judah was so helpful after Charles passed on. You weren't here then, Yael. You don't know what a god-awful wreck I was those days. Judah saved my life."

"He saved your life. He comforted you. And then. Then. He…"

Charlotte shot off the couch, elbows first, practically leaping in the air. "Well, you don't have to imply that! Why does everyone draw those filthy conclusions? He was kind to me, then he fell in love with me. Is that so shocking to you, Yael?"

"Please, Charlotte. Please. Sit. I apologize. I'm not judging you. I just want to, to understand."

The secretary sat back on the couch, but stared angrily. "You don't know me, Yael! Three years here, and you don't know me. You didn't even know about Charles until just now, did you? You didn't even know his name."

"I didn't," Yael admitted. "You're right."

Charlotte shook her head. "Three years, and you never asked," she said softly. "No business of mine telling you how to do your job. But you never asked."

Yael nodded. She never asked. She didn't understand. She didn't *know*. By now she was used to the accusations, all coming from women who had either slept with Judah, or had wanted to. As she had wanted to. They were right, those women, and they were wrong. She would deal with that issue later.

"But, Charlotte," she said, "*he* was married. You were a widow, but he was married."

"Oh, Yael! Come on! That was a marriage? Even you knew about that marriage! Didn't he tell you, didn't he tell all of you, at that board meeting?"

"Yes, he told us," Yael said. "He told us about his marriage." After someone murdered his wife, he told us, Yael thought. He told us about his marriage, after it was over. After she was dead. That's when we heard from him. From him, not from her. We never heard her story, and we won't. Because she's dead. But what was the point of arguing now with Charlotte? For her, there was a happy ending. God had looked out for her. Aviva was dead. Judah was coming home, in fact, he'd be at the synagogue in a matter of minutes for a tearful reunion with… his secretary. A bereaved widow. His lover. A woman he'd counseled in his own office, at a synagogue, a house of God. Yael felt an overwhelming urge to flee. Or puke. But first, one more question.

"Charlotte, that night. The night Aviva was killed. Choir rehearsal. What were you all doing here that night?"

"He *loves* me!" she said, as if in answer, as if that was all the response Yael needed and, anyway, all she was going to get.

"Okay, Charlotte," she said. "I don't want... I just need to know..."

"Don't you judge me!"

"I don't."

"You wanted him too, Yael," she drawled. "You think we all didn't notice that? You think I'm blind? Just 'cause y'all don't know a thing about us, you don't think we were watching you, you don't think we saw what you were feeling? You think I don't know what *you* wanted?"

Anger, black and bilious. How close it lingered to the surface. Yael struggled to keep her hands from folding into fists. "Please get out of my office," she said softly. "Now."

"Don't you judge me!"

Yael shook her head. "No," she said, shutting her eyes, trying once again to control her tremors, this time from rage, not fear. "I don't judge you," she said. But, she thought, why not? Why not judge Charlotte, judge Addison, judge Tzipporah, judge Judah? "Please leave," she repeated, sharper this time. Charlotte bolted up and out of the office. Yael sat for a moment, then slowly rose from the couch. She pushed open her office door and, without looking back, left the synagogue through her favorite rear entrance. She walked home quickly, but instead of going inside, she headed straight for her car. Then she drove to the airport.

CHAPTER 8

Rabbi Gold, Yael's father, was dressed in a brown sports coat, light-blue tie, the knot perfectly placed, white oxford shirt, tan slacks, and black loafers. Yael had no idea who dressed him, or who placed him in the chair next to the bed, making it look like *he* was the visitor, paying a sick call on an invisible patient. For all she knew, he'd done it all himself, the getting out of bed, shaving, tooth-brushing, dressing instincts all functioning perfectly, even as the rest of his brain – the thinking, feeling, interacting parts – had turned to mush. Yael stood by the lone window, keeping the hospital bed between herself and her father. He looks like a rabbi, she thought, a counselor, a pastor. He even tilted his head in her direction, as if he were listening, which, in fact, he was, though not to the words but just to the sound of her voice.

"See, Dad, no one asked about *my* trial. I don't mean the big trial, Judah's trial, the trial that took over the whole town. I mean my trial, when I was on the jury. No one asked. Or, if they did ask, they changed the subject quickly because of the big news. Or I changed the subject because, you know, there was my trial, but, my God, Aviva was *murdered*. So I never got to talk about it. To anyone."

She watched him scrunch up his forehead, as if listening closely. He, his intense, interested face said, would listen, even if the others wouldn't.

"It was a child abuse case. The girl was five years old. The defendant was this, uh, this scumbag. Fat guy, bald, in his fifties. He worked at a toy store; he was just a clerk, worked behind the register. The girl's parents took her to the store three times in a week. They were searching for the perfect present for her fifth birthday. They let her wander, her in this cute red dress with a gold bow in her hair, they let her wander through the store looking for the right Beanie Baby or Powerpuff Girl or box of Silly Bands, or whatever. She would lead them to exactly the right place. Except these parents, they were kind of kids at heart. They let the girl wander, and they wandered a little themselves, looking at, I don't know, the Lego sets, or the elaborate dollhouses, or the plastic pools that everyone in Desert County eventually puts on their patios. So they didn't watch their girl – her name, by the way, was Julie – they didn't see Julie 100 percent of the time. Oh, they felt bad about that. Of course. But what are you gonna do? What's done is done. Anyhow, here's the part everyone agrees about. The parents. Julie. The scumbag. The prosecution. The defense. Everyone's on the same page about this. Each time little Julie, with her golden bow, each time she began wandering away from her parents, each time, that is to say, her parents lost track of her, the scumbag crooked his scummy finger and summoned her behind the counter, to stand next to him, at the cash register. This happened three times. Everyone agrees. Little Julie scooted behind the cash register and spent at least five minutes standing next to the guy. Everyone agrees this happened. Oh, and that the scumbag touched her. Each time.

"The defendant, he says – well, he didn't testify – but he told the police he just patted her head each time, and then he patted her shoulders, and maybe, he said, just once, her rear end. That's it. Friendly. Like an uncle. Now, he told the police he *wanted* to show her his penis. That's what he wanted to do. But he didn't. He just patted her head and shoulders, and maybe her rear end.

"Julie remembers it differently. She also didn't testify, but we watched a video of her describing everything to a social worker. It was funny, because her little-girl voice sounded a lot like the prosecutor's voice. Anyway, she says, little Julie that is, with the red dress and golden bow. She wore the same outfit each time to the store, she loved that outfit. She said the Toy Man – that's what she called the guy – she said the Toy Man patted her head maybe once, her shoulders several times, but that he mostly put his hands beneath her underwear, putting his fingers up her vagina and anus. She says he did this each time. Three times.

"Now, remember, Julie's standing behind the counter, which is made out of solid wood. We visited the store. I spent a lot of time staring at the counter. There's a little gate where you can walk in. The Toy Man opened it for her. But once you close the gate, you can't see her. And you can't see the Toy Man's hands. So, even though the store always had shoppers, no one saw the Toy Man do anything to Julie. No one could even testify that he patted her head, which, of course, he admitted to doing.

"So it was his word versus hers. An adult versus a child. And neither of them testified. A policeman – a guy named Epstein, tall, Jewish guy with a shaved head – he read the police report out loud, and that included the Toy Man's statement that he wanted to show her his penis. And Julie's video, where she acts out where the guy put his fingers with one of those dolls, those anatomically correct dolls. Oh, by the way, Julie also said on the video that she saw the Toy Man do magic. She said she saw him turn a Beanie Baby into a Powerpuff doll. She said Toy Men are magic, they can turn toys into other toys.

"There were two actual witnesses, but all they testified to is that the Toy Man's face turned bright red around the time he was allegedly fondling Julie. But that's all. And remember, they couldn't see Julie, so they couldn't swear that she was even back there when his face was turning all red.

"Sounds like reasonable doubt, doesn't it? No one saw anything. Julie said what happened, but the defense didn't get to cross-examine. And she's only five years old. Plus, there's the nonsense about magic. So, maybe she made the whole thing up, just imagined it. And maybe not. But the point is: reasonable doubt. No witnesses. None. Just a girl on a video. And a red face. And a strange, sick statement about wanting to show her his penis. Reasonable doubt.

"Except, come on! I mean, there's no solid evidence here, but do we really have any doubt that he did it? I mean, why isn't he testifying? No, we're not allowed to use that as an inference of anything, but it's so obvious. He's not testifying because he has a record. I mean, who admits to the police that he wanted to show a little girl his penis? Who admits that? A psycho. A psycho with a record. If he'd testified, the prosecution would have found a way to tell us about other children, other times the Toy Man wanted to flash his penis.

"That's what I told the jury. Most of them were set to acquit, even though they sort of thought he did it. They just didn't think there was enough evidence. They didn't think you can send someone to jail because of what a five-year-old says about a Toy Man. Our first vote was eight to one for acquittal, with three folks not yet ready to vote. I was the one for convicting.

"And that's how it stayed for the first day. Eight to one to three. That whole day, I mostly talked about how believable Julie sounded on the tape. Forget the stuff about the magic Toy Man; all five-year-olds believe that stuff. But why would she make up a story about fingers inside her rear end? That's not coming from a normal five-year-old's imagination. She would only say that if it were true. That seemed obvious to me. And, strangely enough, most of them agreed with me. Yes, they said. It is *unlikely* that she would make that up. Not impossible, no, but, yes, unlikely. Still, they didn't think it was fair. You can't judge a witness for sure unless you can cross-examine her. That's the only way to find out if she was making up that part, too.

"So, I brought up the red face. He got turned on by this girl. Two witnesses saw it. He was stimulated sexually. We know little girls turn him on, because he wants to show them his penis. He admitted that to the police, for God's sake. So even if he just patted her head, isn't that enough? Isn't that sexual abuse or, actually, sexual assault? That was the crime he was accused of.

"And they sort of agreed with me on that one, too. In fact, for some reason, the red face was a stronger argument for most of the jury than Julie's video. That, together with the comment about his penis. But, still. It was just a red face. The witnesses didn't even see Julie. Red face can mean anything; it can mean indigestion, allergies, a trick of the light. One of them, an old lady, Mom's age, kind of looked like her, gray hair in a bun, wore a long-sleeved blouse and a gray jacket even in the hot weather, she kept saying she wouldn't want anyone to convict her of a crime because of the color of her face.

"That's how the argument went the first day. I stuck to the evidence, the stuff we were *allowed* to talk about. The video. The red face. It was funny, the others spent a lot of time trashing the mom and dad. What kind of parents let a five-year-old wander off by herself? The old lady, the one who reminded me of Mom, even complained that the parents came by the store three times. Just pick a present and get on with it, she said. I didn't talk about the parents. Not that I approved – I didn't – but what was the point? We weren't there to judge the parents; we were there to judge the scumbag who assaulted the little girl. So every time someone brought up the parents, I got them back on track. No, I wasn't the foreman, but I pretty much took over. I have to admit that. I do that sometimes. I take over.

"I didn't start talking about the Toy Man not testifying until the second day. I just felt like I had to say something. The foreman tried to stop me the first time. And the old lady looked like she wanted to tackle me. But I had to ask the question. No one else was asking. Why didn't he testify?

Why? And once you asked, the answer became obvious. Because he was a child molester. He had a record – if not convictions, then arrests. The Toy Man was a child molester. It's the only answer that made sense. And that meant if we acquitted him for this, he went back on the street. Back to being Toy Man at some toy store. Back to doing what he does. I didn't even have to spell that one out. Because they knew. They knew what these guys do. They saw Julie do it with her doll.

"So, by the end of the second day, most of them—"

"Most of them voted to convict. Congratulations."

In tone, inflection, stress, and timbre, it sounded like her father. But it was her mother. Thirty years after the divorce, and she still spoke like him. Or maybe it was the other way around. Yael turned and saw her mother standing at the open door.

"How long have you been there?" Yael asked.

"Long enough to hear about the old lady juror who looked like me. Gray hair up in a bun. Business suit, even in hot weather. You're right, I probably would have voted to acquit. It does sound like reasonable doubt."

Yael studied her mother. She did, in fact, resemble juror 4, Marcy Jones. Same build, similar walk, similar frowning visage, though her mother's was certainly more bitter, and more intelligent. "But he did it," Yael said. "I knew he did it."

Her mother nodded slowly, frowning, really scowling. She walked to the bed and brushed it vigorously with both hands before sitting down. "I'm sure your father was fascinated by your story, Yael."

"At least he didn't interrupt."

"No, he wouldn't be able to do that. Except by peeing in his pants. He does that now, every so often. That might have put a crimp in your storytelling." She extended her hand, and, as if it contained a flesh magnet, her father's left hand slowly rose, and the two gripped hands, like young lovers.

"Do you want to hear the rest?"

"Are you talking to me, dear?" her mother asked.

"Mom."

"I already know the rest. I read it in the newspaper. The *Desert City Journal*. I read it online. You were the one angry woman. You convinced that bunch of pansy liberals to convict the scumbag. Creative nickname, by the way. Did the judge say anything in his instructions about referring to the defendant as scumbag?"

"He did it."

"Well, you're certainly convinced. And you convinced a jury of his peers. Who am I to argue?"

Who are you argue? Yael thought. Arguing is breathing for you. You argue, therefore you are. But Yael didn't want to argue. Not about this.

"You *know* why this trial knocked me for a loop. I had nightmares. Asthma. I hadn't wheezed in twenty years, but I needed a prescription for an inhaler in the middle of the trial. You know why."

"I imagine anyone would be upset at such a trial. An innocent little girl. A creepy, predator Toy Man, working in a toy store. Sets off all sorts of primal fears."

"More like primal memories. Childhood memories."

"Are you accusing me of something, Yael? Can you get to the point? After awhile my hand gets numb, and I have to shift positions. I have to do it quickly because he panics when I let go."

"You know. You know what I'm talking about."

She sighed, but it was an act. If a sigh can be sarcastic, this was a sarcastic sigh, a sigh that communicated that there was really nothing to sigh about. "You're referring to Cantor Weinman."

Yael's heart raced, and she felt the familiar rush of blood to her face. Just hearing her mother say the name scared the hell out of her. Talk about primal fears. "Yes," she said softly. "Cantor Weinman. And me."

"And what exactly do you suspect?"

"Please! Please. Just tell me."

"You're so sure there's something to tell," she snapped. She brushed imaginary dust off the blanket. "But surely you understand that sometimes there's nothing to tell. Sometimes we just don't know the story. There's a limit, after all, to our capacity to know."

Thank you, Madam Philosopher. What, after all, is *knowing*? Who can know what we know? Yael looked for a pillow. Her plan was to smother her mother. Probably not kill her, but, who knows, she may get careless. Instead, she shut her eyes tightly. "Tell me what you *do* know," she said.

Beth sighed, but this time for real. Yael opened her eyes and was surprised to see her mother had closed hers, though her face was pointed at the ceiling, as if she were searching the heavens for answers with eyes shut. "Yael," she said. "You were just three years old."

"But I *remember*. I remember something."

"He used to babysit. Not just for you, of course. For the two of you. He volunteered. Actually, he implored us. Insisted."

"Okay."

"I know this is hard to believe, but he struck us – both of us – as, well, as a *kind* man. Good with kids. Good with people."

"Kind."

"Of course we misjudged him. That much is obvious. I freely admit to that. But, at the time, well, it doesn't matter. We misjudged him. Listen, Yael, if anything happened, and believe me I still don't know, it only happened once. We're fairly certain."

"Okay."

"There was no evidence, really. We had you examined, thoroughly. You may remember some of that. Doctors probing in unpleasant places."

"Okay."

"No physical evidence. And even what you told us wasn't particularly damning. You said you'd been playing nurse. Not doctor, nurse. Yes, you told us there'd been some touching, but you didn't say where. And you were crying, but he swore that was only because we came home late. Which we did. You see, the only evidence, if you could call it that, was, well, Arthur."

Yael remembered suddenly. Not the incident itself, but Arthur. Arthur, her older brother, appearing out of nowhere, like magic, standing there, hollering at Weinman. And the scumbag – they didn't call him that then – they called him, what did they call him? – Bozo! They called him Bozo, like the clown – Bozo was yelling back at him, shaking his finger, his face was… "Red," Yael said. "His face was red."

Mrs. Gold stared at her daughter, her mouth open. "Yes," she said. "That's all Arthur could tell us. He'd burst in on you two, you and Weinman. You were in our bedroom. He didn't see anything incriminating. No fingers in the wrong places. Your clothes were on. No nurse, no doctor. But Cantor Weinman's face, he told us, was the brightest red he'd ever seen. He didn't think a face could be that red."

Yael shut her eyes and tried desperately to remember. Nothing. A block. "Why," she asked. "Why did Arthur yell at him? Why were they screaming at each other?"

"Well, the scumbag, as you call him, claimed that he'd merely scolded Arthur for bursting in without knocking, and Arthur just yelled back. But Arthur told us… he told us that Weinman had hurt you. That he heard you, well, he didn't say scream, or even cry. Just a noise, coming from you. A – I don't know, a whimper? He didn't know what it meant, but it didn't sound good. So he burst in, and… and… I don't know. We don't know. You don't remember?"

"I don't," Yael whispered. "Honestly, I don't. But the red face." She shook her head, then looked at her father. She was surprised to see a frown. Had they been shouting? Maybe loud voices agitated him. Her mother touched his cheek and the frown disappeared. Like pressing a button, Yael thought.

"Yael," her mother said, "we did everything we could to see what happened, and then to protect you. Of course, we never invited Weinman to our home again. We made sure you were never alone with him."

"Did you call the police?"

"Why? Because of a red face? What would we say? Anyway, think for a second, Yael. Think. You were three years old. What else was happening around this time?"

Yael thought. "Daddy got fired."

"Well, yes. Yes. Daddy got fired. In fact, that happened exactly six weeks after this maybe-incident. But, remember, why did he get fired? The funeral for his mobster cousin."

"The affair," Yael said. "The affair with his cousin's wife." She looked accusingly at her father. He tilted his head slightly, looking puzzled, but happy to be left out of the conversation, happy just sitting, holding hands with the love of his life.

"Yes," Mrs. Gold said. "So, another scandal. When we didn't know *anything*, nothing at all."

Yael nodded. In fact, she understood. It wasn't as if he'd bragged about wanting to show her his penis. Truly, they didn't have grounds to accuse him, to bring in the police. "But," she said. "But now. Now we know."

"What do you mean? Do you remember?"

"No, but Weinman. We *know* about him. He's a killer. He's evil."

She thought back to the phone call she got from Epstein as she was driving from the Cleveland airport to see her father. "He's talking again," the cop told her. "We think we know why he did it."

"Why," she'd whispered.

"To screw everything up," Epstein answered. "That's a quote. That's exactly what he told Dumanis. 'To screw everything up.' He did it for the scandal. For the attention. I don't know. For fun."

"He's evil," Yael had told the cop.

"Yeah, well, he's not the only one." Then he'd asked when she was coming home.

Home? Desert County? What was home? "Soon," she'd answered.

"You mean because he killed poor Aviva?" her mother now asked. "He killed someone, so that proves he molested you thirty years ago?"

"It's not just that he killed her, Mom. It's why. There was no reason, except to screw everything up. That's the evil." She exhaled deeply, slowly, trying to expel his scummy image from her brain. The smell, she thought, would always be with her, also the sound of his voice, a smooth baritone, musical, sickly reasonable; she'd always see his bald white head. If she could vomit it all up, purge her senses, she would, even if it took weeks. If an exorcist would help, she'd find one. "And his red face," she told her mother. "His big, fat, red face."

She had dinner that evening at her brother's house. She'd planned to confront him as soon as he opened the door, ask him about that night, what he saw, what he yelled, why he screamed, what the scumbag hollered back. But the twins answered the doorbell, leaping up and down, one after the other with synchronized precision, their equal-length blond ponytails flopping up and down, pure, pink delight coloring their freckled faces. They yelled, "Yaelie! Yaelie! Yaelie!" She hugged one, then the other, then both at once, a thrilling reunion, as if she'd returned safely from Mars.

"My favorite nieces!" she cried, in between hugs. It was how she always greeted them; it's what she'd whispered when she first saw them, sleeping side by side in twin bassinets. But now, five years later, they cackled with glee, finally getting the joke. "You're my favorite aunt!" they exclaimed in unison, exploding in laughter, twin engines of mirth. Each girl grabbed an arm and pulled their favorite aunt into the living room. Yael smelled chicken and garlic, her two favorite smells. "What did you bring me?" she asked her nieces. It took a little longer than one second, but the laughter again erupted, this time knocking the twins to the rug. They rolled and tumbled, bouncing off each other like atoms in a collider. Jokes, Yael thought. They love their favorite aunt's jokes. She took two gift-wrapped packages out of her bag, handed them over, and watched as the girls tore through the wrapping, revealing identical Bratz dolls. The twins sang, they danced, they cheered. There was no end to their delight.

It wasn't until the girls ran off, after the banana cream pie, after two glasses of wine, that Weinman entered their conversation, and it was Arthur who pronounced his name.

"So it was Weinman after all. He did it on his own. Your boss didn't hire him."

Yael studied her wine glass, wondered if she should ask for more. "I guess. There are still a few mysteries, but, yeah, that seems to be it. Judah, he was, he was innocent. It was the scumbag; on his own."

"But why, Yael? Why would he just kill someone?" It was Arthur's wife, Toby. Yael looked at her, noticed the worry wrinkles lining her forehead. Toby had aged noticeably since giving birth to the twins, but she still wore her thirty-nine years well. Six years before, she'd resembled a teen cheerleader, with long, straight hair, scrawny build, angled cheekbones, smooth complexion, forced smile always on display. Yael was now embarrassed that she didn't like Toby at first. In fact, she'd suggested to Arthur he rethink getting married. The excuse she used was that Arthur and Toby had been high-school sweethearts, dating since the age of fifteen; they'd met in fourth grade. You can't marry your first love, she'd told her brother. You'll always wonder who else is out there. That's what she'd told him (her parents had said exactly the same thing, but never directly to Arthur), but really, she just didn't like Toby. Too bubbly, jumpy, outgoing, a high-school-cheerleader type all the way through college.

Now, she adored her sister-in-law, and not just because the twins added a few pounds to her bony physique, or because she'd cut her hair and actually sported a few gray strands among the brown. Toby, she'd discovered, was wise as well as extroverted, a combination Yael hadn't thought possible. She'd always been the cutest person Yael knew, but Toby had taught her that raw cuteness can coexist with genuine warmth.

"Honestly? I think he did it just to mess up the community."

"What do you mean?" Toby asked.

"He knew about all of Judah's affairs, the open marriage, the one-night stands, the long relationship with his secretary. Judah was stupid enough to tell him. The scumbag — Weinman — wanted everyone to know. So he created a scandal."

"But, Yael, my God!" Toby said. "He didn't have to kill that woman just to create a scandal. He could have, I don't know, told a reporter, or written a letter to the board, or just hid out and took some pictures."

"Yes, but he wanted to harm Judah. To frame him for the murder. To send Judah to prison."

"Then why change his story in the middle of the trial?" Arthur asked. "Why not keep up the charade that Judah had hired him? He could have sent your boss away for life."

"I'm not sure," Yael admitted. "Obviously, I've thought about it. Maybe he realized that Judah would be acquitted anyway. The evidence against him was pretty weak to begin with. Epstein – I mean, a cop, a friend of mine – told me the police never really bought Judah as the killer, but the DA insisted. But my theory is that he was dispensing his own sick brand of justice. He wanted Judah to experience the humiliation of being arrested, of being revealed as an adulterer, as a phony, but it wasn't really necessary for him to go to prison for the rest of his life. I think the scumbag enjoyed playing God with Judah. First taking away his reputation, then his freedom. Then giving him his freedom back, after his reputation was gone for good."

"Yes, well, I think you're missing something." Arthur said. "Or, you're just not telling us."

"Would you like more wine, Yael?" Toby said, shooting her husband an irritated look.

"What do you mean?" Yael asked.

"Well, obviously this has something to do with you. How did he end up at your congregation to begin with? I mean, let's face it, what was he doing in Desert County? He was looking for you."

That night, she thought. Her parents' bedroom. She couldn't even pretend to remember. But she could ask. She could ask right now. Instead, she said, "You think he killed Aviva because of me? I did consider that. Did you know I was a suspect for a while? At first, I thought that was his plan all along. To frame *me*. But if that was the point, why not just go ahead and tell the police that I'd hired him? Why point them at Judah?"

"No, no," her brother insisted. "You're missing the point."

"You were a suspect, Yael?" Toby asked. "Really?"

"Okay, what's the point?" Yael said. "What am I missing?"

"He did it to get back at Dad."

Yael leaned back in her chair. She turned to Toby. "More wine. Did you say there was more wine?"

"I'll get the bottle," she said. "But nobody says a word until I get back!"

Arthur corkscrewed open the bottle. Two-Buck Chuck, from Trader Joe's. They sipped silently.

"Okay, Detective," Yael said finally. "He did it for Dad. I think I get it."

"I don't!" Toby said. "Somebody! Please."

Arthur sighed. "Yael, you may not know this whole story. I don't know what Mom or Dad told you. Toby, you certainly don't know. But Dad fired Cantor Weinman from Temple Emanuel. He never said why, but it happened so suddenly, everyone assumed it was sexual misconduct." He looked closely at Yael. "And, actually, it *was* sexual misconduct. I happen to know that." He shut his eyes. "I can't tell you right now, how I know, I just do."

"I know," Yael said softly. "I know about it. I didn't know Dad fired him, but I do know what you're talking about." She turned her eyes from her brother. She was surprised to find that she also, suddenly, didn't want to talk about that night. It was enough.

"Arthur, what the hell are you talking about?" It was Toby, sipping her wine.

"Doesn't matter. Let me just continue. Dad fired Weinman. Sexual misconduct. Then three weeks later, what happens?"

"The funeral," Yael said. "His cousin's funeral. The gangster."

"Yes, but more significantly, the affair – his affair comes out. Dad gets fired. So put yourself into Weinman's diseased brain. Dad fires him for sexual misconduct, but for the scumbag, it was nothing. Some harmless touching, really just a game. I heard Weinman defend it exactly that way. Just a game. But that's the end of Weinman's career. As far as I know, he never worked as a cantor again. But now, Dad, he's caught in a real sexual affair. Adultery, with a mobster's wife. So right away, Weinman figures, what a hypocrite! He fires me, for nothing, but look at him! Then, even worse, Dad gets another job right way. He remains respected, successful; he goes on to become one of the great rabbis of his generation. But Weinman? He never works again."

Yael nodded. Toby gaped at her husband.

"A sick brain could do a lot with a grudge like that. And, look, let's admit that unless we're willing to go interview the

guy in prison, we're never really going to know. But I imagine it went something like this. Yael, maybe he followed you
around for years. Or, more likely, he was gambling and
drinking away his life in the desert, and he saw an article
about you in the local newspaper. He finds you, screws
up your head a little with newspaper articles, but then he
really starts to plan. He sees this relationship you have with
your boss."

"What do you mean?" Yael said. Do *not* blush, she told
herself.

"Well, Rabbi Loeb was obviously a mentor to you. I
mean, you've told me that. Like a teacher, a pastor. But for
Weinman, Loeb probably seemed like a father figure to you.
So he gets to know the guy, and he finds out he really *is* like
your father, in one significant way. He screws around. Just
like your real father. So he tells himself this time he's not
going to get away with it. And it's not enough just to write
the board, or even a letter to the editor, because he knows
that Dad got away with it. So he has to truly humiliate the
guy. Demolish his career. Get Loeb arrested for murder, but
then release him into a life where he'll end up just like the
scumbag. Never hired again. Broken. Because, really, who's
going to hire Judah now? A guy arrested for killing his wife?
Even with the judge dismissing the charges, he couldn't get
hired on Pluto. Now, he's finally got his revenge. It's on
the wrong guy, but Dad wasn't available. So he picked the
next best thing." He sipped his wine, grimaced, then took
another sip. Yael heard the twins screeching upstairs, bed-
springs groaning. They were bouncing up and down. Did
they ever stop?

"So," Arthur said, "am I right?"

Toby stared at her husband. "I think you're insane," she said.

Arthur smiled. "Don't worry, Yael. She says that a lot."

Yael didn't smile. She didn't look up. She stared at the cheap white wine, then downed the rest of her glass – still half full – in one gulp.

"Well? Only thing that really makes sense, huh?" Arthur asked.

"I've got to call Peter," Yael said.

"Yael," Arthur said.

"Of course you do," Toby said.

"I haven't spoken to him all day."

"Do you want to you use our phone?" Toby asked. "Use the one in our bedroom. It's private."

"Peter's tried to call me. Actually, he calls me every ten minutes. I finally turned off my BlackBerry."

"Use our phone," Toby urged. "Upstairs. On the night-stand. I'll get the girls to shut up."

Yael turned to her brother. "He killed an innocent woman," she said. "I mean, Aviva never did anything to him. To anyone. To get back at Dad?"

"You've got a better theory?" Arthur asked.

"She had nothing to do with Dad! She didn't even know Dad."

"I know."

"The thing with Dad happened almost thirty years ago."

"Listen, the guy's a fucking lunatic."

"No!" Yael said. She looked at her brother and then at Toby. They both stared back, wide-eyed, expectant, as if she were a teacher dispensing real wisdom. She'd seen the look before, on the face of congregants when she was on a roll in her teaching, expressing herself with full abandon, her face glowing red. She always feared the look, resisting the expectation, the responsibility. "No," she said. "He's not a lunatic. He's not crazy. He's *evil*."

She ran upstairs into the master bedroom and picked up the phone. She thought briefly about Peter, then checked her BlackBerry for the number and called Southwest. There was a flight through Chicago leaving in three hours. Yael checked her watch, did a few quick calculations, then bought the ticket.

CHAPTER 9

Her flight landed at precisely 5 a.m. An hour difference either way and she would have abandoned her plan, and driven home. Instead, she exited on Desert Boulevard, drove the mile and a half through strip malls, cacti, and Joshua trees, then pulled into the synagogue parking lot. It was nearly six by the time she arrived, the summer sun already bright, and just beginning to heat the cool desert air. If she guessed correctly, Judah would be there in another hour.

In three years she'd never tried it, but she wasn't surprised that her key fit the lock. Manuel had told her it was a master key. Over the years, it had opened the sanctuary, youth lounge, various classrooms, and Tzipporah's office, so why not Judah's? The only challenge now was the computer. She sat at his desk, identical in every way to hers – essentially two long, dark, wood platforms at ninety degrees to each other with no drawers, just space – except all his surfaces had been cleared of papers, photos, pens, coffee mugs, scissors, paper clips, everything except his computer; a laptop connected to a docking station, with matching keyboard and 12-inch monitor. It was on. She jiggled the mouse to clear the black screen saver, and encountered a familiar screen asking for a username and password. She took one breath and typed in "rabbi" then "shalom," – her username and password. It had been Judah who suggested she use them, so she wouldn't forget. No one was big on computer security at the synagogue; this wasn't the defense department. Still, she was mildly surprised when Judah's settings loaded quickly in front of her: the files of an accused wife murderer, now acquitted. She was sure the police had already combed through everything in there, but she was looking for just one item on his calendar. She clicked on Outlook and found the date, February 28th, the day of the murder. At 7 p.m., Judah or Charlotte had typed "Deborah and Charlotte." So that was it. Not choir rehearsal. A scheduled meeting, with his lover and the president of his congregation.

Yael leaned back in the soft leather chair, reclining so her face was parallel with the ceiling, and checked her watch. 6:30. She hadn't slept at all on the airplane, hadn't slept well in weeks. She shut her eyes, breathed through her nose, and waited. She heard herself snore once or twice before falling asleep.

"Yael."

She opened her eyes, and found herself staring at a water stain on the ceiling. The back of her neck felt like someone was pinching it and holding on for dear life. Slowly, Yael brought her chin forward and sat up straight.

"What are you doing here?"

It wasn't his kind, pastoral voice. Nor was it his patient, mentoring tone. It was irritated, arrogant. She stared at him. He needed to shave. His hair was uncombed. He looked more unkempt than he had in prison, but he also looked meaner, more confident. He looked great.

"I asked you what you're doing here."

Had she ever heard this tone of voice from him? She didn't think so. In fact, this time she sensed a further edge. Threatening? Yes, he sounded threatening.

She made no move to leave his chair. "What were you doing here that night? The night Aviva was killed. Outlook says you had an appointment with Deborah. And Charlotte."

"You looked at my calendar?" he asked. "*My* calendar?"

There it was again. An edge. Without thinking, she moved back in her seat. What do killers sound like? she wondered. That is, people who hire killers. She knew the voice of the scumbag, confident, clean, crazy, evil. But regular folk, non-criminals, non- scumbags, who one day get it in their screwed-up heads to end another human being's life. How do they speak once they've accomplished the act, once they did it, and got away with it? "Why don't you just answer the question?" she said.

He smiled. He'd had such a wonderful smile, she thought. Before. Every part of his face had joined in that rabbinic smile, his jowls, his forehead, his nose, his ears. And the actual mouth – nothing but white, straight teeth, the light reflecting off of them in a transcendent gleam. He could blind you with that smile. Now it took up just half his face, so it was more scowl than grin. And his teeth somehow had yellowed. "You don't think Epstein asked me that on the first interview? What are you doing, Yael? Investigating the crime now that it's been solved? Can you please get off of my chair? Get away from my desk, my computer. Those are still mine, at least for another day."

She looked around, as if surprised to find herself in Judah's chair, in his office. She quickly got up, straightened her T-shirt, and walked out from behind the desk. He brushed her gently as he squeezed past to take her place.

"Yael," he said, as he sat down and clicked off the computer screen. There it was, she thought. The old voice, warm like a milk bath, mentoring. Who was this man? He smiled. It filled the room, filled her insides. She took a step back, had to steady herself to keep from stumbling. She found a chair and collapsed into it.

"Obviously, I wasn't here for choir practice," he said. "That was – well, not quite a coincidence, as I later discovered, but not why I came that night. You know me. I would go through an appendectomy to avoid hearing our choir practice."

"Okay."

"Of course, the damn choir practice became a prime piece of evidence. Just another reason for me to despise choirs. It was so obvious that the only reason I'd look in on the choir would be to establish an alibi. They probably got a hundred witnesses, including yourself, to swear that I *never* came to choir practice, that I avoided it like the plague."

"Yes." She would, in fact, have testified to that herself, if she'd been asked.

He sighed. "Yael, I would have told you all this. I *intended* to tell you before – well, I mean I would have had to. I came that night to talk to Deborah. To tell her."

Yael waited.

"Tell her that I was quitting."

"What!"

"Yep. That I was quitting. And that Charlotte and I were going away together. I was leaving Aviva. We were planning on driving to Tucson the next day. I was going to write you a letter that night. You see, that was one of the points of the reorganization. Obviously, it was mostly a fraud. I knew I wasn't sticking around. But I wanted to show the board how much I trusted you. Let them know how much authority I was willing to give you. So they'd hire you after I, well, after I ran away. Also, Yael, I really wanted to show *you* how much I trusted you. I wanted to build up *your* confidence. So you could take over. Anyway, that's what I told Deborah that night. That I quit. That Charlotte and I were going away together. And that, while I certainly couldn't tell them what to do, I recommended they hire you to replace me."

Truth, Yael thought, staring at her boss. What does truth sound like? Most people, she imagined, would answer that it sounds precisely like the voice Judah just shared with her. Everything about it bled sincerity. Still, she wondered. Would she ever know? "But Aviva," she said. She suddenly remembered Aviva, crying and trembling in her office the day before her murder. Agitated, certainly, even crazed, but nothing about Judah leaving. "Did Aviva know yet?"

"No," he said, shaking his head. "You see, I decided—"

"Coincidence," Yael said. God, she was tired. She longed for home, for bed. But words, against her will, popped into her mind and then out her mouth. "You said it *wasn't* a coincidence that you set up this meeting the same night as choir practice. What did you mean?"

He looked down at the clean, shiny desk. Yael noticed a penny-shaped bald spot smack in the middle of his scalp. How long had that been there? "It wasn't my idea to choose that night. It wasn't Charlotte's either."

"The scumbag's," Yael said.

He smiled again, all warmth. Her *partner*. "Well, I guess I'll have to adopt that name now. After all, he killed my wife, and then accused me. But, yes, it was Edgar's idea we pick that night to meet with Deborah. And he *did* know about the choir practice, and he knew how that would look. Edgar and I had become quite close over the years. Closer even than I think you suspected. You see, the plan was that Charlotte and I would tell Deborah. And, while we were at the syna- gogue, Edgar volunteered to pop by my house and, well…"

"Oh my God."

He shook his head. "Yes. Well, that was the plan. He was going to tell her. He volunteered to do it."

"But, Judah! He would be alone with her. And you *knew* him!"

"Yael, you have to calm down. He'd been alone with her before. Several times. And, yes, of course I knew him. He was my friend. I mean, you're right, *yes*, he fooled me. I thought I knew him."

"No, no, you *did* know him. You knew his past. I told you! Why do you think we called him the scumbag?"

"Yes, of course, you're right. It was a dreadful, a terri- ble… mistake."

"A mistake?"

"Okay, bad choice of words. But listen, Yael, you're missing something. I wasn't the only one who was fooled by him. You know that. You must know what I'm talking about."

"Judah, I haven't the slightest idea what you're talking about. Remember, part of your plan seems to have been to tell me nothing at all, ever, about you and your life. So please, assume that the plan worked. Because I don't know *anything!*"

He leaned back in his chair. Yael watched him. For her, when she sat in it, the large leather chair was a thing that enfolded her, that took her in, gave her a few minutes of rest. For him, the chair was a thing to dominate, another object on which he could impose his will. He gripped the armrests with both hands. "I guess I'm not the only one not to tell you things, Yael," he said evenly, his blue eyes focused on her face. "There was another guy who became close to Edgar this past year. They shared some interests. In bluegrass music and its Jewish variations. And weird conspiracy theories."

"Peter," she said. The truth. That's what it sounds like.

"You know, it wasn't Edgar who suggested I look in on the choir that night."

"Oh God."

"Being seen at choir rehearsal. It got me arrested. It was such an obviously contrived alibi that the police immediately became suspicious. So, whoever told me to show my face to the choir that night framed me for murder. And that *wasn't* Edgar."

She blushed. For no reason she could think of. She just fucking blushed.

"Don't get me wrong. Edgar did it. He strangled Aviva, and then he swore that I paid him to do it. But *looking in* on the choir? Making sure I was seen? That wasn't Edgar's suggestion. You don't know about any of this?"

She stared at him. Deviant. Sociopath. Blunderer. Teacher. Mentor. Egomaniac. But killer? Probably not. She said nothing.

"You'd better speak with him, Yael."

She nodded. She trembled, then sat up, and tightened her fists into balls to steady herself. Judah stared at her, not flinching, as if daring her to slug him. She rose slowly from her chair and turned toward the door.

"Yael," he said, his voice soft, empathetic, rabbinic. She turned around.

"I'm done here. Charlotte and I are leaving tomorrow. This will be your office."

She looked around the room. Light red carpet. Desert views across from the desk chair through three contiguous skylights; it was the eastern wall, so Judah could watch the sunrise over the hills every day. But mostly she saw books. Dark-stained, walnut wood shelves filled every wall space, but there were still not enough for all of Judah's volumes. Books covered the tops of the shelves; in most rows they were double-stacked. Packing crates with books lay in every corner. More than anything, more than his charisma, his teaching ability, his empathy, Yael had coveted Judah's books; not the physical objects themselves, but the fact that Judah had *read* them, had imbibed their secrets. He was putting their teachings to use in his rabbinate. Now, the thought of sitting in his leather chair and reading even a single volume disgusted her. "Please take everything with you," she said.

Walking home along the bike path – she needed the walk, she'd pick up her car later – Yael considered all the people in her life who had withheld significant information from her. Her mother, father, and brother, of course, who hadn't told her about the incident with the scumbag or, for that matter, the truth about her parents' divorce, and her father's career. There was Tzipporah, her good friend, who never mentioned that she'd slept with Judah. There was Addison, not a friend, more an enemy, but she also hadn't told Yael about her liaison with Judah. Then there was Charlotte, and her long-time affair with her boss. And, of course, there was Judah himself, propositioning everyone but her. And Epstein and Dumanis, who always knew more than they told her.

And there was Deborah. Deborah hadn't told Yael anything about that night, the night Aviva was killed: that Judah had resigned, that he was running away with Charlotte, that Judah wanted Yael to replace him.

None of these people had lied to her; they just hadn't told her the truth. Because? They didn't want to hurt her, or they didn't think she needed to know, or they figured it was none of her business. And yet, here she was, badly hurt, and clearly needing to know because, quite literally, it had become her business.

Then there was Peter.

She slowed down, but just a bit, as his name crossed her brain. The morning chill had burned away entirely. Yael sweated in her black jeans and green Land's End T-shirt. The sun, reflecting off the white boulders, nearly blinded her; she'd left her sunglasses in her suitcase. Two lizards scurried in and out of cracks in the hard, sun-baked path. She'd neglected to bring water for the walk home, and she felt as if she hadn't sipped a cool drink in days. The desert, she thought. How the hell had she ended up living in a desert?

She heard the music as she emerged from the path, the bike lane giving way to the road. She was still a hundred yards from her front door. Peter disliked air conditioning, and kept it off when Yael was away, preferring fans, or just open windows and doors. The canyon they lived in amplified sounds in weird ways so that, depending on the wind, or time of day, you could hear arguments from families several blocks away. Still, Yael had a hard time believing that the mandolin music she was hearing – the quick, ringing, major scale notes – wasn't amplified by the most precise speakers. But she knew that Peter never used electric amplification at home. It's just Peter and his instrument, she thought. And the desert canyon. Music for the whole neighborhood, for the lizards and coyotes too, for the whole desert.

For the first time Yael could remember, the music stopped as soon as she walked in the door.

"Yael!" he said brightly, placing the five-thousand-dollar mandolin on the rug.

It had been slightly longer than thirty hours since she'd seen him. But his beard looked extra scraggly. And, she wondered, is it possible to lose twenty pounds in a day? He looked scarecrow-skinny, his arms suddenly matching the long, thin boniness of his fingers. But maybe she just hadn't been paying much attention lately.

She kissed him on his beard, and sat across from him on the sofa. "There are some things I need to know," she said softly.

"Okay. Me too," he said. He was smiling, but Yael recognized it as a nervous smile. He tended to smile through their worst arguments, a tic that had only recently stopped infuriating her. She cocked her head and studied his toothy grin.

"You and Weinman," she began. "You, uh, had a relationship with him?"

"Yes," he said immediately.

She glared at him. He held his smile. "And?" she asked. "Can you tell me more?"

"Sure. Uh, welcome back, by the way."

"Thank you."

"Next time, maybe tell me before you go?"

"Maybe."

He nodded and glanced longingly at the mandolin lying on the rug.

"Okay. Well, you know I introduced him to Judah. Mostly, I was trying to get him away from you, but I also thought – I don't know – maybe Judah could help the guy. So, one night, Judah invited me over. It was about a year ago. You had a late meeting. I guess Aviva was, I don't know, out. He told me Edgar – I mean the scumbag, whatever – had a collection of Bill Monroe 45s from the early '50s, when they first started making 45s. He wondered if I had some way of playing the records. So, of course, I brought over my turntable. And, yeah, we got to talking. Turns out, he knew a lot about bluegrass music. And swing, and bebop.

And he had lots of records. So, yeah, we kind of hit it off. The three of us."

"And you didn't think you might want to inform me about this? About your new playmate?"

"Whoa, Yael. This was the scumbag. No one could talk to you about Edgar. Judah knew it too. Best thing was to keep it quiet." He smiled. It's all good.

Yael wasn't sure what was causing the pounding headache – anger, confusion, lack of sleep, or all of the above. But she knew truth and she knew lies and, if anything, the headache only clarified which was which. "No one could talk to me? I talked to you all the time about Weinman. Besides, I'm your wife. You're my husband."

The smile went out. He peered at her through rimless glasses. Between the thick lenses, the beard, and the suddenly blank look on his face, it was hard to see what was going on in his head. But Yael knew that somewhere in that complicated brain, a switch had just turned on. "Is it time for truth, Yael?" he said quietly. "We could just go on, you know. Judah's leaving town. Edgar's in jail for the rest of his life. You'll be senior rabbi. I'll play my music, teach my classes. We'll have kids now. As many as you want. Do we really need the truth? We've done alright without it up to now."

"Peter."

He picked the mandolin off the rug, but just set it face-up on his lap, stroking the wood, leaving the strings alone. "Or, I could tell you some of the truth. Enough to satisfy you, probably. At least for now. Or, there's always the option of the whole truth, nothing but the truth. I could do that, too. Problem is, I'm not sure I know the entire truth, even about what I've done. Denial's a pretty powerful force." He looked at the mandolin, seemed to consider placing it sideways so he could run his fingers across the fretboard. He reached for a pick, but then changed his mind and looked at Yael.

She took a breath. "Did you hire Edgar to kill Aviva?"

The mandolin fell from his lap, snapping several strings. It made a surprisingly loud noise for such a small, delicate instrument. Peter ignored it. "Wow!" he said. He looked genuinely amazed, even impressed. "Wow! Is that what you think? Whoa! Is that what's bothering you? Jesus!"

She let out the breath, relieved. "I just thought I'd get that one out of the way."

"Wow!" he said. "I guess we should talk more often!"

"Peter."

He looked at the broken mandolin, and then back at Yael. "Maybe I should just tell you the whole story."

Now she smiled. "Okay."

He told her. It began when he realized that Yael had fallen in love with Judah. And please, he said, don't deny it. If there were an award for not hiding emotions, for displaying on her cheeks, with total accuracy, everything she was feeling, she would win it. And he, after all, lived with her, slept with her. He knew. Coincidentally, he'd figured it out the day before Judah had invited him over to listen to Edgar's 45s. In fact, he went over that night with the thought of confronting Judah, of asking him if anything had happened, or if he even had a clue that his wife had a crush on him. But instead, they got drunk and listened to music.

And afterwards, Edgar walked him to his Toyota and told him about Judah's secret life. His open marriage, his one-night stands and, mostly, the affair with his secretary. "You can imagine," Peter said, "how those revelations made me feel. Not only did you have a crush on him, this was a guy who wouldn't hesitate for a moment to act on your fantasies. And that would be the end of our marriage. I couldn't stay married to you if you'd slept with Judah. And you would have. I know it." That moment, Peter said, when Weinman whispered those awful truths in his ear, that's when he began formulating his plan, the plan to save their marriage.

You see, he said softly, he knew Edgar was up to something. He could sense it in the bitter eagerness with which he spilled Judah's secrets. Weinman was going to expose Judah, and it sounded like he would do it in a spectacular fashion. But that was fine with Peter, because exposing Judah meant Judah leaving Desert County, which meant that Yael would get over him. Because she always did. She always got over her crushes, as long as the guys weren't around to prey on her.

A week later, he phoned Edgar. Count me in, he said, on whatever you're planning. Peter understood that Weinman had his own inscrutable reasons for wreaking havoc on Judah's life. It had something to do with Yael and her father and Edgar's sick, wounded vanity. Peter gathered that much. But it didn't matter. They wanted the same thing: Judah exposed, expelled. They traded ideas. Edgar suggested private detectives, hidden cameras, prostitutes wearing wires, blackmail, threats from local gangsters. Peter thought he'd dissuaded him from these mad schemes. Look, he told

Edgar, every one of those shady ideas will just bring attention to *us*, he said, which is exactly what we don't want. Bring the cops in, and Judah will point them in our direction. The guy's no dope. We want to live our lives, but see Judah run out of town. Peter came up with a much more sensible, subtle plan. Get Judah to sabotage himself. Talk him into leaving his wife, running off with his secretary. Peter had assured Edgar that after a scandal like *that*, Judah would never work again as a rabbi.

"Wait a second," Yael interrupted, for the first time. "What do you mean he'd never work again? Rabbis work all the time after scandals. Look at my dad."

"Yes," Peter agreed, still staring mournfully at the busted mandolin, "but the plan was to convince Judah that if he tried to work again as a rabbi, Aviva would blow the whistle on all his affairs, all the open-marriage stuff."

"And how would you get him to think that?"

"Well, actually, we – that is, not me, Edgar – were actually going to talk Aviva into making that threat. The plan was to persuade her – for her own good – to blackmail Judah."

"To persuade her," Yael repeated.

Peter finished the story. For six months, the three of them met once a week, to drink wine, listen to music, and feed suggestions into Judah's surprisingly malleable brain. It was like having an affair, Peter said, only it was *me* and Judah, not you. Making excuses every Tuesday night. Inventing gigs, faculty meetings, dinners with out-of-town musicians or visiting professors. All that time, he was working in concert with Edgar, convincing Judah that he'd be better off without the hypocrisy, without the whiny, needy, gambling addicts in his congregation; he'd be better off with a woman he really loved and who really loved him. We were relentless, Peter said. Every week. We didn't let up.

"Persuade Aviva, you said," Yael again interrupted. "The scumbag was supposed to persuade Aviva. When and how was that supposed to happen?"

Peter folded his hands together and brought his chin to rest on his fists. He focused intently on his own knees, as if praying to them for guidance. "That night," he said. "While Judah was meeting with Deborah. Edgar was supposed to drop in that night."

"Drop in?"

Peter's fists, still pressed against his chin, started shaking. Soon his whole body was vibrating. Yael could hear his teeth chattering. He blinked three times quickly. "I didn't know," he said softly, his voice steady but sad. "He tricked me. Outsmarted me. Or, I guess, out*eviled* me. It never occurred to me that he would... He had his own plan, all along, to expose Judah by murdering Aviva. Because he didn't care if the police suspected him. He didn't care if he went to jail. He wanted a humongous scandal. And what's bigger than murder? So he created it himself."

Yael watched her husband with something like pity. He'd encouraged the scumbag, a guy he knew to be psychotic, to "drop in" on Aviva. And that was only the worst of what he'd done. He'd also conspired – there was no other word for it – to ruin Judah's life, a conspiracy that, willfully or not, ended in Aviva's death. And yet – and this was somehow the hardest part for her to understand, and yet, still the thing that redeemed him in her eyes – he'd done it for *her*. To rescue their marriage. And rescue it from what? From her. So, in a way, she shared some responsibility for Aviva's death. Odd, she thought, how she'd felt guilty almost immediately after hearing the news, feelings that undoubtedly revealed themselves to Epstein and to Deborah, feelings that made her a genuine suspect. But there had been no reason to feel guilty. She had nothing to do with the crime. At least that's what she'd thought, back then. Now, she knew differently. It was her crush on Judah that set the whole thing in motion.

"He would have killed her anyway, you know," Peter said, as if reading Yael's mind. "He wanted that scandal. He wanted Judah disgraced, in jail. Me coming along was just a bonus. That allowed him to involve you. He used me to get to you."

Yael nodded. It was true. It all came back to the scumbag, and his evil. So, why the guilty feelings? Why did they persist even now, when she *knew* that what Peter was saying was true? She shook her head, shuddered, shut her eyes. She wasn't sure she'd ever understand.

"You told all this to Epstein?" Yael said.

He looked up, surprised. "Of course," he said. "You think I could lie to the police? I was the guy who convinced Epstein to arrest the scumbag. You know, I actually wasn't sure at first. There was clearly a lot I didn't know about either of those guys. Or maybe… maybe… I didn't know. Maybe, I thought, somebody else did it."

"Somebody else."

"Hmm."

"Somebody else. Okay." She thought for a second. "But Peter, if you told Epstein, why not tell me?"

"Because telling you a part meant telling you all of it. It meant admitting that I didn't trust you. And then you'd have to admit that I was right not to trust you. We'd have to acknowledge that thing we've always managed to ignore. And, frankly, I think we've been better off ignoring it."

Yes, she thought. They had been better off. Until a woman got killed.

One more thing she needed to know. "Judah told me it was your idea that he stick his head into the choir room. Why would you do that?"

He blinked again, twice. He was frowning, near tears, as far from smiling as she'd ever seen him. "Because *I* wrote several of the pieces. I thought he might want to hear them. He was interested in my music. At least he said he was."

"Okay."

He blinked. "Judah always loved my music. I mean, that's what he told me."

CHAPTER 10

It was actually Deborah who suggested they meet on the bike path, behind the synagogue. Yael assumed they'd order eighteen-dollar lunch salads at Enrique's and that, in between bites of arugula and pumpkin muffin, Deborah would fire her. Instead, she sat on her favorite boulder, unwrapped a bagel and cream cheese, and watched Deborah munch on carrot and pretzel sticks. Two Desert County gals, Yael thought. Out to lunch.

"I've always loved this spot," Deborah said.

"Really! I thought I was the only one who knew about it."

"Oh, no. I used to rush out here after board meetings. I'd always try to end at least twenty minutes early, to give myself some desert time – time to purify myself – and still make it home precisely when I promised. That's important to Michael, ever since I admitted what happened between me and Judah."

"Okay," Yael responded. Deborah had packed a lot of information into those casual sentences. She'd either elaborate or not. Yael was surprised to find she didn't care either way.

"I like it here because it gives me the illusion that I really just live out in the desert. A simple life. You work for water. And food. And appreciate the beauty because, my God, it really is beautiful, any time of day, in any weather.

Out here – just a short walk from the synagogue – you can't see any buildings. You can imagine that there are no casinos, no gambling, no – well, none of that. None of that stuff we all need to make our livings."

That stuff, Yael thought. A billion dollar industry, employing thousands, generating suburbs, subdivisions, malls, hospitals, fast-food joints, fancy restaurants, colleges, churches, mosques, and synagogues – one synagogue in particular which would have a budget of precisely zero dollars without "that stuff." Deborah came out here to forget about that stuff, to pretend it didn't exist. Yael, on the other hand, had successfully ignored that stuff for years. She'd sat on her boulder and lost herself in the red-brown dirt hills, the cactus, the flowers, the big sky – so she could forget about *other* things, other stuff. The synagogue. The murder. Judah. Peter.

At the exact moment her husband's name buzzed through her thoughts, her boulder vibrated slightly. Deborah felt the movement and looked quizzically at Yael, who glanced at the BlackBerry next to her and quickly pressed "ignore." Yael smiled sheepishly. Deborah studied the BlackBerry, then shrugged.

"I have an offer for you, Yael," she said. "From the board. We'd like you to serve as our interim senior rabbi, until we can get ourselves organized. And then – then, we hope you'll apply for the job, permanently. If you do, we won't interview any other candidates until we make a decision about you."

Yael felt herself blush; the first time, she thought, that pure surprise brought on that reaction. "Wow," she said. "That's not at all what I expected."

Deborah nodded, still looking at Yael's BlackBerry. "Yes, well, we couldn't very well offer you the job when you were a suspect. And it didn't seem right until after the trial. But now – Judah's gone, and everything seems to be getting…" Her voice trailed off. "I guess 'back to normal' isn't really the right phrase, but, anyway…"

The boulder again vibrated. Yael glanced at the display and again pressed "ignore." "Sorry," she said quickly.

Deborah smiled stiffly. "I need to share something with you, Yael."

"Okay." Here it comes, she thought. Deborah's reservations. The board's doubts. Yael's faults as a rabbi, as well as, frankly, a person. She doesn't *understand* them. She's not warm. She doesn't love their… stuff. Yael steeled herself. If she was going to continue in this profession, she'd have to get used to this. And, in fact, there was quite a bit of truth in this critique, so sooner or later she'd have to start working on these things. Understanding. Empathy. Warmth. "Go ahead," she told Deborah.

"I was there, that night," she said. "At Judah's house. The night of the murder."

Yael's heart raced, and she looked around quickly. Paranoia, sharp and fresh, stabbed her in the belly. It wasn't over. Was Deborah wearing a wire? Or worse, packing a gun in her purse? Or a garrote? Her hand reached for her BlackBerry, even as she realized she had no idea who to call. Peter? Epstein? Then she nearly laughed out loud. Murder, she thought. It does a number on you. Would she ever get over it? She put her hand around the device, but just to steady herself.

Deborah, studying the one cloud in the sky, didn't seem to notice Yael's crazed reaction. "I found the body," she said weakly. "I was the one who called the police. You see, even though I was never particularly close with Aviva, I didn't think she should be alone that night. I wasn't sure what Judah had told her, how he'd broken it to her. She never struck me as the most stable person. Who knows, she may even have been suicidal. So, as soon as Judah and Charlotte left, I called her home number. There was no answer, so I drove over. The door was unlocked." Her face was now a pure leprous white, and she shivered despite the growing heat. "Have you ever seen a dead body, Yael?"

In fact, Yael had; she'd prepared several older, female bodies for burial as part of the community's burial society. And, as a rabbi, a pastor, she'd watched a few sick folk take their last labored breaths, in hospitals and homes. But she understood what Deborah meant. She'd certainly never seen a freshly murdered corpse; never glimpsed a strangled, broken neck. She couldn't imagine such a sight.

"But maybe you already know all this," Deborah continued. "I don't know what Epstein or Dumanis told you. And anyway, that's not what I wanted to tell you. I need to share with you what I thought the split second I saw Aviva's dead body."

"Okay."

"I thought, 'good.' I thought, now it's really over. With Aviva dead, and with Judah and Charlotte leaving town, we can finally move on as a congregation. You see, the first thing I thought of when Judah and Charlotte told me about their scheme, their plans, the first thing that entered my mind was 'what about Aviva?' Not, how would she feel, although of course I was concerned – even though you know I didn't really like her – but what would she *do*? Would she leave, go back to Phoenix? Or – and this is what I dreaded – would she stay in Desert County, stay in her house? And that worried me. Because if Aviva stayed, we'd never get over Judah. Every time we saw her on the street, in her Lexus, or at the grocery store, or, God forbid, at services, every Shabbat, we'd think about him – the rabbi who loved us, who *made* us. I guess, deep down, or maybe not so deep down, that's why I rushed over there when no one picked up the phone. I wanted to ask her what she was going to do. No, that's not it, really. I wanted to convince her to leave. So the first thing I felt when I saw her bugged-out eyes, when I couldn't find a pulse, was relief. God help me, the relief hit me before the horror. A split second before, but still before. I was relieved that this was over. That this flawed man would no longer control our spiritual lives, our Jewish identities. We wouldn't need this sick guy, with his perverted sense of sexual morality, to love us, to accept us despite all our flaws. We would survive as a synagogue, and we could embrace a new rabbi. Someone who knew the difference between right and wrong, and stuck to it. Someone like, I don't know, like…"

"Like me?" Yael wondered.

Deborah blinked and seemed flustered at the interruption; as if she'd forgotten that she wasn't speaking to herself, that Yael was sitting next to her on the boulder. "Well, at that exact moment, it occurred to me that maybe you were the killer, and that you'd killed her to get her out of the way so you could make your move on Judah. You were one of four or five suspects that rushed through my mind. Not number one, but not number five, either. So, no, I wasn't thinking of you, at the time." She took a breath. "But that's what we're thinking – what I'm thinking – now. Because, now I know the truth."

"The truth?" Yael asked.

Deborah nodded.

"That I didn't kill Aviva?"

"Oh, no, not just that…"

"That I hadn't slept with Judah? That I was one of the few?"

"You say you wanted to. But would you have? If he'd come on to you? You know what? I used to think yes, but now I think no. I think you would have resisted. Or slugged him with those fists you're always showing us."

Yael looked at her open hands, but said nothing. Privacy, she thought. Even under these sordid circumstances, she was entitled to some privacy. Anyway, her BlackBerry again vibrated. She glanced at the number and pressed "ignore." "Sorry," she said. "It's Peter. He calls me every five minutes or so. It's been going on for three days. Ever since, well, for three days."

"Oh, go ahead and answer it. Don't worry about interrupting our meeting. Tell him the news. We want you to stay."

"No, that's not it. You see, if I answer it…"

How much to tell her, this woman who once seriously thought of Yael as a killer and adulterer, but who now, suddenly, thinks of her as a paragon of marital virtue? Tell her that she'd kicked Peter out of the house the night he admitted to scheming with the scumbag, that he'd been living in the Desert County Inn for the past two days, that he called every five minutes from six in the morning to midnight, and that she didn't answer because she knew that if she pressed talk and heard his nerdy, nasal voice, she'd beg him to come back home? She knew this because over the course of the past twenty-four hours, for reasons utterly mysterious to her, she'd developed a new crush – this time on her husband; a cute, brilliant, weird man, who'd betrayed her terribly, but had done it in order to save her.

And Deborah had just raised the stakes. If she answered the phone now, listened to Peter's whiny, musical pleadings, informed him of the board's offer, he'd urge her to say yes: yes to the desert, yes to the synagogue, yes to him. And she would, she'd say yes, yes to it all because… because, well, who knows why? Who knows the inner workings of the heart, the darkness, the light, the compulsions, the evil meanderings, the empathies, the love and the hate? Ultimately, her crushes were as confounding to her as Judah's sins, or the scumbag's sick plotting, or her father's perverse loyalties.

But to confide all this to Deborah? She studied the synagogue president as she pressed "ignore" on her BlackBerry. A good twenty-five years older than her, she was still, in Yael's eyes, the loveliest sight in this lovely wilderness, a kind of desert flower, offering color to a dry and dusty world. The sun shone dazzlingly off Deborah's long, brown hair; her green eyes – now squinting with curiosity – reminded Yael of new grass after a gentle, autumn rain. Even her wrinkles looked beautiful to Yael; they were lines of wisdom, now damp with perspiration, meandering across her face like creeks, giving life to a parched landscape. Yael, with uncharacteristic hubris, saw herself in Deborah – a natural beauty, with intelligence and a growing moral strength. She understood that they would be partners in the coming years, partners in a great work, not just rebuilding their shattered community, but creating something entirely new: tearing down and building up.

Partners, yes, certainly, but not friends. So she told Deborah, "It's just Peter," and left it at that.

Deborah nodded. "Well, then, why don't we…"

The boulder vibrated. Both women looked at the Black-Berry. "Peter, again," Deborah suggested.

"Uh, yes," Yael said. She extended her index finger, and left it floating over the "ignore" button.

"Must be important," Deborah said.

"Oh, well, I don't…" The buzzing ceased, the call shunted to voice mail. But as soon as it stopped, it started again. Deborah laughed. So did Yael, at first irritated, but then, quickly, amused, relieved, happy. She looked at the BlackBerry, all metal and plastic. It trembled, as if in fear, or embarrassment, looking, on solid rock, in this thin slice of desert, as out of place as a thing could be. Still giggling, Yael picked it up and pressed "answer."

"Hello?" she said.

Philip Graubart is a senior rabbi at Congregation Beth El in La Jolla, California. He is the author of *My Dinner with Michael Jackson, My Mother's Song, Planet of the Jews*, and *A Suicide Note, A Murder*. He lives in San Diego.